THE FOURTH CART
III

STEPHEN R P BAILEY

The Fourth Cart III

Copyright © 2012 Stephen R P Bailey

All rights reserved.

ISBN-13: 978-1514651780

ISBN-10: 1514651785

www.stephenrpbailey.com

All characters in this novel are fictitious and any resemblance to real persons, living or dead, is purely coincidental.

The front cover image is provided courtesy of www.freeimages.com in accordance with their terms and conditions.

Novels by the same author:
The Fourth Cart I

The Fourth Cart II

The Fourth Cart III

FORWARD

Amidst the chaos of the Tibetan Uprising in March 1959, monks loyal to their God-King fought to keep treasured artefacts from the clutches of invading Chinese soldiers. Four horse-drawn carts full of gold and precious jewels left Lhasa in the wake of the fleeing Dalai Lama. Three carts were captured by pursuing soldiers. The fourth cart escaped, but appeared to vanish off the face of the earth.

In the early 1970s, the tale of the Fourth Cart was much circulated amongst the farang hanging around the bars of Patpong, Bangkok's red light district. One bar-fly even claimed to be the sole surviving witness to the fate of the legendary cart and would show listeners an enormous ruby which he insisted was part of the treasures still lying buried in Tibet.

For Nick Price, a brash young English lad on the lam, the allure of buried treasure was too strong to resist. With a wife and two kids to feed, as well as his inflated ego, he saw the Fourth Cart treasures as his financial salvation. So he came up with a plan to retrieve the treasures and cajoled his mates to join his mission. Unfortunately, it was a hasty, ill-conceived plan with devastatingly tragic consequences that would haunt him for the rest of his life.

Twenty years later, someone from Nick's past had emerged to inflict brutal, murderous revenge. The killer had been defeated but, in the process, Nick had opened a can of worms that would not go away. Not unless he faced up to his demons.

Chapter One

Kemp Town, Brighton
26th August 1992

As Detective Chief Inspector Jack Magee pulled protective slippers over his shoes, he looked up from the hallway chair he was sitting on and caught the eye of the crime scene investigating officer. 'I really can't thank you enough for contacting me about this.'

'You'll find a way. I trust.' Detective Chief Inspector Ryan gave Magee an unfriendly stare.

'You're sure about the knife?'

'Absolutely. Same as before. I'd put money on it.'

'But it's not stuck in the body, you say?'

'You'll see.' DCI Ryan motioned for Magee and his sergeant, Melissa Kelly, to follow him. 'This way, it's in a room down the hall.'

At the doorway to the crime scene, Magee stood transfixed at the sight of the six foot high bronze Buddha statue that dominated the room. In his experience, regency flats in Brighton were often decorated bizarrely, invariably on a grand scale, but this beat the lot.

He let his eyes roam over the eclectic ensemble of spiritual offerings scattered around the room. Dozens of miniature wood carvings lay near the base of the statue; elephants, tigers, an assortment of farm animals, all intermingled with innumerable coins and bank notes. Plates of stale food, covered in mould, along with pieces of plastic fruit, littered the carpet. Garlands of long dead orchids draped from the huge hands held out by the statue.

He took a deep breath, rubbed his chin and tried to identify the odours lingering in the air; an unpleasant mixture of sweetness and rottenness. 'My god,' he stated. 'What on earth is this all about?'

'It's a shrine, sir,' Melissa responded. 'A Buddhist shrine.'

Magee tutted. 'I can see that, Melissa. I'm not that stupid. I meant, what's wrong with the statue for god's sake? It looks as though it's got some grotesque skin disease.'

Melissa edged forward through the scattered offerings on the floor and rubbed the surface of the statue. 'It's just gold leaf peeling off, sir. It's nothing unusual. Buddhists often adorn their statues with it. It's so light it drifts easily in a gentle breeze. I've come out of many temples in Thailand glittering from head to foot with the stuff. Didn't you visit any temples while you were over there?'

Magee thought twice about entering a conversation involving Thailand with Melissa in public. He'd visited that country with her three months ago, on an assignment to establish the identity of the legendary drug lord, Khun Sa. May hadn't been a good time to pay a visit, not with the political unrest in Bangkok. He hadn't had a good night's sleep since returning. Visions of army soldiers firing on civilian protesters in the street riots still haunted his dreams. 'No, I didn't. You were the one that went off gallivanting with your young beau, Paul Mansell. I had work to do over there.'

'Your loss,' Melissa mumbled under her breath.

Magee ignored the incoherent remark and turned his attention to the objects in the room. The decorative carved animals looked so out of place; a child's toy room would have been more appropriate. The brown and withered garlands caught his eye. 'It's been a while since anyone was here, that's for sure.'

Melissa pointed to a vase of brown stems in the corner and ventured, 'Several months, I would imagine, judging by the state of those dead flowers.'

Magee joined Melissa in front of the statue, bent down and looked intently at a sharp double-edged knife sitting alongside the photograph. It bore an image of a Buddha carved into the ivory handle. He'd had the misfortune to come across nine others during a serial murder case he'd investigated the previous year. He turned to

DCI Ryan who was standing at the doorway and said, 'There's no doubt about it. You've a good memory.'

'I can hardly forget it. The day you came over to interview that suspect we were holding, you severely chastised some of my men. They gave me hell for allowing you to get away with that. The knife, the suspect, your ranting; the whole episode has been painfully etched into my memory.'

Magee's face turned red. 'Ahh!'

Melissa snorted. 'I told you at the time, didn't I, sir? They were just doing their job. There was no cause for getting ratty at them.' She turned to DCI Ryan and said, 'I apologize if you or your men felt I was in anyway responsible for that chastisement.'

'Thank you, Melissa,' DCI Ryan responded. He turned to face Magee who looked rather flustered.

'Alright, I admit it,' Magee acknowledged. 'I was in the wrong. I was uptight that day, but I shouldn't have said anything. I apologize profusely to you and your men.'

'Apologies accepted, Magee. I'll leave it to you to think of an appropriate present to us as a token of your remorse.'

Magee wasn't sure whether DCI Ryan was kidding or not. He nodded, and turned his attention back to the knife. 'Number ten, I make it. That would make the complete set. I suppose we should make a note of this on the file.'

'But the killer's dead, isn't he? Case closed?'

'Khun Sa may well be dead, if that's who you're referring to. But whether Khun Sa had anything to do with these knives is an entirely different matter. All we had was supposition. We didn't even have circumstantial evidence.'

Melissa sighed. 'You mean we're back to square one?'

Magee shook his head. 'No. Not at all. We're just one step further towards enlightenment, as Buddha would say.'

'I beg your pardon?'

Magee smiled. 'We're getting nearer the truth.'

'The truth being, what exactly, sir? I'm lost.'

'The truth being that whoever committed those murders last year is a very sick person. Mentally unstable, I mean.' He wandered over to the side of the room where a cotton sheet lay draped over a long narrow piece of furniture. He turned to DCI Ryan and said, 'I take it the body's under here.'

'It is, yes.'

Magee lifted the sheet with care to reveal a glass panelled coffin. 'Are you sure this is human? It's not a dummy by any chance? Or something knocked up by a special effects outfit for a television drama?'

DCI Ryan shook his head. 'No such luck. The pathologist said it was real.'

'Was he able to say anything about it?'

'No. He said that mummification wasn't his specialty. He said he would arrange for a forensic archaeologist to be sent over.'

Magee took his time to take in the sight before him, at what appeared to be an extraordinarily well preserved mummified body of a young woman. She had a small frame, long dark hair and leathery skin of a brownish hue, dressed in what looked like torn, ragged army camouflage jacket and trousers. He looked into her face; it was not a Caucasian structure. Above the jacket's left hand breast pocket were some stencilled letters. He tried to make sense of them but there were holes in the fabric that had obliterated a few of the characters. There were certainly a P, a G and an S. 'Looks military to me,' he remarked. 'American soldiers have their name printed on jackets just above the breast pocket don't they?'

'I believe so,' DCI Ryan replied. 'Is that your assumption, that she's an American soldier.'

'No, not at all. Sorry, I was just thinking aloud. Is there any hint of a name from the rest of the flat?'

'None,' DCI Ryan responded. 'This place is sterile except for this room. We've found no private mail. There were a few letters in the mail box downstairs in the hallway, but only utility bills addressed to "The Occupier". The managing agent gave us the occupier's contact details from his files. I checked them out, but, well, to be frank, I reckon they're false.'

'What about the owner of the flat? The leaseholder?'

'A company registered in the Cayman Islands. Unlikely we'll get anywhere with that.'

'Any chance the agent's lying about the occupier's name?'

'I don't see why he should. If he had anything to hide, he wouldn't have phoned us in the first place.'

'And why was he in the flat anyway? He shouldn't have any business to be in here.'

'There was a leak from a badly fitted washing machine in the flat above. Water flooded down through this flat into the one below. The people below called the managing agent, and he came here with a plumber, thinking the leak originated in here.'

Magee glanced at the room's ceiling and walls. 'There's no sign of water damage in here.'

'The water flooded down the kitchen walls, not in here. All the kitchens in this block are above each other.'

Magee frowned. 'Then why did the agent come into this room?'

DCI Ryan shrugged. 'Nosy perhaps, snooping around, looking for something to take, who knows.'

'Has he been interviewed?'

'He has, yes. He said he was checking each room for security reasons, since the place looked empty.'

'Is it his normal practice to let himself into private apartments? Did he have a key with the owner's permission?'

'He said he had a spare key from the time of the previous owner, for convenience, like when decorators need to open the windows from the outside.'

Magee looked quizzical. 'So you can't be completely sure that this mummy wasn't just dumped here by the agent?'

'No, I guess not. Though why would he?'

'I've no idea. Not yet, anyway.'

'If he wanted to dispose of it, there have got to be easier ways, surely. Anyway, why phone us?'

Magee stared down at the corpse, a dozen scenarios going through his mind. 'A set up, perhaps?'

'I guess anything's possible. So, how do you want to play this? I assume you'll want to take over the case.'

Magee held DCI Ryan's icy stare for a moment. 'No. Not at all. Before you rang me earlier today, my serial murder case was closed. And I don't see any reason to re-open it.'

'Good. It's just that I'd appreciate keeping this case, if you don't mind. It's been a relatively quiet summer in Brighton.'

Magee nodded his understanding. 'It's your case. My interest is peripheral. Anyway, to be honest, I can't justify throwing any resources at a closed case. Let's wait until the autopsy report. See what that says. Deal?'

'Thanks. Yes, it's a deal.'

'And in the meantime, we need to give her a name. She needs to be identified. This woman was a living human being once. She must have had a family. Someone out there may well be mourning her disappearance. She deserves to be named and given a burial under that name. It's the least we can do. The laying of bones is sacred.'

DCI Ryan sighed. 'I was hoping you'd be able to give me a lead. That's partly why I asked you over.'

Magee gave a thin smile. 'Thinking about the hours of fun your team will be having with missing person files?'

'Exactly. And dusty old files, to boot. This body must be ancient. It takes ages to mummify a body, doesn't it?'

'Does it? I really don't know. These clothes look fairly modern.'

'But she must have been dead for ages.'

'You could always start with a plea in the newspapers. That might get a response.'

'Maybe. Tell me, though, Magee, I don't get it, why would anyone keep such a hideous thing as this in their home? It would give me the creeps.'

'It's no worse than keeping it in a museum, or a mausoleum for that matter, surely? You must have seen mummies before.'

'Yes I have. But I still don't understand why. Why keep a body? Why not bury it?'

'It all depends whose body this is, I suppose,' Magee added in a kindly tone.

'I still don't get it.'

'Well, I guess it could be a collector's item. A famous person, or rather a famous mummy. There have been cases. There's a museum in America, I believe, displaying some modern day mummified bodies. I remember hearing about the strange case of a mummified man inadvertently put on display in a fairground's ghost train ride.'

'Charming.'

'Or, on the other hand, it could be something more sinister.'

DCI Ryan perked up. 'A murderer preserving his victim?'

'Possibly. Not quite sure I was thinking of that, though. You remember the old woman in the hotel run by Norman Bates, in the film?'

'You mean in Psycho?'

'Norman Bates was devoted to his mother, to her memory. He couldn't accept her death. He held on to her body after she died.'

'But that's just a film.'

'True. But such characters do exist in real life. Film scripts are often based upon small truths like that.'

'You'd have to be unhinged, to keep this as a souvenir.'

'Maybe.'

DCI Ryan checked his watch. 'Seen enough, you two? I need to organize the body's removal for Forensics.'

'Yes, thank you. Would you mind if I stay on a few moments.'

'Sure?'

'Yes. I want to sit here and think.'

'I'll get on then.'

Magee nodded in response as DCI Ryan left the room. He then set out to explore the other rooms, opening and shutting cupboards and drawers until he was satisfied that there were no other records in the flat. He returned to the shrine and sat down on a chair next to the mummified corpse. So, a mummified body, in army dress, in a Buddhist shrine, in an anonymous and deserted Brighton flat, alongside a knife linked to a serial murder case he thought was closed. He scratched the top of his head and pondered where he should allow his thoughts to drift.

Chapter Two

'Lunch at the Rainbow Inn,' Magee said to Melissa on the way back from Brighton. 'My treat. It's a beautiful day, we'll sit outside. I don't want to be stuck indoors in this weather. Especially as we won't be missed back at the office.'

'Thank you, sir,' Melissa responded. 'And I don't just mean for lunch. I mean thank you for getting me out of Inspector Jackson's way for a few hours.'

'Getting to you, is he?'

'You have no idea, sir. He's the most obnoxious man I've ever come across. He's so . . . so . . . I can't think of the right word.'

'Irritating? Arrogant? Closed-minded? Obsequious?'

Melissa laughed. 'There's a few to begin with.'

'Stick with it, Melissa. You'll get out of his grasp one day.'

'That day can't come soon enough. Sorry, but remind me, please, just why have I been assigned to him?'

Magee shrugged. 'I'm not in charge of scheduling staff.'

'Can't I come back to your section?'

'I'd be more than happy, Melissa. You know that. Someone must have got other plans for you though.'

Melissa looked miffed. 'It feels like I'm being punished. As soon as I got back from Thailand, things changed.'

'Well, you did stay there for six weeks. You only had three weeks leave entitlement.'

Melissa gave an innocent look. 'I was recovering from my wounds.'

Magee smirked. 'With Paul Mansell on his brother John's luxury boat cruising around the South China Sea, may I add. Not in a hospital.'

Melissa looked alarmed. 'No one knows that, do they?'

'If they do, they wouldn't have heard it from my lips. Jenny's the only one I told. She was concerned when I returned without you. I felt she had a right to know. Anyway, keeping secrets from a wife is not something I do.'

Melissa nodded her understanding. 'But someone's got it in for me. I can feel it in my bones.'

Magee raised his hand and waved it to his left. 'Left lane, Melissa.'

'Oops! My mind was miles away.' Melissa veered to the left and came off the A27 bypass at the Kingston junction.

Magee sat in quiet contemplation as Melissa turned at the junction next to Lewes prison, drove past the Neville Estate, out on the Offham Road and through pleasant green countryside to the neighbouring village of Cooksbridge.

As Melissa was parking outside the Rainbow Inn, she said, 'I don't suppose being so close to Nick Price's house has anything to do with your choice of venue?'

Magee feigned a look of hurt as he got out of the car. 'Am I that easy to read?'

'It's not that, sir. It's just your lack of subtlety.'

'Need I remind you that less than two hours ago we were looking at a knife which bore a striking resemblance to nine others, most of which ended up stuck into Nick Price's old friends?'

'So the reason for your visit today is, what, precisely?'

'I'll think of something over lunch.'

Melissa sighed. 'You're not going to harass him again are you?'

Magee grimaced. 'He deserves it.'

'No he does not. He's suffered enough, don't you think?'

'Not by half,' Magee muttered. 'Come on, we can't stand out here in the car park all day. Do you want a free lunch, or not?'

'I do, it's just that I think you should go easy on Nick. You've hassled him persistently this last year or so. Don't you think his family has had enough with police intrusion?'

Magee thought about it a while. 'If he'd been honest and upfront with me, I'd have called it a day long ago. As it is, he likes to bait me. You've seen that for yourself.'

The Fourth Cart III

'But we've nothing solid to talk to him about today. He'll accuse you of being on a fishing trip again. He's not obliged to incriminate himself.'

'I agree. Unfortunately, he is indeed not obliged to incriminate himself. Still, I can always hope. Lunch? It's really good in here, you know that. It's one of your favourite places isn't it?'

'You're trying to butter me up, aren't you? Trying to get me on your side before we go storming into Nick's.'

Magee held his hands up in a gesture of surrender. 'I was not trying to butter you up, Melissa. It was supposed to be a genuine treat. I'm in a good mood. Still, if you prefer,' he said, turning back to the car, 'we can head back to the staff canteen.'

'Oh, no you don't!' She laughed as she grabbed Magee's arm and steered him towards the entrance door. 'I don't get to come here that often, not on my wages. Let's agree to talk about something else. I haven't told you yet about the scuba diving we did off the boat.'

After a lunch of home-made game pie accompanied by a glass each of chilled Chablis, they returned to the car for the thirty second journey to the gates leading into Price's Folly. As they drove up the hundred and fifty yard long drive, Magee wondered for the thousandth time how he, the so-called good guy, had finished up living in a three bed semi-detached house on the Neville Estate whereas Nick Price, with his dubious past, had landed himself a fifty room Victorian mansion set within a fifteen acre estate.

As Melissa brought the car to a stop outside the glass panelled double doors at the entrance to the double winged, red brick manor house, she said, 'Now then, sir, you promise to be nice?'

Magee muttered, 'I'll do my best, if it will make you happy.'

'It will. Thank you.'

They were met at the front door by a maid who led them indoors, through the entrance hall, through the imposing galleried inner hall and into the lounge. Sitting at a desk was a young woman, a couple of weeks off her twentieth birthday, with long black hair, her skin the South East Asian dark brown of her mother. She looked up and said, 'Chief Inspector. I wasn't expecting a visit from you. Melissa, nice to see you again.'

Magee thought the girl had grown even more beautiful since he last saw her four months ago. 'Sorry, Nittaya, I was just passing. I thought I'd pop in to see how your father was doing.'

'He's not back from Bangkok yet.'

'Really? Is he still in hospital over there?'

'He was discharged a few days ago. He's staying at John's house at the moment. He'll be back in a week or two.'

'Is he still in pain?'

'He's on crutches. The muscles are healing slowly, but he's rather weak. The doctors dug seven bullets out of him. Recovery is going to take quite a while.'

Magee winced. 'Have the doctors said whether they expect a full recovery?'

Nittaya shrugged. 'When I visited him, they told me not to expect anything at all. However, as you know, Daddy's a fighter. He'll pull through. Nothing's going to stop him getting better.'

Magee wandered over to the bay window to admire the landscaped gardens and the views of the Downs in the distance. His mind started wandering, dredging up past conversations with Nick Price, sorting, analyzing and regurgitating subtle, off the cuff comments.

'Did you want to speak to Daddy?'

Magee turned his head back towards Nittaya and said, 'It will keep.'

'There's something you want, though?'

Magee took a few moments before answering, 'Did your father tell you how he got shot?'

Nittaya gave a knowing smile. 'In a battle to the death with Khun Sa and his army of crazed mercenaries. Like a Rambo film, that's how he put it. Him being the hero character, of course, taking on the bad-guys single-handedly.'

Magee chuckled. 'You don't believe him?'

Nittaya paused before responding. 'Well, he did manage to get shot seven times. Ten, if you include the bullets that grazed him. He must have been fighting someone. You were there, and Melissa too, so I've been told, what's your version?'

Magee reflected on the fact that if it hadn't been for Nick Price's selfless courage, albeit somewhat maniacal, he wouldn't be alive today. He still hadn't thanked the man sufficiently. 'Sounds about right to me.'

'Hmm,' Nittaya responded. 'Somehow, I don't believe you. I was hoping to get the truth from you about what Daddy actually did to get shot.'

'He was extremely brave, Nittaya. You should be proud of him.'

Nittaya chuckled. 'I am. It's just that I detect a hint of his normal over-exaggeration on the matter.'

'For once, he's probably told you the way it was.' Magee fell silent for a while as he collected his thoughts. 'Look, did he say much to you about why he was in Bangkok in the first place?'

'Only that he'd gone there to defend his family and business. Why?'

'Nothing. Just idle curiosity. On that subject though, have there been any further odd incidents?'

'Are you referring to the arson attacks on Daddy's properties?'

'Yes.'

'No. Now you come to mention it, there's been nothing since he went to Bangkok.'

'Good.' Magee continued his observation out of the bay window, in silence, for a full minute. Beyond the formal gardens were fields leading down to woods and a lake. Half a dozen horses grazed the fields. It was an idyllic picture of the trappings of a country house squire.

'Is there anything else I can help you with, Chief Inspector?'

Magee jerked involuntary at the noise. 'Sorry, Nittaya, I was away with the fairies. I'd better go. Sorry to have disturbed you.'

'I'll let him know you came. Any message for him?'

Magee took a moment to consider how odd the visit may look without a satisfactory reason. 'I need to catch up with him, that's all. Tell him I'm sorry I missed him. I'll phone in advance next time.'

Chapter Three

Nick Price stepped off the Thai Airways International airplane with a sense of relief at being back in England. With the aid of a pair of crutches, he hobbled along Heathrow's interminable passageways cursing at the pain of each step. Being trussed up like a turkey in a Bangkok hospital for three months was not how he expected his trip to have gone. He now appreciated just how stupid he'd been to believe he could get away with behaving like the leading character out of an action movie.

At forty-two years of age, Nick's body wasn't as fit as it used to be. He would be paying the price for his foolhardiness for months to come, years even. If he ever saw Brigadier Armstrong again, he vowed to wring the bloody man's neck. He still had the last words the Brigadier said to him resonating around his head; "You'll do it because you're Nick Price". He still couldn't work out what that was supposed to have meant. He was no hero, not by a long chalk.

All thoughts of anger dissipated on sighting a smiling face as he approached the airport's exit funnel. 'Nit, good to see you,' he said, throwing half an arm around his daughter.

Before another word could be said, flashes from a dozen cameras dazzled him. 'Jesus Christ,' he snapped at a group of photographers closing in on him like a mob. 'Did you have to do that?'

Within seconds, an array of microphones was thrust in his direction. A television news reporter grabbed Nick's upper arm and demanded, 'Can we have a comment please, Mr Price?'

Nick cringed at the sudden increase in pain in his arm. 'Yeah, that bloody hurt, you asshole! I've been wounded for fuck's sake! Can't you see the bloody crutches? Get the hell away from me.'

'Mr Price,' the reporter persisted, 'Can we have a comment from you on your two hundred and fifty thousand pound donation to the Conservative Party?'

'What the hell are you talking about?' Nick retorted. 'Get out of my way.' He tried to move forward, but got trapped by the unruly scrum of reporters.

'Mr Price, was the money to buy a peerage?'

'No comment!' Nick tried to raise a fist to throw a punch, but his crutch got caught in the melee. He was saved from a fall by his daughter.

'Get away from him,' Nittaya screamed. 'You'll knock him over.'

Nick shouted at two burly men a few yards away, 'Darren! Mark! Sort this bunch of losers out will you? Bring my wheelchair over.'

'Sure, Mr Price.'

The two minders roughly parted the sea of reporters, pushed several to the ground, settled Nick into a wheelchair and made off in the direction of the car parks.

With the muted sound of protests behind him, Nick muttered, 'God damn it. I wasn't expecting that as a reception. What the hell's going on, Nit? How do they know about my donation? What do they want to ask those kinds of questions for?'

'Cash for honours, Daddy. It's the latest political scandal to hit the headlines. Didn't you hear about it in Bangkok?'

'Can't say I did. I had more pressing things on my mind. Like these damn wounds.'

As they stopped by a bank of lifts, Nittaya bent down to kiss her father on the cheek. 'Sorry, Daddy. How are you, by the way?'

'Very well, thank you for asking.'

'And the masseuses in Bangkok?'

Nick returned a warm smile as his wheelchair was pushed forward into a lift carriage. 'Has someone been talking?'

'Paul mentioned on the telephone the other day that you'd been enjoying a few massages out there.'

Nick blushed. 'Well, they told me it would increase the rate of healing. For the damaged muscle, that is.'

'And improve the blood flow, as well, so I gather,' Nittaya said with a cheeky smile.

Nick's face reddened further. 'I think Paul may have been exaggerating.'

'Don't be so shy, Daddy. I was pleased to hear you were enjoying yourself. Paul said he'd never seen you so relaxed. You haven't had a holiday in years.'

A smile returned to Nick's face. A month relaxing in Bangkok after his hospitalization had indeed been exactly what the doctor had ordered. 'That's as maybe,' he responded, 'but what's with this cash for honours scandal? And how come they're hounding me?'

'Oh, it's just normal boring politics. Someone high up let slip recently that peerages are occasionally promised in exchange for donations. The police have been investigating the complaint.'

Nick was shocked. 'Complaint? What complaint? Who would want to complain about that arrangement?'

'Someone got his peerage nomination rejected. A wealthy doctor, I think.'

'And the idiot complained?'

'Apparently.'

'And he got the police involved?'

'No, that came after he whinged on television about his treatment.'

'I'm not with you, Nit.'

'Selling peerages is a crime, Daddy. You know that don't you?'

By the look on Nick's face, it was pretty clear that he did not. 'Bugger!' he responded.

As they drew up level to the car park ticket machine, Nittaya cast a chastising look at her father. 'Don't tell me you fell for it too. Honestly, Daddy, sometimes you deserve all you get.'

Nick did his best to look offended. 'What's that supposed to mean?'

'Those reporters back there. We've had them at the gates back home, asking where you were. The police have uncovered your name as a donor, it's been in all the newspapers and on the television.'

Nick shrugged. 'I've committed no crime. My donation was above board.'

'That's as maybe, Daddy. But don't tell me you didn't expect something in return.'

'Course I didn't,' Nick replied, although the expression on his face suggested otherwise. 'Now, let's get home. I've missed the comfort of my own bed.'

Chapter Four

Lewes, the county town of East Sussex, along with the rest of the South East, was experiencing a rare but glorious few days of warmth and sunshine. Not quite an Indian Summer, but close enough for Magee's mind to wander off his work as he recalled how, as a lad, after school on such balmy summer days he'd swim in the pool his father had created out of the base of an old mill in their garden.

It wasn't long before he found himself staring out of his office window in the Sussex Police Headquarters towards the hills to the west. It was his favourite route for a jog or a walk with his kids, up past the old Lewes racecourse and along to Black Cap. From there, he would be rewarded with a magnificent panoramic view of the Ouse Valley right down to the port of Newhaven. And between the racecourse and the Ouse Valley stood Juggs Hill, on top of which his childhood home sat in splendid isolation, seemingly staring back in contempt at the rest of the town.

He was startled out of his reverie by the sound of the door closing behind him. He turned around to see his boss, Superintendent Vaughan, in full dress, carrying a newspaper and a grim look set firmly on his face.

'Morning, sir.'

'Good morning, Magee.'

Magee could tell by his boss's face that all was not well with the man. 'Anything wrong, sir?'

Superintendent Vaughan slammed a newspaper down on Magee's desk. 'You've seen this, I take it?'

Magee cast a look at the front page headline Brighton entrepreneur in cash for honours scandal. Twice already he'd read the article about Nick Price; a man equally loved and reviled by the press.

Nick the family man, property developer, pillar of society and knight in shining armour famed for his very public charitable donations. Or Nick the former villain, once an aspiring gangland boss from London's East End. Good-boy, bad-boy, bad-boy-turned-good; take your pick. The jury was still out. He nodded and said, 'Yes, sir, I have.'

'Did you know Price was after a peerage?'

'I didn't. It doesn't surprise me though. A title would go well with his manor house. I'm sure he'd love the villagers over at Cooksbridge to doff their caps and say "Morning, m'lord" as he passed them by.'

Superintendent Vaughan crossed his arms. 'If it's true, he'll be in trouble. Buying a peerage is a crime.'

Magee snorted. 'Odd that, I'd always hoped to nail him for a less classy crime. Still, they got Al Capone for tax evasion, so it's par for the course, I suppose. Do you want me to look into it, sir?'

'No I don't,' Superintendent Vaughan said irritably. 'That'll be up to the Serious Fraud Office.'

'So?'

'So, Magee, what I do want is for you to explain to me why the author of this scurrilous article is not content with casting aspersions on Price's motives for a donation, but is also implying that his money may have come from "dubious sources". I assume the implication is drug money.'

Magee nodded. 'I guess so.'

'Specifically, from dealings with that monster Khun Sa?'

'That would be my guess, sir.'

'And where on earth would that information have come from? Did someone on your staff talk to the press?'

Magee's eyes bore maliciously into Superintendent Vaughan's. 'My staff are loyal, sir. And discrete.'

'But you don't deny this information may have originated from someone here?'

Magee took a moment to calm down. 'Not everyone in this building is on my staff, sir.'

'Damn it, Magee, they've as good as named you in this article. There's no truth to these allegations of a police cover-up, is there? That we knew of business dealings between Nick Price and Khun Sa and did nothing about it?'

'None at all, sir.'

'There's nothing you're hiding from me, I hope. No secrets about Nick Price?'

'No, sir,' Magee replied. 'Certainly not.'

'They must have a reason for publishing this.'

Magee shrugged. 'No doubt, sir.'

'What possible motive could they have?'

Magee grimaced. 'It's just a story to sell newspapers, sir.'

'But it must have originated from someone who has knowledge of your investigations into Nick Price. There must have been a leak. So, who would do such a thing?'

Magee had his suspicions. Inspector Jackson was the type who'd wheedle gossip out of staff and use it to his advantage. But to point an accusatory finger at a fellow officer, no matter how much he despised the man, would be unhelpful. 'I really have no idea, sir.'

'What would anyone gain from it?'

'Money, perhaps. Or simply enjoyment from the maliciousness of it.'

'Against Nick Price?'

Magee bit his lip. Against me, more likely, he thought. 'I was obliged to give full details to Brigadier Armstrong. The leak, if there is one, could have come from a variety of sources, not just from this building.'

Superintendent Vaughan rubbed the back of his neck. 'I don't care for these allegations, Magee. There's something very unpleasant behind them. I imagine this newspaper's lawyers insisted on this article being toned down. What worries me is that there's more to come out. We need to nip this in the bud before it gets out of control.'

'I agree, sir.'

'I just wish I could understand why anyone would leak this story.'

'Who knows how warped minds work, eh sir?'

'Well, we need to extract ourselves from this mess with dignity, Magee. I can't have anyone thinking we're responsible for a cover-up.'

'Of course not, sir.'

'And since Nick Price is your bête noir, I'll leave you to sort it out.'

Magee had been expecting such a demand. He nodded his head in resignation. 'I'll try my best, sir,

'Make sure you do,' Superintendent Vaughan snapped. 'I can't have our reputation damaged.'

Magee returned a false smile.

'It's not as though you've got anything better to do. Other than staring out of windows, that is.'

Magee's face turned a crimson colour. 'I do my best work when I'm thinking, sir. Looking up at the hills helps me relax, helps my mind get to the crux of problems. Anyway, I haven't a great deal on at the moment. For the last few months I've done little else but collate court papers and attend domestic disputes. You're not giving me cases that stretch my abilities.'

Superintendent Vaughan gave Magee a contemptuous look. 'You'll have to gain my trust first, Magee. Need I remind you that you were completely out of order whilst in Bangkok? And I still haven't received a satisfactory report on your time spent over there. No doubt you feel protected by sources higher than my rank, like your mysterious intelligence services friend, Brigadier Armstrong, whom I notice you casually dropped into conversation just now to remind me how more important you are than me.' He turned sharply to leave the room and slammed the door shut.

Magee swore profanely at Superintendent Vaughan's back.

Moments later, Magee's door opened and Detective Constable Deborah Collins poked her head in. 'Visitor for you, sir, downstairs in reception. Brigadier Armstrong.'

'Really? What a coincidence. Could you see him through security? Ask him to join me here?'

'Sure.

Chapter Five

Brigadier Armstrong was straight out of the old school. Late fifties, a greying moustache, catholic tastes. Yet Magee knew it would be a mistake to take the man for an old fool. His brain was sharper than any other Magee had come across in his professional life.

As Brigadier Armstrong was shown into his office, Magee gestured to a chair and said, 'Well, this is certainly a surprise, Brigadier. I didn't expect to see you again quite so soon. And I mean that in a nice way. Can I get you a coffee?'

'That's kind of you, Magee, but I've had three cups of tea in the last couple of hours with my old school chum out at Rodmell.'

Magee took a seat. 'I assume you refer to the Deputy Head of MI5?'

Brigadier Armstrong smiled. 'You've a good memory, Magee.'

'Detail is essential in my line of work.'

'Of course it is.'

'So, you're just passing I take it?' Magee asked with a grin on his face. 'Come to chew the fat?'

'There was something on my mind, I have to admit. Something you may be able to help me with. And I would, of course, relay my gratitude for any assistance you can give me.'

Mage snorted. 'I wouldn't bother passing on your gratitude to Superintendent Vaughan. He mentioned your name just minutes ago.'

Brigadier Armstrong's eyebrows rose. 'Not in a good way, I take it?'

'He thinks I'm in cahoots with you, holding back secrets about Nick Price.'

'Really? That's interesting. Is he psychic or just paranoid?'

Magee chuckled. 'I'll stop short of paranoid. Perceptive perhaps. He hasn't forgiven me for putting Melissa in danger in Bangkok. He thinks I'm holding out on him. He thinks I haven't told him the whole truth about what happened to us out there.'

Brigadier Armstrong frowned. 'And you're very wise not to. What with the political repercussions if the truth gets leaked.'

Magee reached into his briefcase and extracted a newspaper. He placed it on his desk and said, 'Talking of leaks, did you read this story about Nick Price?'

'Funny you should say that, Magee. That's actually why I'm here.'

'Really? I'm all ears.'

'Three months ago, you visited me in Whitehall to brief me on what happened to yourself and Melissa in Bangkok.'

'Indeed. I remember it well.'

'You told me that the serial murderer you'd been hunting was in all likelihood Jook, the brother-in-law of Nick Price. You also said that Jook was in all likelihood Khun Sa. Given the seriousness of what happened in Bangkok, we agreed that it was best to keep the whole matter quiet for reasons of national security and diplomatic relations with Thailand.'

'And I've kept my word on that. And because of it Superintendent Vaughan sees me as a failure for not being able to properly conclude a serial murder investigation case. I've closed the file, but the killer's identity was left open. So he's given me little else but trivial tasks since I returned from Bangkok. The most interesting case I've been involved with in the last few months is the identification of a mysterious mummy.'

Brigadier Armstrong cocked an eyebrow. 'In what way can a mother be mysterious?'

Magee cracked a thin smile. 'I meant as in a mummified human body. It turned up in a Brighton flat alongside a knife reminiscent of those used by my serial killer last year.'

The corner of Brigadier Armstrong's mouth curled. 'You certainly live a bizarre life, Magee.'

Magee ignored the sarcasm. 'And Superintendent Vaughan doesn't want Melissa to get involved with any more cases with me.'

Brigadier Armstrong puffed out his cheeks. 'I'm sorry to hear all this, Magee. But we did discuss the implications at the time. But to get back to my point, unfortunately the words "in all likelihood" are simply no longer acceptable.'

Magee blinked. 'Sorry, what's changed?'

'Nick Price.'

'I beg your pardon?'

'Let me make this clear to you, Magee. Nick Price has been a frequent and generous contributor to Conservative Party funds. The Prime Minister cannot entertain the idea that Mr Price is involved in any criminal activity whatsoever, especially drugs. Do you understand me?'

Magee was horrified. 'Oh, god, this is all about Nick Price?'

'Indeed it is.'

'But he's right at the heart of Khun Sa's very existence . . .'

Brigadier Armstrong raised a finger. 'No, don't say it. You have no firm evidence at all of Mr Price being involved with Khun Sa's drug empire.'

'I never said there was, sir.'

'The implication is there, Magee. As it is in the leak to the newspapers.'

Magee looked suitably offended. 'The leak did not come from me, sir.'

'I'm not suggesting it did.'

'So?'

'So, Magee. Three months ago, the Prime Minister wanted absolute proof that Nick Price had no link to the illegal activities of Khun Sa. I could not give him any such proof, or even assurances for that matter, and I didn't think you could either. So we went for silence instead.'

'You're talking about this cash for honours scandal, aren't you? This is why I was silenced? The Prime Minister is worried that Nick Price's money comes from drug dealings with Khun Sa?'

'I told you some time ago that politics is behind most issues in life, Magee.'

Magee thought for a moment. 'Is someone trying to discredit the Prime Minister? Using this gossip about Nick Price against him?'

Brigadier Armstrong inclined his head.

'Oh, Christ,' Magee muttered, rubbing his cheeks. 'I had no idea. I thought the information may have leaked to the newspaper from this office. You think it may have come from a political opponent of the Prime Minister?'

'More likely to have come from one of his own side, I fear. There are many who would like to see the PM go. Mr Price has donated substantial funds to the Party, and the PM would be sunk without the generous support of such individuals.'

'Matched by political sweeteners, no doubt. I assume Nick Price has had help getting his property development projects approved, in return?'

'I couldn't possibly comment on that,' Brigadier Armstrong said with a wry smile. 'What I do know is that the PM is stuck between a rock and a hard place. Nick Price's name has been put forward for a peerage on the basis of his charity work. The PM cannot allow the nomination to proceed if there is any chance that Nick Price received money from Khun Sa. The scandal could ruin the government. On the other hand, the PM cannot decline the nomination because that would have the effect of confirming the defamatory newspaper article.'

'Can't the Prime Minister just return the donation?'

'Life's not as simple as that, Magee. The PM would, of course, be obliged to return the money if it was tainted. However, the Party has a substantial overdraft. Returning two hundred and fifty thousand pounds is not a financially viable option.'

Magee rubbed his temples. 'I thought I had it bad.'

'Quite.'

'So, how are we going to sort this mess out?'

'There's only one solution, Magee. We need to prove Nick Price is innocent of any wrongdoing, especially of any involvement with Khun Sa's drug empire.'

'Prove him innocent?' Magee exploded. 'But I've spent years trying to prove him guilty!'

'Life can be bizarre, Magee.' The brigadier tapped the table with his fingertips while contemplating the issue. 'You know I can't close my files. Not until I can give the PM a satisfactory answer.'

'And in the meantime, I have to keep my silence and suffer the vindictiveness of Superintendent Vaughan?'

'I imagine so. Solve the PM's problem and you're a free man, Magee. I expect he'll even write you a commendation.'

'But where do I start?'

Brigadier Armstrong drummed his fingers on the edge of Magee's desk. 'Ten men, including Nick Price, became overnight millionaires in nineteen seventy-three. You have a photograph showing those ten men celebrating in a Bangkok bar around that same time, presumably celebrating their new found wealth. Jook took that photograph, and he is reputed to have died shortly afterwards. You are short of a provable motive for your serial killings. You are short of an identification of the killer. You are also short of an explanation as to how Jook may have actually survived the accident in which he was thought to have died. You also have no explanation of how Jook, if he did indeed survive, became Khun Sa, or why he would choose to do so. Join the dots, Magee.'

Magee's was flabbergasted. 'Is that all?'

Brigadier Armstrong chuckled as he checked his watch. 'I'd better be going. Thank you for your time, Magee. One last word before I go. Help me write "case well and truly closed" on this damned file. It's your only hope.'

'I'm well aware of it, sir.'

Brigadier Armstrong smiled warmly. 'Good man, Magee. Keep in contact.'

'Yes, sir.' As Magee watched the Brigadier depart his office he wondered how he'd ever managed to get involved with an intelligence officer in the first place and, more importantly, how on earth he was going to extricate himself from the man's devious grip. What the Brigadier had just asked for was impossible.

Chapter Six

Early one morning, two weeks after Brigadier Armstrong's visit, Magee was interrupted during his walk through his floor of the Sussex Police Headquarters building by the sight of a cartoon sketch pinned to the staff noticeboard. His eyes bulged in horror at the sight of a hand-drawn picture of a mummy bound from head to foot in cloth, stumbling around, with the words "I'm in the dark!' written in a speech bubble. Someone had scrawled Magee's name underneath the mummy.

For a few seconds Magee stared at the cartoon in disbelief, his ears burning, his face flushed. He ripped it off the notice board and turned to see if anyone was laughing at him. Inspector Jackson's handiwork, he concluded. 'Prat!' he muttered under his breath as he stormed off to his office. He was not amused.

As he reached his office he screwed up the offending paper, chucked it in the bin and sank into his chair. His mind turned to thoughts of sadistic revenge. He sat brooding for a few moments before a knock on the door brought him back to earth.

Melissa came into the room and closed the door. She pointed to the screwed up paper protruding from the waste bin and said, 'I saw that on the notice board earlier. And I saw your reaction to it just now. I know it was mean of them, but it's only a joke.'

'A joke? I don't think so. I can see that fool Jackson's hand behind this. He hasn't forgiven me for making him look such a prize dickhead for completely failing to spot a set-up at a crime scene last year.'

'Tit for tat, surely?'

'That's not the way I see it,' Magee snapped. 'If I wasn't being pressured from above, that lot out there would think differently, that's for sure.'

Melissa looked stunned. 'What? What do you mean, pressured from above?'

Magee averted his gaze.

'What's happened, sir?'

'I'm not supposed to talk about it.'

Melissa placed her hands on Magee's desk, leant forward and demanded, 'I'm not leaving here until you explain that comment.'

'Bangkok, that's what I mean. When I got back in May, I had a long talk with Brigadier Armstrong. He made me promise not to tell anyone what really happened over there.'

Melissa was shocked. 'Why?'

'Repercussions; national security, stuff like that. I had to promise on pain of death not to reveal what happened to Khun Sa and who I thought he was.'

'What, not even to Superintendent Vaughan?'

'Especially not to him.'

'But . . . you never told me that. You said you'd take responsibility for the incident, not that you'd hide it.'

Magee squirmed. 'Yes, well, now you know.'

'Bugger!' Melissa was incredulous. 'Is that why I'm with Inspector Jackson? Because my dear uncle doesn't know the truth about Bangkok?'

Magee squirmed more. 'Probably. He was angry that you were wounded. He thinks I was reckless, that I was wrong to put you in danger. He re-assigned you to Jackson to keep you out of my way, he thinks I'm irresponsible.'

'Shit!'

Magee winced. He rarely heard bad language from his sergeant. 'Sorry.'

'But my career will go nowhere with Jackson as my boss.'

'I guess your uncle wanted you out of harm's way.'

Melissa rubbed her temples. 'I don't believe this. I've been sidelined by my own uncle. I thought he was on my side.'

'I'm sure he thinks he's doing the best for you.'

'Well, sod that!' Melissa exploded. 'Can't you do something about it?'

'I'd love to. Any suggestions?'

Melissa fell silent. After a few seconds, she wiped away a tear from the corner of her eye. 'I want to be back with you as my boss, sir.'

Magee's face flushed.

'Seriously, sir. I enjoyed working with you. No matter how annoying you are.'

Magee's jaw dropped. 'Pardon?'

Melissa broke into a smile. 'Please, sir. Get me out of Jackson's section.'

'There's nothing I'd like better, Melissa. I just don't know how, or where to even start.'

'You could start with giving Brigadier Armstrong an earful, that's where. He has no right to expect us to be treated this way. I can't continue under Jackson. And I don't want a transfer to another station. My life is here in Lewes, sir,' Melissa choked. 'I'd prefer to stack shelves at a supermarket.'

'Really? You'd resign your commission?'

'Yes, really, sir, I really will resign if I have to continue much longer with Jackson. He's so stupid. I can't learn anything from him. Working for him will finish any career prospects I have. '

Before Magee could respond, the door opened and DC Collins entered carrying a large pile of documents. She caught Melissa's eye, then Magee's. 'I'm saying nothing,' she said, dumping the pile on Magee's desk and leaving the room with a smile on her face.

'I'd better go,' Melissa said at length. 'I think I need a word with Debs before she starts any gossip. Can't have that, you being a married man. Jenny would never talk to me again.' With that, she hurriedly left Magee's office.

Magee turned his attention to the files DC Collins had brought in and dumped on his desk. They were marked as being sent over from Brighton by DCI Ryan. Trying to forget the image of the cartoon, he picked up the top file, settled back comfortably in his chair and began to read.

It was a full hour before he finished the autopsy and forensic reports, after which he looked down at a summary he'd made of key points:

The woman's age was put at between eighteen and thirty.

Clothing and shoes suggested the body was dressed in materials manufactured in the Far East in the early nineteen seventies.

Seeds and pollens extracted from the body's clothes are from Tibet.

CT scan revealed that the body's upper torso contains fifteen bullets.

Cause of death would have been the complete collapse of internal organs after being shot.

Cause of mummification was dehydration combined with freezing temperatures.

Radiocarbon dating leads to best guess of time of death being nineteen seventy five, plus or minus five years.

So, she had been shot dead. He had thought she might have been stabbed. Either way, this was now a murder case and, even though it technically wasn't his case, it intrigued him. Why had a knife identified with a serial killer been found near the body? He crossed to a filing cabinet in the corner of the room and, from the top drawer, extracted a hefty file and returned to his chair.

Clipped to the inside jacket cover of the file was a photograph that had played a central part of his serial killer investigation. He took it out, leant back and stared at the image of Nick Price and a handful of his old friends celebrating in a Bangkok bar in nineteen seventy-three.

Case closed. Yet here he was looking at the photograph again.

And the subject of Tibet had surfaced. It hadn't been the first time either with this old case. He browsed through the file looking for the name of an old lady who may be able to throw more light on the subject.

Chapter Seven

Within the hour, Magee drove up the quaint, narrow road named The Street, in Kingston, a village just outside Lewes, pulled his car into the driveway of Cherry Tree Cottage, walked up the path and rang the doorbell hoping his unannounced visit was not to be wasted.

As the cottage's front door opened, an old lady cried with excitement, 'Good Heavens! It's . . . now, don't tell me . . . it's Chief Inspector Magee isn't it?'

'Spot on, Mrs Gibson.'

'Well, well, fancy seeing you again, Chief Inspector. What can I do for you?'

'I'm afraid I need to talk to you again about your son, Keith.'

Mrs Gibson nodded her consent. 'Well don't just stand there, it's chilly out here. Do come inside. You look as though you're in need of a cup of tea.'

Magee knew this game well. As with many an old person living alone, the opportunity of a cup of tea with company was not one to let go without a fight. He allowed himself to be drawn in, submitting to the knowledge that it would probably take a couple of hours to leave the old lady's house.

'How have you been keeping, Mrs Gibson?'

'Very well indeed, thank you for asking,' Mrs Gibson replied as she headed for the kitchen. 'And yourself?'

'I took your advice, I've been trying to spend more time with the kids.'

'I'm so glad to hear that, Chief Inspector. You just never know what's going to happen to them. I don't mean that in the sense of losing them, like with Keith. I mean in the sense of them going off to lead their own lives.'

'University, a career in London, that sort of thing?'

'Exactly. They won't be around your ankles forever.' The old lady fussed around for a minute, getting out her best bone china, wiping the cups, putting sugar in a bowl. 'Would you like a chocolate biscuit?'

'I'd love one, Mrs Gibson.'

'Really? That surprises me, Chief Inspector. You're what, in your early forties? Most men your age are either running to fat or on a doctor's diet. You don't seem to fit into either category. How so?'

'I try to keep fit, Mrs Gibson. I love jogging over the hills; up around the old racecourse is my favourite route.'

'Indeed? It's a beautiful view from up there, isn't it? I wish Keith had been more active in that way. I think exercise is healthy for both the brain and the soul. It could have been a diversion for him, kept him off drugs.'

Magee stepped forward to take the tray of tea off the kitchen worktop. 'I understand what you're saying, Mrs Gibson, but don't let it prey on your mind. What's happened can never be changed.'

'I know that, Chief Inspector,' Mrs Gibson said as she walked into the lounge. 'But I can't help dwelling on it occasionally. It's a grieving mother's prerogative. Now then, sit down and let's talk.'

'Thank you.'

'First of all, I heard nothing more of those dreadful murders last year. Was everything resolved? I don't remember hearing anything more about it on the news.'

'You're quite right, Mrs Gibson. The case was concluded, over in Bangkok in May actually. We were able to keep it out of the newspapers. Fortunately, so far, there have been no repercussions in this country.'

Mrs Gibson let out a sigh of relief. 'I'm so glad to hear that. It would have been the death of me if Keith's name had appeared in the newspapers in a less than desirable light.'

Magee nodded. 'I think we should be able to keep it that way.'

'But?'

Magee frowned. 'Excuse me?'

'You can't fool me, Chief Inspector. You're here to dig into Keith's past again, aren't you?'

Magee smiled warmly. 'I never could get anything past you, could I, Mrs Gibson?'

Mrs Gibson returned the smile. 'I may be old, Chief Inspector, but I'm not stupid. Now then, how may I assist you this time?'

Magee took a sip of tea and settled back in the armchair. 'The murder case I was working on last year has been concluded, as I just mentioned, in the sense that I am no longer looking for the murderer. However, I am left with an anomaly. A quite serious anomaly at that, and I need to get it resolved before I can properly close the file. There are potential repercussions if I can't close that file, Mrs Gibson, some involving national security, others involving, well, Keith's name, for instance.'

'National security?' Mrs Gibson said with a startled look on her face. 'Good heavens, that sounds like something out of a spy novel.'

Magee nodded his agreement. 'I don't mean to frighten you, Mrs Gibson, but a certain government intelligence officer is refusing to allow my case file to be closed until I can give him a satisfactory answer to this anomaly.'

Mrs Gibson stirred her tea an unnecessary long time before posing a question. 'This national security issue, does it involve the Home Secretary? Not the current one, I mean the last one, Geoffrey Rees Smith?'

Magee bit his lip. He had to tread carefully. 'What makes you think that, Mrs Gibson?'

'I told you last time, Chief Inspector, I was following that spate of murders very closely. Especially after you visited me last year.'

Magee shook his head in wonder. 'Really, Mrs Gibson, you could out-smart Miss Marple. I do hope you haven't said anything to anyone else.'

'Of course not. I knew there was something queer about what happened to that dreadful man Rees Smith, but who would have believed an old woman like me?'

'I trust you don't want details?'

'Certainly not, Chief Inspector. That would be vulgar. So then, how can I help you this time?'

'The subject of Tibet has cropped up in a current investigation. It's critical for me to get an understanding of what a certain person was doing in Tibet.'

'You think Keith might have known this person?'

'It's possible, yes. It's certainly what I'm hoping for.'

'What is that person's name?'

'I have no idea.'

'Oh? But . . . now you've confused me.'

'I'm sorry, Mrs Gibson. It wasn't intentional. I need to identify this person, a young woman as it happens. I know she was in Tibet. I know that Keith was in Tibet. I have an inkling that their paths may have crossed. If so, Keith might have made a note of it. I was hoping to read through his old papers, see if I could spot her.'

'Good heavens, Chief Inspector. You sound as though you're clutching at straws.'

'I am indeed, Mrs Gibson.'

'Well, you're welcome to look. I've still got that old box full of Keith's papers.'

Magee smiled. 'That's exactly what I was hoping you would say.'

Five minutes later, Magee looked down at several stacks of papers spread out over Mrs Gibson's kitchen table. He picked up a manuscript. 'This is what I was after. The Fourth Cart. Last time I was here, I asked if I could borrow it. By the time I came to leave I was so overwhelmed at finding that photograph that it slipped my mind.'

'Keith's book? Does it interest you, then?'

'It does today, Mrs Gibson. Very much so. My Tibetan woman may well be in it. If I may, I'd like to take it back to the office and read it there.'

'Of course, Chief Inspector. May I would remind you, though, of what I said last year. The last time I saw Keith alive, he was in a highly agitated state. He'd been typing that day, presumably on this book. It's therefore likely to contain something that affected him very deeply. I have never wanted to know what it was. I would like you to keep it that way, it would be far too distressing for me.'

'I understand.'

The Fourth Cart
By Keith Gibson

i. Oxford, January 1951

The winter scenery was straight out of a Gothic fairy tale. Glancing out from the window of my university digs, I sat entranced at the magical picture of snow and ice, glistening in the January sun, packed several inches deep yet precariously hanging on to the multitude of spires that was Oxford. I looked downwards at the papers on my desk, appalled at what had taken me all morning to write.

Tibet, the legendary Shangri-La, the Land of the Snow Leopards. Known by many names, its lands and mountain passes are known to but a handful of explorers. Isolated and cruelly cut off from the rest of the world by nature and man, Tibet lies surrounded by the impenetrable Himalayas on one side and exposed to the vast sprawling expansionist empire of China on the other. The country has lain vulnerable, defenceless and forever at the mercy of marauding Asians from the bloodthirsty Genghis Khan to the idealistic Mao Tse-tung.

I was studying Oriental studies at Corpus Christi College and it was the start of an essay on the subject of foreign influences on Tibet. It was also the start of one of my many day-dreams about the country, for I have never quite been able to get Tibet out of my system. It was my very own private fantasy world, and it has been so for as long as I can remember. I can still vividly recall sitting on my grandfather's knee listening in awe to heroic tales of the old man as a corporal in the British Army marching from India, over the Himalayas, through to Lhasa, the Tibetan capital city, arriving awestruck at the sheer magnificence of the Potala Palace.

It was his connection that had got me a visa. I received the priceless document from the monk Changkhyimpa, one of the four emissaries that had been hand chosen by the boy-king Dalai Lama to go on a world tour to promote Tibet's independence. I had been one of the small handful of people invited to attend a formal party to meet the delegation for lunch one day during their visit to London. I'm still not quite sure how I got away with it. I remember well the pompous words I'd written in a letter to the Foreign Office, ". . . the grandson of an old soldier who served her Britannic Majesty's army during Younghusband's campaign of 1904 would be privileged to meet . . ."

ii. Shekar Monastery

I had fulfilled my ambition. Despite my tendency to daydream, I had sailed through university, managing to obtain a first class degree. After that, there was only one course of action for me to follow. I needed the highest academic qualification possible if I were to achieve my ultimate aim of becoming the foremost knowledgeable professor of Tibetan studies in Great Britain. I needed a PhD. With my doctoral thesis sketched out in my mind, all that remained was to get on with it.

So, in September nineteen fifty-four, I paid a tearful farewell to my parents and took a cheap passage to India on a P&O ship. On arrival, I journeyed by train to Darjeeling at considerable leisure, for I enjoyed many a stop-off. From there it was a simple matter of slipping over the border dressed as best as I could as a native Indian. Mind you, it may have helped that I was buried underneath half a ton of silk at the bottom a of a trader's cart.

I found my way to Shekar monastery, not far from the city of Shigatse. It was rather out of the way, but it had been recommended to me by Changkhyimpa, the revered monk. It was a good choice; I found the location to my suiting. The monastery was quiet enough to study without being disturbed and the libraries were full of remarkably detailed ancient scriptures unknown to Western academia.

I had originally planned to stay three years at the monastery, but life was to take a different course. Within six months of my arrival, I was struck with the most unexpected good news. The Dalai Lama had heard of my studies and wanted to meet me in person.

iii. The Potala Palace

I had read about the Potala Palace, and its dominance over Lhasa, but nothing prepared me for the spectacular vision I was to see as we neared the city. As I approached on horseback, I couldn't help feeling awed by the architecture and extraordinary feat of engineering it must have taken to construct the palace in medieval times. It seemed so bizarre to have what could be regarded as one of the most magnificent buildings in the world nestling amongst native houses constructed of little more than mud and stones.

I was led straight to the Potala Palace, yet I wanted to ride slowly to absorb the sights, smells and sounds of the streets, for this was the Forbidden City where only a few dozen westerners had ever set foot. My grandfather must have trod these very streets. I wanted to dismount and savour the moment, to ask the local elders if they recalled Colonel Younghusband and his party. Maybe someone even remembered my grandfather, it was not impossible for it had only been fifty years ago.

I had no idea what to expect inside the palace, and was more than surprised to be led up endless ladders and steps, past dark and dingy rooms and passageways, until I reached the top floor. There, pausing outside the Dalai Lama's chambers, I felt extremely lightheaded, my mind seemingly detached from my body. It was a very spiritual moment.

The Dalai Lama granted me the honour of being allowed to stay and study at the palace. I was given quarters in the Tsedrungs school in the east wing and, over the years that followed, I become an occasional tutor to the Dalai Lama himself.

Life for me seemed perfect until the morning of seventeenth March nineteen fifty-nine. The day started the same as any other for me, with chores and prayers. Yet it changed rapidly for it was that ominous day when the Dalai Lama had been invited by the Chinese to a theatrical concert outside the palace. It was considered a sham, a ruse to remove His Holiness from safety. Hundreds of thousands of ordinary city folk packed the streets that day to protest against Chinese aggression.

After much discussion, the Dalai Lama decided to flee the country. The plan was that he would travel light; others would follow behind with the palace treasures. I was one of those chosen to help the evacuation of the treasures.

iv. The fall of the palace

The date of the seventeenth March nineteen fifty-nine will never be forgotten by Tibet. It was the country's blackest day. It was the day Tibetans lost the battle to remain an independent nation. In scenes of utter chaos, armed with little more than farming and household implements, Tibetans pitted themselves against Chinese cannon and gun. From the top of the Potala Palace, I stared transfixed at the events unfolding before my eyes. This was history in the making. I hoped never to see such sights again.

Inside the palace, the scene was of utter chaos as hundreds of saffron robed monks ran frenzied, plundering chapels and crypts that had probably not been disturbed for centuries. We were all occupied with just one single, loathsome thought, to remove anything valuable.

We did this because, in his final address to courtiers, the Dalai Lama had issued an order. All the ancient relics amassed since the monastic dynasty had been founded in fifteen forty-three, were to be removed. It broke my heart to see monks stuffing priceless treasures into linen sacks like burglars on a looting spree. They were weeping, wailing, begging for divine forgiveness, yet we knew there was no alternative but to obey the order. Nothing of value was to be left for the despised godless Chinese.

I watched the pillaging in despair. Yet there was no alternative. Irreplaceable treasures were snatched from altars, ripped from covings, wrenched from mountings. Cupboards were smashed open in the hope of unearthing forgotten treasures. Cabinets were turned over in the rush to disgorge their contents. Walls were hacked with axes where secret panels were believed to lay hidden. Sacred chapels and holy shrines were desecrated, wrecked in the obscene search. But time was of the essence, we gave scant regard to the recklessness of it all. The Potala Palace was plundered by its own custodians. And I aided them. I felt nothing but shame. I felt like a thief.

I was acutely aware that time was running out for us, yet the monks' act of vandalism seemed to last forever. By late afternoon we were growing weary with the strain of destruction, but the Potala Palace was, finally, completely and devastatingly ransacked. All that was left was emptiness. The majesty of the Potala Palace had gone. Its very soul had been gutted.

Our final hurdle was to flee unseen. In a courtyard, I watched as a group of monks struggled to hitch four horses to each of four large wooden carts. Other horses were saddled for the bodyguards. Some thirty-two horses reared and kicked, spooked by the din of protesters and cannon fire outside the palace walls. The horses were not trained well. Some had not been ridden for years. Our task seemed hopeless.

Outside the palace walls stood two hundred thousand Tibetans, chanting, wailing, screaming in despair. The unending roar of human voices confused and frightened us all, not just the horses. No matter how much we tried to calm them, they would not settle. I watched these events unfolding with ever increasing restlessness. I had dressed in the attire of a local peasant, with the hope of blending in once outside. I paced anxiously, infuriated at being unable to control events around me, my brain impaired from thinking clearly because of the ever rising crescendo of noise outside the gates through which I knew I soon had to pass.

The roar of the peasants reached deafening levels. Although I could not see, I knew instinctively what they were doing; goading and provoking the despised Chinese soldiers to advance against their shield of human souls. Their bravery was truly astonishing. The peasants seemed to have no fear of death. They would have happily faced the menacing rifles and die if Fate demanded such action, for they were protecting their God-King. Each inch the soldiers advanced, the more resolute the peasants became, for the soldiers were insulting the country's most holy of buildings by their mere presence.

I heard, rather than saw, the attack come. It seemed almost welcomed by the peasants, for it gave them the sudden boost of adrenalin so needed to withstand their ordeal. Soldiers fired indiscriminately at the unarmed crowds and the peasants fell by the dozen, bloodied and mangled in the ensuing stampede. The peasants paid heavily for their rebellion against the invading soldiers, yet they stood firm that evening despite the ever present threat of death. The life of their God-King was at stake, they would protect him until there was no one left standing, they would sacrifice themselves, dying in the belief that they had saved their spiritual leader from the clutches of Communism.

One by one, the hundred or so monks that had been charged with the gathering of treasures emerged from the depths of the plundered palace and deposited their linen sacks in a huge pile in the forecourt. Each sack bulged and lay heavy on the ground with the weight of gold, silver and jewels. Then, with even more reckless abandon, the sacks were thrown up into the carts and haphazardly bundled into large wooden crates. I recall each crate being well over eight foot long, two feet wide and the same in depth, about eight crates to each cart. Above the deafening roar of close cannon fire, I shouted at the monks to open the gates. We were ready. It was time to go. I was to leave first. The three other carts would depart immediately behind me.

I was not prepared for what I witnessed next. No man could be. I can only describe it as hell on earth. The scene before me left an imprint in my mind I shall never forget. As the gates opened, I was standing up on the cart and so had a bird's eye view of the carnage. One face that epitomized the atrocities wrought on the peasants belonged to that of a man I would later come to know as Lieutenant Tchen. He was pure evil; he was responsible for the deaths of hundreds of monks that day.

v. Buried Deep

The sun burst over the brown hills to the East sending shimmering fingers of dawn light probing the darkness of the valleys. I sat crouched against the laden crates, reins in hand, swaying with the rhythm of the cart and watching the sun gradually rising higher to expose the parched and barren deserts of ochre sand and rock. The night had been freezing again and it had sapped my strength to an all-time low, but not my resolve. We had been traveling for three days, pushing the horses against their will, resting them one hour in every three. I was hungry, tired, thirsty and angry that we had left the palace at such a late stage in the Chinese takeover. Why hadn't we fled the previous week, in comfort, with provisions and with hope?

With nothing else to do but worry, I surveyed the countryside that passed us by. It was bleak, as bleak as can be imagined. Except that the landscape possessed a myriad of softly brilliant colours that warmed my heart. Deep red brown shadows were cast under the cloudless blue sky and, in the thin air, the sun's rays burned my exposed skin. I had rarely been outside for such long periods of time and I suffered terribly for it. Only the occasional patch of shadow yielded shelter and a welcome frosty chill.

Yet I had always loved this countryside, for all its coarseness. Usually, that was. On this particular trip, in my moment of crises, I was cursing it. I doubted the sanity of any man living in this hell-hole. I even doubted the existence of man inhabiting this place at times. The environment resembled the surface of a distant planet on occasions, and appeared equally hostile to man. If it wasn't for the presence of small cairns and prayer flags dotted around the high passes, I could easily have assumed that no humans lived in the arid hills above the valley floors.

Our trek was long, hazardous and far too slow. Four of the Dalai Lama's most trusted men, two courtiers and two bodyguards, rode alongside the cart. They tried to inspire me with confidence, but from the very outset I had felt defeated. It was an impossible task. There had been no sight of the other three carts since leaving Lhasa. Maybe they had been stopped by the Chinese already, or maybe they were just being slow. It was maddening not to know. But what we did know was that if the Chinese followed in the same tracks, it couldn't possibly be long before we were caught. Yet we had to try. The country's only hope may well depend upon the success of our mission. What would the God-King of Tibet be without his treasures?

Without money, I knew that the Dalai Lama would fare no better than the dozens of ex-kings of Europe who lived in exile around the Mediterranean without money and without hope. The Dalai Lama would be a mere symbol of a previous power. He would no longer be wanted. He would have no country to rule and no place in the redefined arena of world politics. Each additional mile that we travelled I sunk further into depression. The weight of the country's burdens rested firmly on my shoulders. It drove me to despair.

We must have looked like a group of renegade bandits. Our clothes were covered by the all-pervading yellow dust that billowed up from the dry dirt roads and our faces were masked by tatty, dirty silk scarves. Yet we were received as heroes by the peasants we encountered. Word had been left behind by the Dalai Lama's small group as they fled several days in front of us: help them, nourish them, protect them, give them chang and tsampa, lay out hay for their horses and, most importantly, give them news of the Chinese Army.

News of the army came to us at the worst possible time. We had travelled two hundred miles since leaving Lhasa, but still had hundreds of miles to go to the border on the Thongla Pass and the safety of Nepal and India. Fate had caught up with us. We stared upwards as a lone shepherd rushed down the hillside frantically waving his arms, shouting for us to stop.

'Soldiers! Soldiers!' the shepherd shouted frantically whilst trying to catch his breath.

We brought the cart to a halt and squinted backwards. We could see nothing but our own trail of dust. We waited until the shepherd approached the cart. 'What have you seen?'

'I see a cloud of dust. From the top of the hill I see army trucks. Dozens of them. Maybe three hours behind.'

My heart sank. The soldiers must be searching for the Dalai Lama, or us, or both. Theirs was an easy task; there were not that many passes we could have taken. Our horses were too tired to make a mad dash anywhere. There was no chance of success now. We had failed. I had failed in my mission. We would now have to abandon our journey and concentrate on the agreed fall-back plan. We would ditch the treasures safely and return later when the Chinese had given up their search.

'Where are we?' I asked, tentatively.

'Shigatse is two hours away.'

Shigatse? That was familiar territory. I'd been there once, years ago. It was a busy city, the second largest in the country. Too busy though, many Chinese lived there, along with many locals with pro-Chinese attitudes. Secrets could not be kept in that city. We needed a small town, or village, with a close-knit society of peasants. It came to me in a flash; Shekar. Of course. I'd spent several months at the monastery at Shekar over five years ago. A few peasant shacks, just a handful of families. High above the town was the castle, Shekar Dzong, the perfect hiding place.

'How do we get to Shekar from here?' I asked the shepherd.

'There's a track on the right, about half an hour away. That will lead you to Shekar.'

We bade farewell to the shepherd and led the cart off. Presently, our dust covered party found the path, steered off, then backtracked on foot to cover up the cart's wheel marks. We prayed that the advancing army would continue straight ahead for Shigatse, assuming that our aim was to head for the border.

Our ruse appeared to have worked. The army did not catch us up. It was little to be jubilant about, for, after all, we had failed in our mission. We could only imagine the fate of the other three carts: their treasures would have been returned to Lhasa.

A few days later, one early morning, we found ourselves casually riding through a cluster of old Tibetan houses heading for Shekar Chode, a Geluk monastery located at the back of the town. I remembered it well. I had found peace and tranquillity here once; I hoped to find it again. We halted our cart in the middle of the monastery's courtyard. I jumped off, smiling, to greet the inquisitive monks who were gathering around us. An elderly monk approached our cart and squinted at me.

'Keith? Is that you?'

'Yes, father, it is me. It is good to see you again,' I replied warmly, re-acquainting myself with the monastery's head monk.

The head monk surveyed the crates, and then turned his attention to the two bodyguards and the two courtiers accompanying the cart. He nodded his head as if in understanding.

'We heard news from Shigatse that the Chinese shelled Lhasa, and that His Holiness has fled to India. We also heard that four special envoys were traveling in his wake. I assume that you are one of those envoys, Keith, and that something has gone wrong?'

I smiled and replied, 'You are as perceptive as ever, Father.' I could well remember that nothing got past this old man's eyes.

'Come inside, you all look exhausted. Share some chang with us. I'm sure you have lots to speak. No doubt you have come here with a purpose. We would be honoured to aid a special envoy from Lhasa.'

'Thank you, Father. You are most kind, as always.' I would have preferred to skip tea and get straight on with our task, but I had learned the hard way that nothing happened quickly in Tibet. It would be considered quite rude to act in a frenetic manner. I had to bite my lip, calm down, and act casually as though I was about to have Sunday afternoon tea with my old aunts. It was maddening, I felt like panicking. I was petrified that Chinese soldiers would materialize any second from behind the stone walls.

We unshackled our horses from their burden and led them into the monastery compound for food, water and a well-earned rest. The five of us, as honoured guests, then joined a small party of around twenty of the more revered monks to partake of refreshment. The need to observe social etiquette seemed absurd in the circumstances.

We sat around for ages, drinking the rancid butter tea that some five years ago had taken my taste buds months to adapt to, and eating our fill of oatmeal cakes. It was half an hour before the subject of the Dalai Lama's decision to flee the country even surfaced. It was another half-hour before we were quizzed on our perilous mission. At last though, I managed to explain that we had a most important task to carry out on behalf of the Dalai Lama. With extreme difficultly, for by this stage I thought I was going to gabble incoherently, I managed to explain that we must complete the task urgently in case the Chinese Army caught us.

'Father,' I finally said, with emotion, 'I don't like to burden you, but we are in desperate need of assistance. The Dalai Lama's task is too onerous for me and my four colleagues alone.'

'My dear Keith. You are trembling. What ails you? Of course we'll help. What do you want us to do?'

'The eight crates in our cart. They contain religious artifacts and relics removed from the Potala Palace. The Dalai Lama has fled, to take his fight for freedom from the Chinese to another country, but he could not take these relics with him since they are too heavy. We hoped to flee the country as well, but the Chinese nearly caught up with us before we even got to Shigatse. We must now hide the crates from the Chinese. We must not let the Chinese find them.'

'Where do you suggest they are hidden? Somewhere in the monastery, perhaps?'

'No, Father. I believe the Chinese will come here, in time, to search. I was thinking up there.' I pointed upwards in the direction I knew to be the top of the mountain. 'In the castle. There must be dozens of places where these crates can lie undisturbed.'

The head monk snorted with laughter. 'That is indeed true, Keith. The crates can rest there for centuries without being found. The castle foundations are riddled with tunnels. Let us begin this task now. As you say, there is no time to lose.'

The cart was unloaded of the eight heavy crates and then pushed manually by a handful of monks to the back of the courtyard. Rubbish and dirt was thrown in the back to make it look as though it had been unused for a long time.

Sixteen yaks, along with sixteen of the strongest young monks, were assigned to carry the crates up the mountainside path. Unwisely, we took little in the way of provisions, each of us carrying just a knapsack containing little more than a water flask and a handful of dried oatmeal cake. The five hour long trek to the peak was more arduous than any of us expected. Yaks move slowly; even on the flat they travel at little more than two miles per hour. With one crate strung between two yaks, plus two monks to steady their burden, the going was excruciatingly slow. The head monk insisted on leading the way, for he knew the castle's secrets best. Our own party of five walked alongside him. Trailing behind us in a bedraggled, snake-like procession staggered the sixteen young monks each sweating profusely with their exertion and lack of oxygen.

With immense relief, we made it to the eerie old castle by late afternoon. It was deserted, as had been the case for as long as anyone could remember. The yaks were tethered outside and we rested a few minutes before unburdening their loads. As we entered the castle, kerosene lamps were lit and the crates were hauled down into the basement, deep into the foundations where a maze of tunnels existed, cut into the bare rock by unknown workers, and for unknown reasons, centuries ago.

We searched for twenty minutes before finding the ideal hiding place. A recess in a tunnel wall gave access to a small room with a hole carved out of the floor, about ten feet square by eight feet deep, with holes on the edge where once had lain a cover. A shiver went down my spine. The room had obviously been a dungeon in the past, though long since abandoned. Nevertheless, the atmosphere still seemed to purvey a sense of sadness, of centuries of human pain.

The hole was just what we were looking for. We lowered the crates into the pit, and scattered loose rocks and debris over them. Within half an hour the crates had been completely hidden, no one would ever suspect there was anything other than rock buried here. The monks walked back, upwards the way we had come. I remained a few seconds, looking down, satisfied, at our work before turning to join them. All of a sudden, hell broke loose. The very roof above us collapsed, followed by the rumble of an explosion in the distance. I was thrown to the ground, narrowly avoiding a chunk of falling rock that could have done me serious injury.

As the debris settled, I became aware of more explosions and the tunnel walls seemed to shake. It took me several seconds to realize that I was hearing cannon fire. The castle was under siege, it was being shelled. It seemed absurd. It was deserted and disused. It had long ceased to be a strategically important building. So why bombard it now? It was a senseless act. Unless we had been spotted climbing, that is, or unless the Chinese were acting out of maliciousness.

I lay still, in a foetal position, transfixed, for what seemed like hours before the shelling stopped. It was the most frightening experience of my life. I thought I'd be buried alive, trapped for days, alone, starving and slowly dying of thirst. My mind pleaded for a quick death. It did not come.

Eventually, when there had been no noise for a long gap, I wiped the dust from my mouth and called out to the monks. There came no reply. I relit a kerosene lamp and held it up. Ahead of me lay tons of rubble. It was neck high, impenetrable. I heard no screams, no pleas for assistance. I knew their fate. There was nothing I could have done for the monks. I wept for them, wept for myself, it was my fault they were dead.

I stayed in the tunnel all night. It seemed the wisest thing to do, for I didn't know where the Chinese soldiers were. Maybe they were right outside. Perhaps they had followed us up the mountain. Maybe they had seen us from a distance with binoculars. If I moved now, perhaps I'd walk straight into them. The imponderables were depressing. Anyway, by now it must have been dark outside so it was safer to stay put. It was then that I regretted my decision to carry so few provisions. My meagre rations were scant comfort. I ate what food I carried, doused the kerosene lamp and tried to find a comfortable position in which to sleep.

I had a restless night. My mind whirled with the potential horrors of the situation I found myself in. During the night I could hear further falls of rock. Should I try to get out quickly in case the remainder of the tunnel collapsed, or should I wait till dawn in the hope that I could see daylight through a life-saving fissure? One thing was certain, there was no way back to the castle. I would be forced to penetrate deeper into the tunnel.

I eventually determined it must be early morning. Not because of any light, but simply by the fact that my body appeared not to be tired. I used one of the precious few matches left to relight the kerosene lamp and took slow, careful, heel-to-toe steps in the only direction available to me. I shuffled along, wary that my feet could ever so easily slip down a bottomless pit. Alone, it was a frightening experience. I'm no hero in such circumstances; I prefer to follow, not to lead.

I counted off each step aloud. After four hundred I could smell fresh air, after five hundred I could see daylight. After six hundred and seventy-five shuffled steps, my eyes welled up with tears; I stood at the tunnel's exit, staring at the most breath-taking mountain scenery imaginable. Close to the summit, standing on a ledge wide enough for three men to walk abreast, I looked across the steep sided valley to a small waterfall cascading halfway down an ice-covered mountain. The sky was blue, the sun shining; my body warmed at the realization that I would live.

I had the presence of mind to realize that, hopefully, one day in the future I would be back and would need to find this tunnel entrance again. The scene in front, of the beauty of the waterfall and mountain top, though awe-inspiring, could not be relied upon for bearings. There were simply too many similar sights in the neighbourhood, let alone in the country. I took time to relax, and to familiarize myself with my closer surroundings. If, or rather when, I returned, I would somehow have to remember exactly which rock fissure was the tunnel entrance, for there were other similar ones nearby. The entrance was narrow, no more than four feet wide and for all the world looked just like a natural crevice between the rock face. There was nothing to distinguish it from any of the others.

A childhood experience sprang to mind. The first time I had climbed a tree, in my parents' garden, at age five, I had carved my initials in the trunk, proclaiming it to be mine. It was what an adventurer would do; something my grandfather had said he was proud of when I related it to him later. I grinned at the boyish memory, and extracted a sheathed knife from my knapsack. At eye level, on the right of the tunnel entrance, I viciously attacked the rock surface. Within a minute, the knife was blunted. Then it broke. The rock surface was barely more than scratched, but to a close observer the initials KG were unmistakable. The carved letters were less than perfect, yet they would have to do. The sign would at least give me a bearing next time I came, with a rescue force.

For the last time, I turned from the mountain face and stared at the waterfall opposite. It was a picture I would hopefully never forget. I tried to imprint it on my mind, like a photograph. In an effort to remember, I again surveyed my nearer surroundings. I was on the opposite side of the mountain from Shekar town, and therefore out of vision of the Chinese Army if they were still there. I was satisfied that no one else could inadvertently stumble across the treasure by accident, and confident that I could find the tunnel entrance again.

I nearly didn't make it down the mountainside. As I came round the ledge, to the side leading down to the town, I came across a fork in the path. One path forked upwards but then appeared to drop back down again after fifty feet or so; the other path, which deceptively looked to be the main path, continued straight on. I choose the easy route out of sheer laziness. It was the wrong choice. Seconds later I stood on loose scree which caused my feet to slip away. In a panic I hurled myself to the ground and just managed to grab a protruding rock. Fortunately, it held my weight. With exceptional strength, for I have never been particularly athletic, I pulled myself up to safety, and sat panting for several minutes staring down the scree slope which led to a precipice. I backtracked a few paces and took the higher ledge. I made a mental note to avoid the death trap next time I passed this way. Coming round the corner to rejoin the main pathway, I was overjoyed at seeing our yaks still alive outside the front of the castle. I untethered them, but there was little I could do with them, or for them. Hopefully, they'd have the sense to make their way back down the mountain in search of pasture.

It had taken five hours to climb to the castle the day before. It took me only three hours to descend. My pace slackened as I approached what had been the small town of Shekar. I was struck dumb with horror. There was little evidence of any life, just piles of crumbling walls that only hours beforehand had been peoples' houses. And bodies. Lots of bodies. Limbless, headless, bloodied, mutilated, unidentifiable. And the monastery, it was gone; just ruins remained. There were no monks to greet me with kind words or tea. There was only death and destruction. I was alone. What's more, I was alone with a terrifying secret. A secret I had to get out of the country. I wanted to stay and bury the dead, but that was not the Tibetan way. Bodies are usually butchered and left for the vultures. Such a brutal end meant nothing to these people, for after death, with the soul gone, the body has no significance. So it was to be for the people and monks of Shekar. I offered my prayers as I walked away.

I set off on foot for the Nepalese border. Regrettably, there was no sign of our horses. The Chinese soldiers had probably taken them, or maybe they had run off in fright from the exploding shells. My spirits were down, there was a long gruelling trek in front of me; one that I knew not all travellers survived.

The road, or rather dust track, to Shigatse passed by the odd peasants' shack, tent, or tasam house, in which one would normally be able to find lodging. Each habitation I encountered was empty, devoid of life, although not of nourishment. I politely entered each residence, calling out for the occupants as custom dictates, but left full-handed, stealing whatever food or water I could find. As the days wore on, my diet consisted of ever-increasing rotten food. Such looting was not a high point of my life. Eventually I reached the outskirts of Shigatse. I lay low until the sun had set that day, and crept in stealthily under cover of the moonless night.

I had reckoned on completely passing through Shigatse that night. I could not let myself be seen by daylight, for with it came danger. The Chinese soldiers would still be out in force all the way to the border. I had no doubt that many Tibetans would have chosen to leave the country, especially on hearing that their leader had fled. Such refugees would take their worldly possessions with them, which would produce rich pickings for any greedy soldier lucky enough to catch them. Besides, my white skin and European looks were going to be a problem. Even with my face wrapped up in a scarf and speaking like a native peasant, I was unlikely to fool any Chinese soldier. My body was just too far removed from the local model.

Before dawn broke, I slipped into a small farmyard on the outskirts of Shigatse and into an animal shed. I gulped down some refreshing cold water, and collapsed asleep in a corner of straw with three goats for company. My luck ran out long before midday. I was in the throes of waking when I sensed movement near the shed entrance. Muffled voices gave way to shouts. I was painfully prodded in the stomach by a rifle. I opened my eyes to see two Chinese soldiers glaring down at me, yelling at me to stand up.

I was roughly frisked by unkind hands. They found rather a lot of gold coins in my knapsack, for I had taken several handfuls whilst clearing out the palace, knowing I'd need them to purchase provisions. There were still many remaining. No peasant could possess such wealth, any soldier knew that. Accordingly, I was taken for a thief. I pleaded innocence, for I knew the Tibetan punishment for a thief was to cut off the offending hand, but to no avail. I was unceremoniously shoved out into the farmyard in which a peasant and his rotund wife cowered. She looked me straight in the eye, pleadingly. These were dangerous times. She had been fearful for the life of her children. No doubt it was she who had reported that a stranger was hiding in her shed. Maybe she wanted forgiveness. Her anguish was little comfort to me.

I was marched off to the local jail and forcibly thrown into a dark, dank, cesspit of a cell crammed full of other inmates. The cell door slammed and I sank to the floor, clasped my head and cried. I had utterly failed. Not only would the Dalai Lama be denied his treasure, but also the secret of where it was hidden. I was the only living soul to know the location of a vast horde of precious stones, yet looking around the cell I could imagine the secret dying with me pretty soon.

The first week in the cell was the worse, mainly because of the mayhem outside. I could only imagine the Chinese soldiers getting their revenge for not being able to catch the Dalai Lama. From the sound of it, there must have been countless cases of looting, raping and burning of houses, as well as the indiscriminate firing of shells at monasteries and temples. Innocent people were being killed, and I was trapped in the middle of it all.

vi. A living hell

The heavy wooden cell door burst open at six o'clock in the morning accompanied by the usual harsh cry of 'Out! Out, you lazy shitheads!' This was how my life had started each day for nine years. Each guard had his own favourite term of endearment for me and the other dozen prisoners that spent each night in a restless sleep on the straw-strewn stone floor.

I staggered out of the cell and shuffled to the latrines. It was hard to last the night sometimes, especially with the laxative effect of the putrid slops they fed us. Most days the food just went straight through my body's system, scarcely staying long enough inside my stomach to have its nourishment extracted. I managed to catch a glimpse of my reflection in a mirror another prisoner had somehow managed to keep unbroken. I was ragged, dishevelled, gaunt, emaciated, my unkempt beard straggly. I could think of many appropriate descriptions, but didn't like to dwell on them. I knew that, compared to my former physique, I was no more than skeletal. I also knew that I could not survive for much longer in these conditions. There's only so much the body can take before the spirit gives up.

I spooned down the breakfast gruel without bothering to examine what it was. I had ceased caring long ago. I mechanically opened my mouth and swallowed whatever had been thrown into my bowl, grateful that it would temporarily take away the pangs of hunger. I needed my strength. I needed to eat the revolting slops of food to survive. I had no choice, there was not an ounce of fat left on me. I had never been able to conclude whether malnourishment was a good or bad thing in prison. On the positive side, I was allowed to stay in the prison compound all day, where I could occasionally bask in the sun's rays. Those moments lifted my spirits and gave me hope. Beforehand, when I had had the strength, I was forced to go out each day working as slave-labour on the new roads being constructed by the Chinese to open up the country. These days I couldn't even lift the smallest of hammers, let alone wield it.

I had given a false name to the guards on being arrested all those years ago. I had concocted some cock-and-bull story to explain my western looks. It wasn't difficult to convince the guards that my Tibetan servant mother had been the mistress of a bureaucrat at the British Legation, and that my father had denied parental responsibility from the moment of my birth. At the time, I thought it wiser to be arrested as a thief rather than face the consequence of the assumed alternative, a foreign spy. No doubt I would have been executed pretty quickly as a spy. Perhaps I should have told the truth, death would have been quicker and less painful.

My daydreaming kept me alive. It was a characteristic that had infuriated my parents, schoolteachers and university lecturers; they all said I would fail in life because I was a dreamer. But here, in prison, there was nothing else to do. There was no stimulus for an educated brain. Every day was desolate. There were no books, no newspapers, no pens or paper. I wasn't even allowed to make contact with anyone on the outside. I had seriously misjudged the extent of sentence I would be faced with. Before the Chinese invasion, convicted criminals, though usually manacled, would often be free to roam the streets and stay with family, rather than being cooped up. I hadn't counted on the system changing. I had made an error of judgement, and there was no one to appeal to.

The only stimulation we prisoners received was the occasional biased piece of news from a garrulous guard. It was never good news. We were frequently told of the downfall and break-up of the country. We were told of the millions who had lost their lives, been forced into labour camps, shot or starved out of existence. We were told that hundreds of temples had been destroyed, along with every aspect of Tibetan culture the Chinese could find. We were told that peace loving monks had been executed as enemies of the State. For the ordinary Tibetan, there seemed little to live for.

Presumably such stories were told to us out of spite, deliberately to destroy our souls. I tried not to dwell on it. I devoted my brain to dreams, but they alone could not completely save my sanity. I was losing it. I knew that to be true, I could discern it from my odd behaviour. At times I could barely remember why I had been put in prison. As for the events that led up to my arrest, and my association with the Dalai Lama, the story went untold. My secret was locked deep within. I would never tell. That one thought, alone, was my saviour.

The worst news ever to filter through to me was that concerning the Dalai Lama. The guards seemed to enjoy themselves most when narrating negative stories of the country's rightful leader. It was truly demoralizing. The guards gleefully told us how our leader had abandoned his people, and that he had in turn been abandoned by the world as a political embarrassment. It hit home hard. The Dalai Lama had no money. He therefore had no power. And it was me, trapped in a god-forsaken pit of a prison, who was responsible for his financial situation.

Throughout the nine years I remained in prison, I ceaselessly reflected on the fact that, if I'd been on the outside, I might have been able to do something to help Tibet in its plight against China. The millions of pounds that the jewels, now buried deep in the mountain tunnels, could have raised would have had some effect. I blamed myself for failing the Dalai Lama, for failing the Tibetan people and, consequently, I felt responsible for the millions of deaths that had occurred. Each depressing piece of news that filtered through to my prison cell concerning the destruction of Tibet was like another nail in my coffin.

The world continued without my being part of it. The events of the nineteen sixties passed totally unknown to me. As far as I was concerned the world had stopped as of March nineteen fifty-nine. I was a broken man and had become institutionalized. Several prison wardens had come and gone, along with hundreds of guards, and I reckon no one was really sure who I was, where I had come from or why I was there in the first place. No one cared. My destiny seemed to be to die among the filth.

At the end of May nineteen sixty-eight a new warden arrived to take charge of my prison. As usual, on the arrival of a new warden, we prisoners were shuffled out into the courtyard for inspection and an inaugural speech. I stood facing the sun, absorbing the warmth into my skin, virtually oblivious to what was going on around me.

The new warden passed along the straggly rows of prisoners, demanding a name from each and marking that man's name off on a sheet held to a clipboard. There were some one hundred and fifty of us. It took quarter of an hour before he reached me, by which time my weak legs were nearing collapse.

'What is your name?' asked the warden.

I was unaware of the voice. The question came again, only louder and with a little anger. I turned to stare into the warden's eyes. My lips moved, but no sound came out. My brain seemed completely detached from my body, I felt as though I was floating high in the air. I had no idea who I was or where I was. The warden grabbed my bony shoulders and shouted his question in my face.

A distant memory from childhood surfaced. I was at school, writing my name on a classroom test paper. That was it. 'Keith Gibson,' I replied.

The warden surveyed his clipboard. 'What? Say that again.'

I repeated my name. The warden frowned. 'Is that a Tibetan name? The warden turned to a Tibetan guard alongside him. 'Corporal Wangdula, what is this man's name, I can't hear him properly.'

'I do not know, sir. It sounded neither Tibetan nor Chinese.'

'What name does he go by here, then?'

'Norbu, sir,' replied Corporal Wangdula.

'You,' the warden said jabbing his clipboard at me and offering a pen, 'write your name down.'

I did so, just as my schoolmaster had instructed us to on the test paper.

'What language is this?'

The warden's eyes burnt into my own. What had I done to upset my old schoolmaster, I wondered? My lips moved up and down again, silently.

'Where are you from?' asked the warden.

My mind was elsewhere. I was ten years old and battling with the complexity of an exam. My Eleven Plus was only a few weeks away. I had to concentrate on the test questions.

'Can you understand me?' asked the warden. He paused for a few seconds before turning to the corporal. 'This man has either lost his senses or he's playing a dangerous game. Put him into solitary confinement for a week. Let's see if that refreshes his brain.'

With that, I was marched off to the smallest cell I'd ever had the mischance of encountering. There was no window, no fresh air. There was just a rusty bucket in the corner, and a foul smelling, slippery floor. Not even any straw for bedding. I thought it would be the most desolate place imaginable in which to die.

vii. Lieutenant Tchen

I had been released from solitary confinement a month since, and was now back in the relative comfort of my cramped cell. At least I had other human beings to talk to. One morning, out of the blue, the cell door creaked open, a guard entered and pointed straight at me.

'You, come with me,' the guard snapped out the instruction so sharply we all bristled with fear.

The rest of the prisoners stared at me quizzically, no doubt wondering what on earth I could have done to warrant this intrusion. I stared at the guard expressionless, my mind racing for an explanation as to what I could possibly be wanted for. Had I breached a prison rule? I thought not, I rarely did anything at all. I staggered up off the cell floor and stumbled out behind the guard. I was ushered into the warden's office where a smartly dressed army officer stood talking to the warden. His conversation stopped when he realized I was in the room. He smiled and courteously beckoned me to sit. I did so apprehensively. There was something reptilian about him that caused my hackles to rise.

'Please sit down,' said Lieutenant Tchen gently.

I could see from the look in his eye that he was shocked at the appearance of my dirty, dishevelled, skeletal body. Dressed in rags, with a scraggy beard, no doubt I looked sixty years old rather than the thirty-eight I was. I sat down as instructed, fearing reprisals from this cold-eyed army officer. I had long since learned the punishment for disobeying orders, and this man looked the sort not to be angered.

Lieutenant Tchen asked politely, 'What is your name?'

My mouth went dry. It seemed to have been happening a lot recently. It opened and closed a few times, but nothing came out. I stared ahead vaguely, looking neither at the Lieutenant nor at the warden.

Lieutenant Tchen persisted with his questioning. 'How long have you been imprisoned here?'

My mouth repeated its silent exercise.

'Your name is Gibson, is it not? Keith Gibson?'

This time I purposefully chose not to open my mouth. Alarm bells were ringing inside my head. The officer had called me by my proper name, yet I was sure I had not given it to him when asked. Why was this man here? What did he want with me? Adrenaline pumped through me for the first time in years. I was scared.

'This is hopeless,' sighed Lieutenant Tchen. 'Governor,' he said. 'I have questions to ask this prisoner, questions for which the answers are vital to the security of the state. I have authority to do anything to achieve results. I have total discretion. Do you understand?'

The warden sighed even deeper. 'Yes, Lieutenant, I understand perfectly well.'

'Good. Now then, this prisoner is not at his best at the moment. Could you please arrange for him to have a nice meal, plenty of meat and vegetables, hot tea and some fruit perhaps?'

The Fourth Cart III

'He'll vomit,' replied the warden casually. 'He hasn't eaten a decent meal in years. He's had nothing but scraps. His stomach won't be able to take it. Meat's too rich for him.'

Lieutenant Tchen held the warden's gaze for a few seconds. 'Are you trying to defy me?'

'No I am not,' the warden replied. 'I will feed him, but I will not have him vomiting all over my office floor.'

Lieutenant Tchen mollified under the warden's stern gaze. 'Some noodles and a little chicken soup, then? Something that contains vitamins? The man's suffering from malnourishment, can't you see that?'

'That will be no problem, Lieutenant. I know what's best in this situation. It takes time to strengthen them up.'

'Thank you. A shave, haircut, hot bath and clean clothes would help. He stinks and I need to get close to him.'

'We are not a hotel, Lieutenant,' the warden responded with a smirk.

Lieutenant Tchen reached into his pockets, withdrew a few coins and threw them on the table. The warden smiled and nodded his head.

I was escorted out of the warden's office and shunted into the guards' quarters. For the first time in years I was given free rein to wash in peace, with no time limit, no one shouting to hurry up, no one jostling for position. I was even given a bar of soap; I'd forgotten just how wonderful it smelled.

Ablutions done, the guards looked on enviously as I tucked into a bowl of soup and a heap of rice cake. I ate with fervour, relishing each mouthful, and was then left to sleep peacefully, and comfortably, on a mattress for a change. I had no hint of the unpleasantness to come.

Three hours later I was rudely awoken, dragged into a small office in which Lieutenant Tchen stood coiling rope around his fingers, stripped naked and tied to a chair. He set about torturing me with remarkable deftness.

'I said, what is your name?' Lieutenant Tchen advanced towards me, cigarette in hand.

'Gibson. Keith Gibson,' I screamed. My face had screwed up in pain long before I could answer properly. I rocked violently back and forward in the chair, the restraining ropes around my naked body cut into the flesh of my wrists and ankles as I desperately fought to evade the source of pain.

Lieutenant Tchen withdrew the tip of his cigarette from contact with my scrotum. It had been the final straw to break me.

'Very good, Mr Gibson, we're on speaking terms at last.'

I had not spoken up until then. I had resisted speech during nearly ten minutes of torture at his hands. It wasn't that I had refused to answer any of his questions, it was just that this was the first question he had put to me. The sadist had been torturing me purely for fun, singeing my flesh with cigarettes for the sheer pleasure of it. I suppose it may have been his warm up exercise, to get him in the mood. It certainly got me in the mood for talking. I would have said anything to make him to stop.

'Now then, Mr Gibson, let's start properly. Are you from England?'

'Yes,' I replied woodenly, my mind half gone. I uttered little more than monosyllable replies to maybe a hundred questions Lieutenant Tchen put to me during the rest of the day. He seemed to have detailed knowledge of nearly every aspect of my life, whether in England or in Tibet, right up to the moment I left the Potala Palace in March nineteen fifty-nine. It was extraordinary; I couldn't understand how he could possibly have gleaned so much information about me. It was as though he had composed a biography, but one that contained more facts than I knew myself.

By evening, I was exhausted and near to passing out from the mental effort of having to listen and focus my memory. I was left to recover for the night. Lieutenant Tchen was obviously in no hurry, he gave the impression that he was going to stay with me for a very long time.

The next morning was a duplication of the previous day. I was stripped naked and shackled to a chair. Lieutenant Tchen alternated between sitting opposite me behind a desk, on which lay a packet of cigarettes, and pacing the room. I was asked the same questions, but in a different order, and sometimes mixed up together. Each answer was methodically noted by Lieutenant Tchen. I can only assume he was double-checking what I'd said the previous day. For what reason, I couldn't fathom. Maybe that was just his convoluted character.

The crunch came on the third day. It was half way during the morning's interrogation that the purpose of Lieutenant Tchen's visit finally dawned on me. He had been questioning me about the events of the day that the Dalai Lama decided to flee the country.

'Tell me about the Fourth Cart, Mr Gibson.'

'The what?'

'The Fourth Cart, Mr Gibson.'

'I don't understand,' I replied nervously. This was the first question put to me that I couldn't comprehend, let alone think of an answer to. I feared it would lead to more pain.

'Come, Mr Gibson, let's not play games. It seems everyone else in the country knows that phrase, surely you do as well.'

'I don't!' I screamed in panic as I saw Lieutenant Tchen reach for a pack of cigarettes. 'Honestly, I don't. Please don't do that again. I am not lying!'

Lieutenant Tchen's hand paused, hovering over the cigarette packet. He seemed to reflect a moment before continuing to speak in a slow, heavily emphasized manner. 'If you make any false statements, I will burn you for an hour. Do you understand that, Mr Gibson?'

I didn't need to plead. The fear in my eyes as he lit a cigarette was sufficient for Lieutenant Tchen to accept my desire to tell the truth.

'On the day in question, four horse drawn carts left the Potala Palace. We apprehended three of them later that night, but the fourth cart eluded us. We have been looking for that fourth cart for a long time, Mr Gibson. If you really don't know the phrase "The Fourth Cart", then let me tell you that it has come to symbolize Tibetan resistance against our administration. As you can imagine, that symbol is a constant irritation, especially to me personally. Are you with me so far?'

I said nothing. My mind raced out of control. I was in a state of confusion and anguish. I wanted more information of the resistance, but at the same time I didn't want to admit any connection to the cart.

'I see by the whites of your eyes that you know what I'm talking about, Mr Gibson. Good. That will speed things up. Where was I? Oh, yes, The Fourth Cart. There were witnesses who said you were on one of the carts. Now, since you were not found on either of the three captured carts, it stands to reason you were on the Fourth Cart, the one that eluded us.' Lieutenant Tchen drew heavily on his cigarette, causing the end to glow red hot, before continuing with his next question. 'Is that not so, Mr Gibson?'

I nodded, totally petrified.

Lieutenant Tchen leaned back on his chair, exhaled a cloud of smoke, and smiled contentedly. 'What was in that cart, Mr Gibson?'

My forehead glistened with sweat. This was the moment of truth I had to bluff out, or all would be lost. 'Books. Documents. Ancient copies of the Tibetan Bible. We couldn't leave those things behind, they were too precious. We feared you would burn them.'

Lieutenant Tchen said nothing. He stood up, came round the side of the desk and jabbed the red hot end of his cigarette into the tip of my penis. I screamed so loud an anxious guard burst through the door. The whole prison must have heard my piercing cry of pain.

'Out!' Lieutenant Tchen shouted at the intruding guard. He then turned his attention back to me. 'Oh, Mr Gibson. Dear, dear, foolish Mr Gibson. I did warn you, didn't I? Would you like to change that last statement?'

'Yes! Yes! Alright! No more, I beg you. Please don't do this to me.' I told him exactly what the cart contained.

'And what happened to this cart of yours?'

'We spotted your army tailing us, just before we reached Shigatse. We realized we were never going to make it to the border.'

'So what did you do?'

'We put in action our fall-back plan. We veered off the main route and headed for Shekar. I had lived there some years beforehand. We hoped to find help there.'

'To do what?'

'To hide the crates. That was the fall-back plan. Hide the crates then get word of their location to the Dalai Lama. We would come back later, once the situation had calmed down.'

'And you hid the treasure in Shekar? I do not believe that,' responded Lieutenant Tchen.

'Yes. No! Not in Shekar. Up the mountain, behind the village. We buried it under the castle.'

Lieutenant Tchen's frown deepened. 'How did you get eight crates full of treasure up the mountain?'

'As I said, I had lived there earlier. The monks at the temple were more than happy to help. They carried the crates for us.'

'So, you buried the crates. Then what did you all do?'

'We buried the crates in the castle basement. Then all hell broke loose. Your army shelled the village and the castle. The roof of the tunnel we were in collapsed. I think all the monks with me were killed. I was the only one who walked out.'

Lieutenant Tchen barely seemed to be able to disguise his excitement as he steeled himself for his next question. 'And what became of the treasure?'

'I don't know.'

Lieutenant Tchen sighed and his hand instinctively moved forwards, edging the cigarette towards its target.

'No!' I screamed, even though the cigarette had not made contact. 'I really don't know what happened to it. I was arrested and put in here soon after. I've been here ever since. Please believe me!'

'Please explain,' Lieutenant Tchen said withdrawing his hand.

'I had planned to escape the country, but I got picked up by guards in Shigatse. They assumed I was a thief because I was carrying a lot of money. I gave a false name, they threw me in here. I have never been able to return to Shekar. There's no way I could know what's become of the treasures.'

Lieutenant Tchen smiled. 'Mr Gibson. I have just one more question for today. Then you can eat and rest. Can you remember exactly where those eight crates are buried?'

I knew now what was going to happen to me. I would be forced to reveal the precise location of the crates. Then I would be shot as a looter. I had lost the battle. My body was too weak to fight. I had finally failed the Dalai Lama.

I surrendered to the inevitability of the situation. 'Yes,' I replied. 'I remember very well.'

viii. Release from prison

The prison gates creaked open and I walked out with an almost nostalgic feeling, for I thought I would not be returning. The decrepit building had been my home for nine years. I yearned to turn around and go back inside, especially given my current predicament. But that was impossible. Right behind me stood Lieutenant Tchen, with an expectant look on his face. I was to lead him to the treasure buried deep at the top of the mountain.

There was a loud banging sound as the gates slammed shut behind us. I turned and faced Lieutenant Tchen quizzically, taking in one last glimpse of the depressing grey walls of the prison.

'Over there, Mr Gibson, to your right,' said Lieutenant Tchen gesturing to a dusty old army jeep.

I stood motionless for a few seconds staring in the direction of the jeep. It was an inconspicuous vehicle. There was no one inside. There was no other Chinese soldier nearby. There was also no other vehicle around. It was at that stage that I noticed a gleam in Lieutenant Tchen's eyes. 'I take it we're going alone,' I stated, rather than asked.

'Correct, Mr Gibson,' responded Lieutenant Tchen. 'I wish to check out your story first. I will report it to my commanding officer once I have determined the facts. I would not like to lead my superiors on a wild goose chase.'

That confirmed it. I now knew exactly what the man intended. 'Very wise, Lieutenant,' I muttered as I climbed inside the jeep. In the back lay several bags of provisions, an army rucksack, two kerosene lamps, fuel, water, blankets. 'You're well prepared, I see.'

'Yes I am, aren't I?' Lieutenant Tchen reached inside the dashboard locker and pulled out the keys. 'Thanks to you.'

'You're going to steal the treasure aren't you? You're not going to tell your superiors about it are you?'

'Now why do you think that, Mr Gibson? Do I look like a thief?'

'No, but there is a certain look in your eye. I'm not sure what, but there's some resentment, isn't there?'

'Resentment!' Lieutenant Tchen screamed. 'Have you any idea what I've been through this last nine years? I've been victimized, cast aside, denied promotion, given the shittiest of work to do by that bastard commanding officer of mine, Colonel Tsim. And all because of you!'

'Me?'

'Yes, you, Mr Gibson. You and that bloody Fourth Cart. That's all Colonel Tsim ever talks about. He wants to get his hands on those treasures. Then he'll run off, flee the country, somewhere warm, with a sandy beach, that's what he dreams about. And boys! Oh yes, he dreams of slim, tender young boys, I know. He has a reputation for it, always eyeing up the new cadets, he is. I'm sure he dreams of a nice warm bed where a boy will carry out his fantasies. His kind makes me sick.'

'I take it you don't get on well with your boss?'

'Too right I don't. He gets promotion, frequently. Me? I get nothing. I've been a lieutenant for eleven years, he'll be a general soon, I'm sure. Curse him! I want to get as far away from him as possible. And you, my dear Mr Gibson, are going to help me achieve that. I fancy escaping to America. Lots of tall blonde women. That's my dream. And the treasures of the Fourth Cart are going to finance those dreams.'

'But what if the treasures are no longer there? Maybe they've been looted. It has been nine years after all,' I said in as dispiriting a manner as possible. I wasn't keen on the greedy look on his face. 'Who knows how many people have been up that mountain.'

'Come, Mr Gibson, you know as well as I that no Tibetan would climb up a mountain just for enjoyment. That's solely a western pursuit. Plus, I do know sufficient Tibetan culture to understand that mountain tops are sacred. Tibetans do not go wondering around mountain tops, they would worry about disturbing the gods. Is that not right?'

I said nothing. It was difficult to contradict the truth. We drove off, my mind searching for delaying tactics. Maybe I could somehow alert others to my peril, and get them to come to my aid. But how?

As we made our way towards Shekar, Lieutenant Tchen talked of little else except his hatred of Colonel Tsim. There's always two sides to any story, but the impression I was given was that he was being punished by his boss for an indiscretion. He proudly told me of his involvement with the storming on the Potala Palace, and how our paths must have crossed as I made my escape. Given the vast number of deaths that day, and Lieutenant Tchen's predilection for violence, I can imagine it had something to do with over-zealousness on his part in carrying out his duties.

Lieutenant Tchen seemed to be taking a tortuous route, driving at odd times of day, unnecessarily resting for lengthy periods, occasionally doubling back. No doubt he was avoiding being seen by any passing patrol. I took advantage of the delays by sleeping, and eating as much as I could stomach. I needed to build up my strength if I was to climb a mountain.

We eventually reached Shekar. It had grown quite considerably since I saw it last, but it was still a village rather than a town. We drove along the main track noting the inhabitants were no more than the poorest of peasants. A handful of old monks were idling around in the former monastery grounds. The jeep ground to a halt.

'If you want to live, Mr Gibson, then you will follow my instructions precisely. We need to get the villagers consent to go up the mountain. I do not want their suspicions aroused, do you understand? We will calmly get out of the jeep now, and you will talk to those old men over there.'

'It may take a few hours of conversation. You know what these villagers can be like for social pleasantries,' I replied, hoping to false-foot the man. Should I alert these old men? Would it be of any benefit? As if in answer to my thoughts, Lieutenant Tchen pulled out a revolver from a jacket pocket.

'If you say something wrong, Mr Gibson, I will shoot everyone that hears you. Maybe I'll have to shoot everyone in the village. Frankly, I don't care. It is your choice. Do you want their deaths on your conscience?'

My mouth gaped at his words. Ruthlessness showed in his eyes. I was resigned. I shook my head.

'Good. Then we understand each other.' Lieutenant Tchen replaced the revolver.

We got out the vehicle, strode over to the old men and I started to engage them in conversation. As expected, we were soon invited to take tea. I spent a couple of hours chatting with them, enjoying their hospitality and passing the time of day. I was in no hurry. It was getting late, we would not be able to start our quest until the next morning anyway. Lieutenant Tchen had remained impassive throughout the social pleasantries, but as dark descended he caught my eye and patted his jacket pocket where the revolver was. It was time to abandon social gossip, and to start inquiring.

'I visited here once, about nine years ago, just before the crises,' I casually mentioned, 'I left four of my friends here. It would be nice to see them again. Were any of you here then?'

Lieutenant Tchen shot me a sharp look, but relaxed as all the old monks shook their heads in unison. 'No, my son,' came the reply. 'It is sad, but no one survived from that period.'

'No one?' I gasped in despair. 'What happened?'

The Fourth Cart III

The eldest monk responded. 'The Chinese soldiers came. They took away all the monks living in the temple, then blew it up. They also blew up the village. Retribution, they called it.'

'What happened to the monks? My friends would have been amongst them.'

The eldest monk sighed. 'I am sorry to hear that, my son. It is not known what happened to them. Most would have been sent to labour camps, or would have been executed.'

It was my turn to throw a sharp look to Lieutenant Tchen. The Chinese had certainly lived up to the barbarism I had warned others about during my days living in the Tsedrungs school. I remained silent for a few minutes, reflecting on so many unnecessary deaths. It seemed appropriate. The monks joined me in the silence.

'Last time I came here,' I eventually said, breaking the sombre atmosphere, 'I was on a pilgrimage with my friends. We travelled to the castle ruins, up there, where the views are magnificent, to offer prayers to the guardian god, Kangchenjunga.'

The monks all nodded their understanding.

'At the time, we vowed that we would return someday. Sadly, my friends cannot now do that,' I continued, rapidly thinking of a plan. 'I would like to go up there tomorrow, to offer a silent prayer to those dear departed friends.'

'We have all lost close friends, my son. These last few years have indeed been cruel. Go with our blessing,' the old monk said, then added, 'No one has been up to the castle in our living history. I will give you some candles and matches, will you please hold a prayer ceremony for us. We are too old to climb.'

'I will do that father,' I replied emotionally.

Lieutenant Tchen smiled at me enthusiastically. I did not share his mood.

Come the morning, we had a hearty meal with the monks, bade farewell and set off on the trek up the mountainside. I found the going really tough, my body was in no condition for strenuous exercise. I was still not much more than skin and bones, even though I'd had nearly a week of wholesome food since Lieutenant Tchen had intruded into my life. Fortunately, he realized my plight and did not force me to carry the provisions.

We had to climb just over two thousand feet, at a reasonable incline that did not necessitate ropes. I remember it had taken five hours on the last occasion with yaks carrying the crates. This time it took a little longer as I had to rest frequently. The gruelling ascent nearly finished me off. In fact, I yearned for a heart attack, anything to stop Lieutenant Tchen reaching his goal.

Eventually the time came to split off from the main track which leads to the castle, to a side track which leads round the mountain towards the tunnel exit. My heart gave a leap as I remembered it was along this path that I had fallen and only just managed to avoid plunging over a precipice. My mind raced. Could I turn it into an advantage? Adrenaline pumped fast and furious as we came nearer and nearer to the path that could lead to tragedy. Within minutes I had made my mind up. I would keep walking and leave the outcome up to God.

I was leading the way, Lieutenant Tchen a couple of yards behind. I bit my lip as I stepped on to the fatal path. The ground beneath me held. Maybe it was because I was nothing more than a bag of bones, several stones lighter than nine years ago.

'Ahh!' Lieutenant Tchen cried out as he slipped on the loose scree behind me. He landed hard on the ground, burdened by the heavy weight of the rucksack. He started to slip and he shouted to get my attention, 'Help me!'

I continued to walk, praying intently, not looking back.

'Help me,' screamed Lieutenant Tchen as he scrambled trying to get a grip on loose rocks. 'Mr Gibson, please, for the love of god, help me!'

I had made it to safety. I turned round to see Lieutenant Tchen slide faster and faster down the slope towards the precipice. His screams were strangely comforting. He was getting his just desserts. I doubted if anyone would grieve his loss. I watched dispassionately as his body disappeared over the edge. I was free.

Liberated from Lieutenant Tchen, I sat down for a rest and to contemplate my position. I really had no idea what to do. I'd only come up the mountain because I had been forced. It seemed logical that I should now go back down. But to what future? I couldn't go back to the prison, and it didn't seem a good idea to stay in the country. Questions would be asked about Lieutenant Tchen. But how was I to get out? I had no money, no hope. And then something stirred inside me. Distant thoughts resurrected themselves; my mother, my father, my previous life, happiness, friends. There had been good times, I had loved life before. Other people had loved me. Something told me I wanted that life again. I needed that life again. I struggled to my feet with determination. I would fight for life again. I just needed some money.

I concentrated hard and dug deep into my memory. Gradually I formed a picture in my half-dead mind of leaving the tunnel and seeing the sight of a beautiful waterfall in the distance. I knew what I had to do to survive.

Five minutes later I stood near a crevice fingering a scratch on the rock face. Despite the severity of weather in the area over the last nine years, there was no doubt about it; my initials were still there, inscribed in the rock. This was it, but my future would now depend on what I found inside the tunnel. If the treasure was gone then it was likely that I would not survive much longer, a matter of days perhaps. I stepped inside the tunnel, my stomach knotted in anticipation.

From memory, I recalled having to walk six hundred and seventy-five heel-to-toe paces. I set off at an agonizing slow pace out of fear for what I may find. The tunnel grew darker and darker as the daylight faded. I had walked this way before, I kept telling myself, I could do it again.

I was quite shocked to find the recess exactly where it was supposed to be. At least my feet hadn't shrunk over the years. I rummaged in my pocket and brought out the candles and matches the old monk had given me that morning. I lit three, placed them to the side of the entrance, and a very dim orange glow lit the former dungeon. As my eyesight adjusted, to my absolute shock and incredulity, I found that the floor inside the room was still covered in debris. It was obvious that no one had been here. No one had dug up the treasure.

I had almost convinced myself that a pit would be there, that I would have found nothing but a big empty hole where the treasure had once been. Yet it was intact. The floor looked exactly the same as it did the day I had left it nine years ago. The back of my neck shivered involuntarily. The room possessed a creepy, ghost-like atmosphere. Maybe the souls of the monks who had died trapped under the rock-fall haunted the place, trying to offer protection to its valuable contents. As the orange candlelight shimmered, casting eerie shadows across the walls, I could almost hear their whispers.

I gently lifted a few rocks and wiped away dirt from a corner of the pit until the top of one of the wooden crates was revealed. One good yank and the lid opened with a loud creak. I looked around nervously, half expecting the noise to have attracted someone's attention. Maybe it had woken the dead. I held a candle above the opened crate and gazed in awe at the multitude of ancient gold and silver coins, rubies and diamonds scattered haphazardly. I knelt for what seemed like hours, lifting handfuls of gems and letting them run through my open fingers. In those moments I realized I had been reborn, I had been given the opportunity to live again. Yet at the same time a twinge of guilt came over me, for it wasn't my treasure, it belonged to the Dalai Lama.

I fought a long hard battle with my conscience. I eventually reasoned that I would need ample resources to flee the country, to find the Dalai Lama and to mount an expedition to return to salvage the crates. So, slightly apprehensively, I emptied a linen bag of its contents then refilled it with a selection of jewels and gold coins that I reckoned would be the easiest to exchange for hard cash or to bargain with.

Rummaging through the treasures, my gaze fell on to the largest ruby imaginable. It was enormous for a gem, the size of a small plum. It was beautiful, sheer perfection. It shimmered in the candlelight, sparkling magically amongst its companions. I reached over, picked it up, held it aloft and let the candlelight dance off its surfaces. I just had to possess it. It was the most striking work of nature I'd ever seen.

I reasoned that the Dalai Lama would not begrudge me the one bag of treasure. I was sure there would be a large portion of the bag's gems still left when I located him. My conscience reconciled, I closed the lid, sprinkled dust and debris over the crate and left the floor as I had found it. Despite the eeriness of the room, I curled up in the corner and spent the night there. I slept surprising well, given that the remains of so many men still lay buried, without ceremony, just yards away. They came to me in my dreams, all of them, each telling me I was doing the right thing. It was a comfort.

I woke refreshed and backtracked my way out of the tunnel. It was mid-morning. I was hungry, yet used to having to go without nourishment. I could survive the trek down to the village. I had survived worse foodless days of hard labour.

The Fourth Cart III

Back in Shekar the villagers came out to greet my return, and enquire about my pilgrimage. I spent a few hours entertaining them, describing the wondrous views from the castle ruins of neighbouring valleys and snow-clad mountain peaks and, more impressively, of the peace and calmness I had acquired by praying to dear departed friends. I was asked about my companion. The lies came easy. I explained that he had resolved to stay another three days to fulfil his pilgrimage, in quiet solitude. No one would have thought this odd.

The villagers fed me well, each villager hoping that their alms would elicit a new tale from my lips. When I decided it was time to leave, to the villagers' astonishment, I repaid their kindness. I made a big show of pulling a gold coin out of a pocket as though it was the only object inside, and presented it to the eldest monk. He immediately showed it to everyone. The children in particular were in awe. No one had seen such a coin before. I asked the monk to spend it wisely, to buy something to benefit the whole village. This produced a rapturous response. I would be well remembered in the village.

I bade farewell. As I headed out of the village I spotted the jeep. A thought occurred to me. If only I could get it to work, I could escape that much quicker. I opened the driver's door and reached into the dashboard locker. My fingers touched a bunch of keys. I was right. Lieutenant Tchen had placed them there without thinking about it, an automatic action.

I set off in the jeep, kangarooing down the road for I had not driven since my youth, destined for Shigatse where my plan was to ditch it and barter a lift in a caravan headed for India.

As I crossed the border, a feeling of deep sadness came over me. I bade a fond farewell to the country that had, in an earlier innocent life, fulfilled my dreams. I knew I couldn't return. I knew it would be madness to attempt to return. The country had punished me with incredible cruelty, and would punish me even more severely if I dared to show my face within its borders again.

All went well until I reached India. Having said goodbye to the caravan, I was on my own. I was in a big, big world, yet I felt like a lost child without any adults to tell me what to do. The outside world frightened me terribly. I couldn't cope with decisions. There was no order, no routine, no one to give orders and no one to obey.

Worst of all, my life seemed to fall apart when I eventually caught up with the Dalai Lama. He was pleased to see me, shocked that I had been in prison because of the escapade with the Fourth Cart, but pleased that I had survived the ordeal. I told him where the crates were buried. He nodded his head and thanked me. But that was it. I asked if he was going to retrieve the treasure, and whether he wanted me to go back with a team, but he said no. I didn't understand. He tried to explain that he didn't want anyone to risk their lives, or to risk the treasure being captured by the Chinese. He said he would make a note of the treasure's location, and retrieve it once he had won back his throne.

I was dumbfounded. I realized that my suffering had been in vain. The treasure would remain buried forever, lost for eternity. I might just as well have shown Lieutenant Tchen where it was buried. I reckon he would have fled the country in his jeep. He might even have taken me with him, as a hostage, or as a guide once we'd got out. I wouldn't have had his death on my conscious.

In fact, I realized my nine years in prison had been a waste. I might as well have told the prison warden on the first day what I'd been up to. From what Lieutenant Tchen had said, the Chinese Army knew about the Fourth Cart from the outset, that they'd been looking for me almost from the moment I left the palace.

Those thoughts really stung me; nine wasted years. I left the Dalai Lama feeling as though I had wasted my whole life. There was nothing left for me. Somehow I reached Calcutta, and just drifted in a vague hope that somebody would put things right for me. It wasn't long before I was offered hashish.

One day I woke up in Bangkok. I don't remember how I got there, let alone why I had gone. All I do remember is that it was very easy to obtain every type of drug possible. Perhaps that's the reason why I had gone there.

My love for Tibet had been destroyed. It was nineteen sixty-nine when I crossed the border, out of the country for good for I had dismissed the thought of ever wanting to go back. Yet how strange life turns out, for I did indeed return, just four years later. And my next visit would change my destiny, leaving me in a hell far greater than that ever experienced in prison.

Chapter Eight

It was late afternoon by the time Magee finished Keith Gibson's manuscript. A dark gloom had descended outside. He swivelled his chair round to stare at the distant dullish outline of the hills.

He had found no mention of a woman that could help identity the mummified corpse. Nevertheless, he was heartened by Keith Gibson's recollections of life in Tibet which had been an insight into another world. And it had left Magee with the intriguing question of how to explain Keith Gibson's last day on earth. What demons had the author conjured up in his mind? Magee shook his head clear. It was no good, what he needed was inspiration. Perhaps a good night's sleep would help.

Rubbing the tiredness from his eyes, he chanced to see the three hands of his wall clock coming together around five twenty-seven. He heaved a sigh, grateful that another day had ended, that he would soon be home with his kids, helping them with homework, getting them off to bed so he could have a few quiet hours with his wife, Jenny. He leaned forward to tidy the files on his desk and did a sharp double-take at the clock. Hands coming together. Convergence.

A nauseous feeling grew in his stomach. He leant forward, picked up Keith's manuscript, and re-read part of the last paragraph:

It was nineteen sixty-nine when I crossed the border, out of the country for good for I had dismissed the thought of ever wanting to go back. Yet how strange life turns out, for I did indeed return, just four years later.

And then it hit him. Nineteen seventy-three. The same year the photograph was taken of Nick Price and his friends celebrating in a Bangkok bar. And Keith, the author of the manuscript, was in that photograph. He gasped as his head span dizzily. With an alarming clarity, he recalled a conversation he'd once had with Nick Price:

'You did pull off a job, right?'

'No, we did not. We simply found something that had been hidden years beforehand. That's the truth.'

Was this the origin of Nick Price's wealth? Was this how he and his nine old friends in the photograph became millionaires overnight? A fortune in gold and jewels, buried in the ruins of a Tibetan castle?

'Well I'll be buggered!' Magee muttered as he slipped on his coat and left the office.

Chapter Nine

Early on a bright morning late in November, Magee's office door opened wide and in strolled Brigadier Armstrong, snappily dressed in a dark suit. 'Well, Magee,' he said quietly, 'I've done all that you asked. Everything has been set in motion.'

'Thank you, sir.'

'You're taking a big risk today. You know that, don't you? This could all come crashing down in one giant cock up. You could easily end up with egg on your face.'

Magee sighed wearily. 'I'm well aware of that, sir. But I've no choice, have I? There doesn't seem to be any other approach to the problem.'

Brigadier Armstrong shook his head gently. 'I'm not sure about that, Magee. This route you're taking is very confrontational. It's not too late to try a more softly, softly approach.'

'I've tried that before with Nick Price. It got me nowhere. Anyway, I need to do this, or my career is over. I can't bear the atmosphere in the office any longer, nor the pettiness of the casework coming my way. I've had six months of triviality. It's time to put an end to it.'

'Very well. It's your call. So then, let's get going. It's likely to be a very long and difficult day.'

Magee drove over the Phoenix Causeway and up Lewes High Street, pulling over opposite the Law Courts where Melissa had been waiting looking at pictures of houses for sale in an estate agent's window. As she climbed in the front passenger side, she glanced at the occupant in the back seat.

'Brigadier Armstrong? What on earth are you doing here?'

'And a good morning to you too, my dear sergeant,' Brigadier Armstrong replied breaking into a broad grin.

'What are doing here in Lewes, sir?'

'Tagging along behind you, of course.'

'Why?' Melissa asked, as she closed the door and tightened up the seat belt. 'Where are we going?'

'Cooksbridge, of course,' Magee replied as he drove off.

Melissa's jaw dropped. 'What's this about, sir? You didn't say anything about going out to Cooksbridge to me before I went home last night. You're not going out there to harass Nick Price again, are you?'

'No, Melissa. I'm not going to harass him. What I'm going to do is much more than that. It's a make or break day for him and me. Brigadier Armstrong has pulled a lot of strings to make today happen.'

Melissa looked shocked. 'Is Nick expecting you?'

'Too right he is. Well, to be honest, no, probably not. But he's certainly expecting an official visit from the Brigadier.'

The colour disappeared from Melissa's face. 'You kept this all very quiet from me. Why?'

'Because you like Nick, that's why. And, what's more, you have an even softer spot for Paul Mansell. He's come over from Bangkok with John, especially for this occasion.'

'Oh God! What are you planning to do?'

'I need the truth from them about their past. So does the Brigadier. Today, it's all coming out. I admit it may not be a pretty sight, but it's got to happen for all our sakes. Yours included.'

'Stop the car,' Melissa cried. 'Let me out, I'm not going.'

'Yes you are, I'm afraid.'

'You've set me up, sir. I can't be forced into this.'

'Possibly not, but you're very much part of this. Do I have to remind you that six months ago you shot a very prominent person in the head at point blank range, from behind? Would you care to explain that in front of a court? Any reasonable prosecutor will make a jury think it was a cold, calculated execution. You'd get a life sentence for that. Probably worse if you were extradited to Thailand to face a court there.'

Melissa winced. 'Do you have to put it so bluntly?'

'That's not being blunt, Melissa. It's being truthful. I know I agreed to take the flack for that fiasco in Bangkok and we've been able to keep it pretty quiet so far. But the Brigadier has got the Prime Minister breathing down his neck, asking questions about the origins of Nick's money. And the only person who can possibly save us from our current predicament is the Brigadier. Therefore, it's in our best interests to help him. So please, let's just do this now, today. Let's get it over with as quick as possible.'

Melissa looked quizzical. 'You said the Prime Minister is involved? Why?'

'Because Nick has been nominated for a peerage and the Prime Minister is concerned that the donation he took from Nick is money from Khun Sa's drug dealing, that's why. The Prime Minister wants Nick's name cleared of any association with Khun Sa. Brigadier Armstrong is tasked to achieve that. We're just pawns in the game.'

Melissa sat clutching her knees in bewilderment. After a few seconds of contemplation she said, 'If this works out badly, sir. I'll resign. Today.'

'Trust me, Melissa, so will I.'

'You mean that?'

'I certainly do. Look, please, just trust me. It's going to turn out alright. I promise you that. Come on, we need to get out there quickly, it's going to be a long day.'

Chapter Ten

As Magee approached the final bend in the driveway leading up to Price's Folly, he frowned at the sight of a welcome party standing outside the front door. There was not one friendly face to be seen. 'This is indeed going to be a long day,' he muttered as the car came to a halt.

'Magee,' Nick Price spat out. 'The Brigadier didn't say anything about you being here today.'

'No?'

'No he did not,' Nick Price spat back. 'Hey,' he said, turning his attention to the Brigadier as the man stepped out from the back of the car, 'You didn't tell me Magee would be coming.'

'My apologies, I'm sure, Mr Price, but he's part of my investigative team. Anyway, he's here now, so perhaps we can cut the moaning and get on with this.'

'I'm not sure I want to cooperate with Magee around. I don't want anyone thinking I've turned into his snitch.'

'Oh for goodness sake, Mr Price,' Brigadier Armstrong muttered. 'Do you really want me to carry out my threat? I will have your business closed down within the hour, if you don't cooperate with us.'

Nick Price seemed to consider the prospect for a moment then stood to one side. 'Just watch it, Magee, that's all.'

'Some introductions would help, Mr Price.'

Nick Price pulled a false smile, yet complied with the request. 'Brigadier Armstrong, you've met my daughter Nittaya and my son Somsuk already. And Paul Mansell too. This is Paul's brother John.'

Brigadier Armstrong shook hands and said, 'Well, thank you for all for being here.'

The Fourth Cart III

Nick Price grunted, 'I don't remember been given a choice.'

'You weren't, Mr Price, but I'm indebted to John and Paul for making the effort to come over from Bangkok. It can't have been an easy journey, emotionally, that is, for John.'

'Magee said this was necessary for Nick's liberty,' John Mansell replied. 'It's the least I could do.'

'I'm still very grateful, Mr Mansell. There's much I need you to help me with. Shall we go inside?'

Melissa sidled up to Paul Mansell and gave him a peck on the cheek, whispering 'I had nothing to do with any of this.'

'That's okay,' he responded. 'You up for a meal tonight?'

'Of course. But let's get this over with first. I've got no idea what's going on.'

They walked into the imposing red brick Victorian mansion, through the galleried inner hall and into the spacious lounge. Within the minute they had taken a seat, Nittaya holding her father's hand on the sofa.

Nick asked innocently, 'So, what's this all about then?'

Magee perked up, and resorted to an old favourite line. 'I need to ask you some questions concerning a current investigation.'

'For god's sake, Magee,' Nick snapped. 'Why is it that whenever you have a case on your hands, you come knocking on my door?'

Magee bit his lip. He had vowed not to make today personal. 'I need to know about your past.'

'Excuse me?'

'Your past, Nick. I need to know about your past. In particular, I need to know about Khun Sa.'

Nick sighed deeply. 'Oh for Christ sake Magee, we've covered this ground before on many occasions. I don't know who Khun Sa is. I don't remember ever meeting him.'

'And I accept that. But you've never told me the whole truth about your life in Bangkok in the early seventies. I think I may be able to find Khun Sa lurking there somewhere, so I need to know it all.'

'Hah!' Nick guffawed. 'You have got to be joking, my old sunshine. No way!'

Brigadier Armstrong stepped in with an authoritative voice. 'Mr Price, as I told you recently, the press allegations about your involvement with Khun Sa are serious and may have a profound effect on your hopes of a peerage. I need to be satisfied that those allegations are false. Please do not think I was bluffing about closing your business down in order to get to the bottom of the problem. And if you refuse to cooperate, well, I'll assume the allegations are true.'

'Bully for you,' Nick responded.

'The problem won't stop there, though, Mr Price. I'm sure you know the powers of Customs and Excise are wider, and less restrictive, than Magee's. A Value Added Tax audit could mean the end for your property empire. If Customs find something suspicious in your paperwork, they would freeze your assets. They would confiscate everything you have if they found evidence that you'd been dealing in, how shall I say, restricted substances.'

Nick snarled contemptuously. 'You wouldn't dare do pull that one!'

'You'd better believe me, Mr Price. I would. And I'd make it my duty that Customs found something very suspicious. It would kill off your nomination for a peerage, and the press would have a field day dragging your name through the mud. '

Nick looked into Magee's eyes with a burning hatred. 'This is blackmail.'

'Nick,' Magee replied. 'I also need to know about your involvement with Tibet.'

Nick's jaw dropped. 'What did you say?'

'You heard me. Tibet.'

'What of it?'

'I know you went there. It's where your wealth originates from, isn't it? It's what led to the murders of your colleagues last year. And, in all probability, the origins of Khun Sa are tied in with the same events. The Brigadier won't leave you alone until he knows all the facts. So, I need you to tell me everything from those days. And the reason I've asked John to come over from Bangkok is so that he can fill in any gaps you're not clear about. I wouldn't want you to think you can get out of this by claiming memory loss.'

Nick turned a ghastly puce colour. 'Don't do this to me, Magee. Not with my children here, I'm begging you.'

'Sorry, Nick. It's crunch time. You've done your best to confound me over the years. I need to hear what really happened to you in Bangkok and Tibet. No more lies, no more half-truths, no more bullshit.'

Nick exchanged a glance with John before replying. 'What's this really all about, Magee.'

'The truth will always out, Nick.'

'You're talking in riddles. What the hell does that actually mean?'

'It means I could take you down to a station now, hold you as a suspect, interview you at length. You know the drill.'

'Yeah, I do know the drill. And you'd need a charge to keep me there. So, what are you going to charge me with?'

'At the moment, I'm not accusing anyone of anything, let alone charging them. What I want is your cooperation for a few hours.'

'But if you don't accuse me of something, I won't know what it is you're after!'

Magee allowed a smile. 'It's a perfect situation for me, Nick. You won't know what not to say. Hopefully, for once, that will enable me to get somewhere near the truth with you.'

'You're a pain, Magee,' Nick spat back. 'You're wasting my time, as usual. Whatever your problem is, I am not involved.'

'Keith Gibson says otherwise.'

'What the hell has Keith got to do with it?'

'He was writing a book about his life in Tibet.'

'Bully for him.'

'Keith's manuscript was entitled The Fourth Cart.' By the pained look on Nick's face, Magee had struck a nerve. 'Look, Nick, I'm not going to go away. I'm determined to get to the bottom of the whole Khun Sa issue, and I am going to do that right here, today.'

'Excuse me,' Nittaya interrupted, 'But who is this Keith Gibson?'

Magee was thankful for the interruption. 'Keith Gibson was a friend of your father in his days in Bangkok.'

Nittaya nodded her understanding. 'But you just said he wrote about his life in Tibet.'

'That's very observant of you, Nittaya. Yes. You see, Keith Gibson spent many years in Tibet before he went to Bangkok. You need to know about his life there.'

'No she does not,' Nick spat back.

'She's an adult, Nick,' Magee responded. 'She needs to know.'

Nick stared menacingly at Magee. 'Is that what this is about? You just want to know what I got up to in Bangkok? Trying to get one over on me, is that your game?'

'I need to know, Nick. So does Brigadier Armstrong. As I said, your peerage depends upon it. That's why he's here. Do you really want to defy him?'

'Fuck you, Magee!' Nick rose from his seat.

'Daddy!' Nittaya cried out, and pulled her father back down.

'Do you really want to take on the Brigadier, Nick? Is it worth it? Sooner or later your antics in Bangkok are going to come out. You might just as well get it over with here, today, where at least you can control it.'

Nick looked in desperation at his daughter. 'This'll destroy us, Nit. A peerage isn't worth that. Tibet is a subject best left unspoken.'

It was John Mansell who intervened. 'Actually, I'm not sure I agree with you, Nick. I think Magee's got a point. Somsuk and Nittaya are adults now. I think it's about time it came out. Time to let it all go. Time to move on.'

'Please, Daddy,' Nittaya said, laying a hand on her father's knee, 'tell me about it.'

Nick choked back a tear. 'It involves your mother, Nit.'

'I imagined it would, but please, I want to know.'

'When you were young, I told you she died in a traffic accident, along with her brother, Jook. That wasn't strictly true.' Tears cascaded down Nick's cheeks.

Nittaya took her father's hand and said, 'I'm not stupid, Daddy. You suffer so much with guilt over her death, it had to be more than a simple car crash.'

Nick wiped away the tears on his face. 'You're so like your mother, Nit. Every time I look at you, I'm reminded of her. Can you imagine how hard that is for me? Every morning, to see you enter the dining room for breakfast, to be reminded I lost the most precious thing in my life?'

'I understand, Daddy. I also understand you need to let her go, for the sake of your health. This may help.'

Nick fell silent for a few moments before facing Magee and saying, 'You'll let me handle this my way?'

'Absolutely.'

'I'm here for you, Nick,' John put in.

Through gritted teeth, Nick said, 'You'd better be right about this, Magee. I'll fucking kill you with my bare hands if this goes wrong for Nit and me.'

'Trust me, Nick. For once, just trust me. Treat it as therapy.'

'Okay, you win,' Nick replied in resignation, 'I give up. What exactly do you want from me?'

'Just the truth about Bangkok and Tibet. That's all.'

'Dear God, we'll be here all day.'

'That's why we've come early,' Magee replied.

'Where do you want me to start?'

'At the beginning, perhaps?' Magee replied with a hint of sarcasm.

'Which is?'

'I recall you just vanished from my beat in Limehouse in the summer of nineteen sixty-nine. No one knew what had happened to you, it was as if you'd disappeared off the face of the earth. Why Bangkok? What made you go out there?'

'Why did I disappear? Huh!' Nick grunted. 'You, of all people, should know the answer to that, Magee. It was your doing.'

'My doing?' Magee asked perplexed, 'What do you mean by that?'

'The seventeenth of July, nineteen sixty-nine. The day after my nineteenth birthday. Don't say you've forgotten what happened that day. The subject came up earlier this year.'

Magee turned red. 'Ah! I wasn't actually expecting you to go back that far.'

'Why not, Magee? Are you saying you don't want to be embarrassed in front of everyone?'

'Well, yes, but ...'

'Tough shit! We started this together, Magee. Like it or not, it's where I'm starting the story. Back in the days when Sean and I lived in Limehouse. Your beat, as you well remember.'

Magee glanced at Brigadier Armstrong. The Brigadier shrugged and said, 'I did warn you, Magee, that you could get egg on your face.'

'But this isn't necessary, sir.'

'Oh, I don't know,' Brigadier Armstrong replied, 'if it helps Mr Price relax, get into the swing of things, it's fine by me.'

Nick Price grinned. 'Right then, Magee, you've probably guessed what I'm going to talk about ...'

****

Limehouse, 17th July 1969

A bright shaft of sunlight broke through the central parting of a pair of garish, floral-design curtains, landed on the edge of a dishevelled bed and inched sideways onto a pillow yellowed by years of a sleeper's involuntary night time dribble. Malevolently, the sunlight pounced upon its unsuspecting prey.

Nick Price's youthful, roughly chiselled, unshaven face twitched in response to the irritation of the unwelcome heat. Drowsy, and with his body still trying to overcome the previous night's alcoholic excesses, he could barely summon the strength to mount any sort of defence.

'Oh, for Christ's sake,' he mumbled incoherently into his pillow.

A minute later he wrenched his body on to his right hand side in a futile attempt to escape the unrelenting heat. Unwittingly, his stomach made contact with the back of the girl he'd met a few hours beforehand. As if by instinct, his left arm fell across her pert young breasts, and his loins stirred.

'Nnn . . . No. No, Nick, not again. Let me sleep, please . . .'

He managed a lazy smile and sighed contentedly. His mind conjured up pleasant memories of two hectic hours of frantic lovemaking, from the early hours to the break of dawn. Sweet sixteen, and never been kissed before. Well, so she'd said, anyway. A not entirely truthful statement, he'd thought at the time. She hadn't been able to get enough of him. Not quite what you'd expect from a virgin.

The girl had been a wonderful birthday present. He made a mental note to thank whoever had put her up to it. He smirked as he reflected on his dawn performance. Was he a wonderful lover, or just the best in the world?

The girl moaned. 'Nnn . . . Nick?'

'Mmm, what?'

'Could you turn the light out please?'

'Yeah, sure, just a second,' he replied. Silly bitch, he thought after a moment's hesitation. She's far too spaced out to even realize what time of day it is.

The Fourth Cart III

Nick lay where he was, gently caressing the girl's breasts, and drifted back to sleep for a few minutes before the shaft of sunlight caught up with his eyes again.

'Nick? Please?' This time the request was accompanied by a jab from the girl's elbow.

'Jesus H. Christ,' Nick huffed in resignation. 'Bloody stupid curtains.'

He threw back the bed sheets, swung his legs down to the floor and sat up, groggily, and for a few seconds tried to focus on his surroundings. He scooped up his underpants from the floor and slipped them on before staggering over to the window. With each step he winced as an acute pain hit him harshly behind his eyes. He had never liked mornings, and today was no exception.

Contrary to the girl's request, he yanked the inadequate strips of curtain fabric aside. An unwise move, he realized a moment too late, as the mid-morning sun's glare hit him squarely in the eyes. He reeled back in agony. 'Fucking hell,' he cursed, his body flinching in shock. Out of habit, he cupped his hands against his face and rubbed vigorously to stimulate the flow of blood. Wiping the sleep from the corners of his eyes, he screwed his face up and squinted over at the girl, lying naked in bed, exposed from the knees upwards.

His mind involuntarily replayed the scenes of the previous night. Him, throwing the girl all over the bed. Her, screaming in ecstasy. Jesus, what a tart she was. And so hungry for more! With his eyes and mind firmly fixed on the pleasures of young flesh, a noticeable bulge appeared in his underwear. A bulge he knew wouldn't go away without attention.

He staggered back to the bed, slunk back under the sheets, ran his fingers over the girl's stomach and tickled her sides to elicit a response as he pressed his bulge up against her buttocks.

'Ahh, no. No, please, not again,' the girl begged. A short burst of giggles gave him a different impression.

His intentions were short lived. A loud series of knocks on the door, accompanied by muffled shouts, called a halt to his desires.

'Nick? Are you up yet, Nick?' came the voice from the other side of the front door. 'It's ten o'clock already. It's time to do the rounds.'

Nick sighed wearily. His anticipated enjoyment ruined. He looked down at the inviting patch of black curly hair between the girl's legs and groaned inwardly. That cute little thing seemed to be screaming for his attention, and he really would have liked to have had one more go. Still, business had to come first.

'Yeah, yeah. All right. All right. I'm coming,' Nick shouted back. 'And for Christ's sake, Sean, stop hammering the fucking door, will you. You'll knock it off its hinges.'

Nick grimaced as he lifted the sheets and threw them over the girl's nakedness. Another day, perhaps, but not now. He had work to do and, in his books, money was more important than fun.

He dragged his heels to the door, muttering vulgar oaths under his breath. With his tired eyes firmly shut, he turned the handle of the lock and opened the door a fraction. 'Come in, Sean. Make yourself useful, will you, and put the kettle on.'

'Sure, Nick.' Sean Fitzpatrick headed for the kitchenette like a faithful dog keen to do his master's bidding.

Nick yawned loudly and headed for the bathroom. 'Coffee for me, Sean. I've a feeling it's going to be a long day. We've got to sort out Garnet Street good and proper this time. Those Paki bastards have got it coming to them. Bloody coons told me to piss off last month. Fucking cheek of it.'

'You want to hit them first thing?'

'Nah, late afternoon will be fine. They know I'm coming today. Let the bastards sweat it out. They'll be twitching like mad by the time we get there. And they'll be sick as dogs. They'll have had a dozen visits to the bog before we show up.' Nick snorted as he accidentally splashed water up his nostrils.

'Shall I round up some help? Terry and Bob aren't doing much these days.'

Nick exited the bathroom and snapped, 'Fuck off!' He advanced menacingly towards Sean, raised a finger and stabbed the air. 'I'll take care of it myself, Sean. As always, right?'

'Sure, Nick. Sorry, I didn't mean anything by it. Just trying to cover your back, that's all. That's what you want me for, isn't it?'

Nick nodded in satisfaction at the half-apology, then accepted the steaming mug of low quality, instant coffee Sean was holding out as a token of subjugation. He smiled contentedly. He liked people to know who was boss. He walked back towards the bathroom carrying the cup of coffee.

'Yeah, okay.' He could smell the girl strongly, the stickiness of their passion still clinging to him. 'Do us a favour, mate. Wake the tart up and kick her out, will you. My wallet is on the hall table. Give her a fiver out of it for a taxi or whatever. Tell her I'll see her tomorrow, maybe, if she's lucky. I need a shave and a bath before we go out.'

An hour later, they were driving down Cable Street in a rented silver sprayed E type Jaguar. Sean at the wheel, Nick looking the height of coolness, elbow perched on the window sill, hand tapping the roof in time to the Beach Boys I Get Around blaring from the car's radio. His eyes surveyed all that they past, in self-admiration. This was his territory. His manor. He would own it all one day, along with everyone living and working within it. Land, property, pubs, businesses, maybe even a nightclub and casino. His business would be bigger than that of the Krays. He had no doubts about his future, he was going to hit the big time with a vengeance. He could feel it in his bones.

'Go down to the docks, Sean. We'll stop off at Greasy George's. I'm famished. I need a fry up before we tackle Garnet Street.'

'Sure, Nick.' Sean swung the Jag ninety degrees left and pulled up sharply outside a run-down cafe.

Nick swung the passenger door open wide, catching the leg of a young uniformed police officer coming out of the cafe.

'Oi! Do you mind? That hit me,' barked the young officer.

Nick broke into a smile. He ignored the officer and edged past him to get into the café, mumbling 'Can't win them all.'

'You cheeky bugger,' the young officer exclaimed. 'You watch your lip.'

'You're a bit green behind the ears aren't you, mate? What happened to the "sir" bit?'

The young officer gave Nick, Sean and their flashy car a slow once-over look. Something very unpleasant seemed to have got under his nose. 'And your name is?'

'Price. Nick Price. And don't you forget it, mate.'

'Well, Mr Price, since you look the type that I'll be meeting again, you'd better know my name as well, because you'll soon learn to respect it,' the officer retorted. 'I'm PC Jack Magee. Sir, to you.'

'Magee, huh? Well, Magee, do you want something, or are you just going to hang around here all day pissing into the wind?'

The two men glared daggers at each other, each priming themselves for an attack like two rutting stags ready to battle over the last doe in the herd.

Eventually, PC Magee sneered contemptuously and said, 'I've got more important things to do than chat to scum.'

Nick laughed loudly as PC Magee moved off on his beat. 'Pathetic crud. What a prick. Come on, Sean. Let's eat.'

The day deteriorated rapidly from that moment onwards. Once Nick had finished his breakfast, he walked up Garnet Street to the Costcutter store only to find Mr Patel behind the counter flanked by two of his heavyset cousins. Seconds later, he was physically thrown into the street.

'You shit bag scum Paki,' Nick shouted, as he picked himself up. 'You're dead meat, you know that? You and your whole fucking family are dead. I'll get you bastards. You can count on that. Nick Price keeps his word, and I mean to get even.'

Mr Patel crudely gestured with the middle finger of his right hand. 'No one collects insurance premiums from me, kid. Now fuck off, I've customers to look after.'

'You fuckhead!' Nick screamed.

'Fuck you, too,' Mr Patel shouted in childlike response.

'Right, you bastard. I warned you. You've got it coming now, you Paki dickhead.' He strutted off down the road and round the corner towards his Jag, muttering under his breath.

'What's the problem, Nick? Do you need me to help?'

'No, Sean, it's nothing. I can take care of it myself. Open the boot, I need some gear.'

Minutes later, Nick strutted back to the Costcutter, took a back swing with a brick in his hand and hurled it at the shop's window. To his amazement a shout came from behind him.

'Oi! What the hell are you playing at?'

Nick turned to see PC Magee not twenty yards away. 'None of your fucking business, mate. Clear off if you know what's good for you.' He picked up a bottle with a rag stuffed into the neck, lit it, and hurled the bottle through the newly created hole in the shop's window.

'Jesus Christ!' As flames leapt through the window, PC Magee hurled himself onto Nick Price saying, 'You're nicked, sunshine.'

'Get off me, you fucking great oaf,' Nick screamed. He lashed out as they crashed to the ground. 'This is nothing to do with you. It should be your job to get rid of those fucking wogs from our country.'

'You bigoted little scum,' PC Magee swore. He aimed a particularly good right hook at Nick Price's jaw.

'Ow! You bastard. I'll teach you to lay your pig hands on me,' countered Nick as he swung an unsuccessful fist at PC Magee's left eye.

'Christ, you're a foul mouthed thug, Price. You deserve to be taught a lesson.' Using a two stone weight advantage, PC Magee pinned Nick Price to the ground, turned him onto his front and trapped his arms with his legs. He reached behind for the handcuffs on his belt.

'Okay, mate, you win,' Nick spat through blooded teeth. 'Look, just let me off and I'll cut you in.'

'What did you just say?'

'Come on, mate, they're all at it down at your station. Everyone's skimming off a bit on the side. It's no big deal.'

'Are you trying to bribe me?'

'God, you're slow aren't you. Of course I'm trying to fucking bribe you. All you pigs are bent, so don't come innocent with me, mate. Just turn a blind eye and I'll give you a cut from my manor.'

'Your manor? Who the hell do you think you are? Some crime lord?'

'I'm Nick Price, that's who. And if you don't get off me right now, you're a dead man. I'll have you taken out before the end of this week, right? And your family. Just let me go, for Christ's sake.'

'You little shit,' PC Magee growled as if something inside him had snapped. He stood up, grabbed the thug off the ground and proceeded to give him a thorough beating.

Nick Price didn't have a chance. The best he could do was to try to defend himself as PC Magee lashed out like a demon possessed. Punches landed everywhere on his body, on his face, in the kidneys, in his groin. Over and over, he fell to the ground, only to be dragged up and hit again. For three minutes, Nick Price suffered a nightmare at the hands of a man gone berserk.

To make matters worse, local residents emerged from their houses and shops and gathered to jeer at the ever-so-tough Nick

Price being beaten to pulp by a fresh-faced policeman. Chanting "Kill him, kill him", the crowds cheered every time Nick was hit.

By the time Magee stopped, Nick was little more than a bloodied mess groveling for mercy. 'Oh my God,' PC Magee muttered looking down at the bloody wreck of Nick Price. 'What have I done?'

Mr Patel moved forward to speak. 'You'd better go, Officer. I won't be pressing charges against him. The fire's out now, and there's very little damage to the shop. Price had this coming, he won't be back here again in a hurry. He's history. You'd better go before anyone else comes along.'

'But . . .'

'It's okay, really, just go.'

PC Magee stared trancelike at the shopkeeper. Surely he should stay, call an ambulance and wait for more police to arrive? He stood motionless for a few seconds before nodding his head and walking off.

Nick had finally been granted his wish. PC Magee had let him go. Scot free, except for the puffy eyes, bruised cheeks, blood dripping from his mouth, a few loose teeth and what felt like a multitude of internal ruptured organs. He just wanted to die. He was in agony. He had been humiliated beyond endurance. His career was ruined. He just wanted the ground to open up and swallow him. He forced opened a small crack in his swelling eyes and, despite extremely blurred vision, he managed to focus on a familiar face bending over him.

'Sean. Christ, Sean,' he whimpered. 'Just get me the hell out of here, please.' Seconds later he passed out unconscious.

Chapter Eleven

'Now just a moment,' Magee said in a raised voice, interrupting Nick's lurid description of their encounter some twenty-three years ago. 'I asked you to stick to the truth. You can't possibly know what I was thinking that day.'

Nick smiled in Magee's direction. 'You don't deny it though.'

'That's not the point. I need you to stick to the facts. You're embellishing them out of all proportion. It's a gross exaggeration to portray me like that, you make me sound bigoted. You were the bigot, not me.'

'You were arrogant then, Magee. Even more so than now.'

'And you weren't?'

Nittaya gripped her father's hand. 'Please, Daddy, don't start a bickering match now. This is getting interesting; you've never spoken of your youth in this way before. It's fascinating. Casual sex, petty crime, racist language. It's the real you isn't it? The real Nick Price I've never known, but clearly the one that the Chief Inspector remembers.'

'You wouldn't have been proud of me, Nit. I'm certainly not proud looking back on it. But it was life as it was. You see, I never knew my Dad, and my Mum died when I was five. I was dumped on my Uncle Reg and Aunt Liz. They treated me like dirt, so I grew up in a hostile environment with no love around. It was inevitable that I turned into a young thug.'

Brigadier Armstrong sighed and interjected, 'My heart bleeds for you, Mr Price. But perhaps we could get back on track. You've explained how you'd been beaten up by Magee. It sounded as though you deserved it. Please continue. And perhaps you could tone down the colourful language. I'm not sure it helps paint an accurate picture.'

'Yeah, well, bloody PC Magee, is all I'll say. I swore I'd kill him once I got out of that sodding hospital Sean took me to . . .'

****

Hospitalization, July 1969

As Nick's unconscious body was carted off into an emergency operating theatre, a rather plump, formidable ward sister marched straight up to Sean Fitzpatrick. She frowned in scorn at his flashy, wide-boy clothes, shook her head, tutted as though in frustration at the hopelessness of modern youth and demanded an explanation.

'What on earth happened to him?'

Sean decided to keep the lie simple. 'He fell down stairs,'

'Fell down stairs? He looks as though he's been sat on by an elephant.'

'Well, there were rather a lot stairs.'

'Poppycock, young man. Absolute rot. He's been in a fight hasn't he?'

'Um . . .'

The ward sister folded her arms as best she could around her ample figure. 'It's no good trying to cover up for your friend. This is a serious matter young man, I'll have you know. Have you called the police?'

'No!'

'Well you should have, he's in a serious condition. We could be talking attempted murder here. The police should know about it.'

'Somehow, I don't think they'd want to.'

'And why didn't you call for an ambulance, for heaven's sake. He's bleeding internally.'

'I thought it would be quicker by car.'

'You thought . . . you thought? Well, young man, you didn't think good enough. He should have had medical assistance immediately. An ambulance team might have made all the difference.'

'Yes, well I'll know better next time, won't I.'

The ward sister looked horrified. 'Next time? There'll be no "next time" for your friend. He's probably ruptured his spleen. The doctor is going to have to operate very quickly. Your friend is lucky to be alive at this very moment. Next time he gets into a fight he'll be dead, it's as simple as that. If your friend is lucky enough to survive the operation, then he won't be seeing any action for a few years, if ever again. His wounds are going to take a long time to heal. He mustn't expose himself to any more fights, do you understand, it could be fatal for him.'

'I'll tell him, Sister. Honest.'

'You do that. Now, out of the way. I've got work to do. You can go and sit in reception if you like. Leave your details with the nurse on the front desk. She'll inform you of any progress. Now, off with you.'

The ward sister strutted off leaving Sean cowering like a schoolboy. 'Yes, Sister. Anything you say, Sister. Right away, Sister,' Sean mumbled as he wandered off in the direction of the reception. 'Wonderful. Bloody wonderful. Now what's Nick going to do for a living?'

It was three days later before Sean Fitzpatrick returned to the hospital. He leaned over Nick's body stretched out on a bed and searched for any vague sign of life.

'Nick? Can you hear me, Nick? Are you still alive?'

'Course I'm alive, you fucking idiot,' Nick barked, sending Sean reeling backwards in surprise. 'And I was enjoying the peace and quiet before you came barging in here.'

'Jesus, Nick. I'm sorry. I didn't know you were awake.'

'I wasn't a minute ago.'

'I mean conscious. I didn't know you were conscious. The nurse outside didn't seem to know.'

'Well I am now, no thanks to you. Where've you been? I've been lying here for days without knowing what's going on. Where's the doctor, for Christ's sake?'

'He said he'll speak to you on his rounds, six o'clock this evening.'

Nick noted the way Sean wouldn't make eye contact. 'Did he say when I'll be out of here? I've got to sort out that bastard Magee. By the time I've finished with him, he'll be sorry he was born. Have you found out where he lives yet? He's the first job on the list, just as soon as I get out of this dump. Maybe I'll get him in the night, storm into his bedroom and give him a heart attack. Yeah, and . . .'

'Nick'

'. . . a sledgehammer through his front door . . .'

'Nick?'

'. . . and an axe into his head . . .'

'Nick!'

'What?'

'No more rough stuff. Doctor's orders. You'll die otherwise.'

'What? What the fuck are you talking about?'

'You know, like a boxer that's had one too many rounds in the ring. You can't fight any more, Nick. You ruptured some organs inside, you've been sewn up but you can't afford to damage them again. The doctor will tell you this evening. Honestly.'

Nick stuck out a finger in Sean's direction. 'You're having me on, right?'

Sean lowered his head and whispered softly. 'No, Nick. Sorry, no messing around. You're out of it.'

Nick made a fist with his right hand, flexed his arm muscles and smirked at his companion. 'Like fuck I am. You wait and see, mate. I'll be back. Nothing keeps me down. Nothing.' And with that, his eyes faded shut.

'Nick? Nick?'

But there was no response. Not a murmur. Not for three more days. Three days in which Sean virtually camped out in the hospital waiting for news.

At the start of the fourth day of Nick's unconscious, a pretty young trainee nurse sat in a bedside chair dabbing at the rivulets of sweat pouring off his forehead. She looked up in response to a question from Sean Fitzpatrick.

'The doctor called it post dramatic shock, sir.' She frowned and added, 'Or something like that, anyway. Are you his friend that brought him in last week?'

'Yes,' Sean replied, appearing shocked at the deterioration of his friend lying in an almost comatose state, drenched from head to toe with his own bodily waste fluids.

'I heard there was blood all over the car.'

'Yes, it was a bit of a mess.'

The Fourth Cart III

'Wish I'd been there. I never get anything exciting to do, just bed baths and bed pans. It's not exactly exciting. Not what I had in mind, anyway, when I took this job.'

'No, I can understand,' Sean replied completely dazed. Nick was so white. He looked as though he was at death's door.

'Is he a famous gangster? I heard he'd been in a really vicious fight. Took ten others on, they say, single handed as well. He must be really brave.'

'How long?' Sean barked impatiently, interrupting the nurse. 'How long before he snaps out of it?'

'I don't know,' the nurse shrugged. 'The doctor reckons maybe a few days if he's lucky. If not, it might be permanent.'

Sean was speechless. Without Nick he would be lost, he would have no future. He stared down at Nick's feeble body. Dark thoughts came to him. Maybe Nick would die. Worse, maybe he would be paralyzed. He couldn't cope. He turned and left the ward.

A week later, Sean Fitzpatrick found Nick sitting huddled up on top of his bed. His body shook uncontrollably. His face was battered, bruised, and purple. His eyes were swollen, puffed up like a soufflé.

'How's it going, Nick?'

Nick appeared not to have heard Sean's question. He sat staring ahead, towards the bottom of the bed. Sean repeated the question, a little more loudly. No response. He sat down and started to pick at the bunch of grapes, untouched since he'd brought them in the day before. He continued to sit, unspeaking.

Nick's head dropped a couple of inches, as if nodding off, then jolted back up. He turned to his bedside companion and asked, 'How much money do you have, Sean?'

Sean frowned as if wondering whether Nick was in need of a hand out. 'About a thousand quid, give or take a few bob.'

'Yeah, I've got about the same. It's not much really, is it?' Nick continued to shake whilst staring intently at his toes. 'I'm going away for a bit. The doctor said I need a rest. He suggested I have a holiday.'

'Where to?'

'Anywhere. Overseas, perhaps. So long as it's as far away from Limehouse as possible.'

Sean looked to the floor as if in contemplation of a life in exile.

'I need to go somewhere else, Sean. Somewhere no one has ever heard my name. And I need rest. Lots of it. Do you want to come with me?'

'Sure. Where though? Any suggestions?'

'You choose. It's all the same to me.'

Sean shrugged. 'I don't know anywhere overseas. I've never even been out of London. It's all the same isn't it? Hot weather and bloody foreigners everywhere.'

Nick broke his stare and gave a look of annoyance to his so-called best friend. 'Don't you know anywhere suitable for a rest?'

'France? Spain? Italy?'

'No! They're too close. I want to go somewhere exotic. Somewhere on the other side of the world.'

'Tahiti?'

'Nah! Elvis has been there, hasn't he? It's too namby-pamby. All that tribal culture crap, there's not enough real action.'

'Bangkok, then?'

'Sounds good. Where is it?'

'Fuck knows. Overseas somewhere. There's an article about it in a magazine I've been looking through down in Reception. It's where all them American soldiers go for rest after they've been shot up in Vietnam. Cheap beer and thousands of girls giving it away for a few bob a time. The article said there are even bars where naked girls wander around giving the customers blow jobs under the counter for free.'

Nick noticeably perked up. 'Yeah? You're joking?'

'Well, maybe not for free. But they certainly do it in the bars while you're having a beer. And on stage. Yeah, that's right. The magazine said there're live sex shows on stage.'

'Really? Sounds like fun. Okay, Sean. Enough. Don't give me a hard-on talking about it, it might damage my insides. Go and book a couple of airline tickets, one way.'

The Fourth Cart III

Chapter Twelve

'So, just like that, you did a disappearing act?' Magee asked.

'Yep. Within a couple of weeks, Sean and I were on our way to Thailand.'

'And you told no one where you were going?'

'No way. I was dead scared that someone might have taken out a contract on me. I just wanted to slip out of the country unnoticed.'

'You certainly succeeded. I certainly thought you must be dead.'

Nick snorted. 'Life's full of disappointments, Magee.'

'I didn't mean it like that.'

'Not much you didn't. I bet you were shit scared that you'd be in trouble if I reported the attack.'

Magee glanced at Melissa then at the Brigadier. He'd never managed to get over the incident. He was still haunted by the feckless way he'd lost control that ghastly day. 'So, you flew to Thailand for a holiday in, what, August nineteen sixty-nine? That must have been quite an eye-opener for someone who had never been outside London.'

'It certainly was. It was unbelievable out there. Bangkok was so different to London, not just the climate but the culture as well. I couldn't possibly have imagined what it would be like before I went. It took me ages to find my feet . . .'

****

Bangkok August 1969

'Christ it's fucking hot,' Nick swore as he stepped out into the tropical heat surrounding the airport.

'I told you it was always hot overseas,' Sean responded.

'Not this fucking hot, though.'

'How hot is "hot", then?'

'Fuck it, Sean. Never mind, let's just get the hell out of here. Taxi!' Nick waved in the direction of a man loitering near a car fifty yards away. The man vaguely looked in Nick's direction, then returned to the pleasures of his cigarette. 'Oi! Taxi! Yes you, you fucking dipstick! Taxi, for Christ's sake. Jesus, don't you speak fucking English? Get your ass over here.'

The taxi driver flicked his cigarette into the road and slowly wandered around to the driver's door.

Sean shook his head in despair. 'Nicely put, Nick. I'm sure he appreciated that.'

'Well, for pity's sake, he could have made an effort.'

As the taxi pulled up in front of them, Nick did his best to communicate his desire for a cheap hotel in the centre of Bangkok. The journey took an hour, for most of the time Nick stared agog at the passing scenery. The colours everywhere were of an extraordinary intensity he'd never have believed possible. The sky, trees, greenery, peoples' clothes, everything was so much more colourful than the grey drabness of London's East End. Yet alongside the beauty was a poverty far worse than he'd ever experienced in the post-war misery of the nineteen fifties. He couldn't believe people lived in rough shacks that made the East End slums look luxurious. Bangkok, the so-called city of angels, both fascinated and horrified him.

It was only on arrival at a hotel in Suriwong Road that his normal irritability returned. 'Jesus, what a stench,' he swore as he stepped out of the taxi. 'Is there an open sewer around here?'

'Don't complain, Nick. The taxi driver says it's the cheapest hotel around. It's only going to cost us fifty baht a night, that's not bad.'

'Really? And just how much is fifty baht in real money, then?'

'Um . . . I think the exchange rate is set at twenty baht to one American dollar. So that makes it, um . . . '

'I thought so. You don't know, do you? Christ, Sean, we could be ripped off and we'd never know about it. We've got some learning to do, fast. Come on, let's get checked-in and unpacked, I want to try out this Patpong place, the taxi driver said it's the next road along from here. I can't wait.'

The Fourth Cart III

By mid-evening, Nick had concluded that he had indeed picked the best place on earth for a holiday. Patpong Road was so vibrant it was mind-boggling. There were dozens, if not hundreds, of bars lining the roadside. Outside each bar stood a handful of touts, bouncers and tarts, all beckoning the passerby to enter. Music blared out into the street. Neon signs proclaimed massage parlours, go-go dancing, live sex shows, cheap beer and cheep food. Anything you could want seemed to be on offer. Best of all though, he reckoned, scantily clad, petite Thai women festooned the place. Everywhere he looked, his eyes fell on the most beautiful girls he had ever seen. He was in paradise.

'Here we go, The British Bulldog,' Nick shouted over the roar of touts competing for their attention. It had taken him no time at all to establish the name of the best bar for unemployed drifters to hang out. It hadn't been a difficult task, what with there being so many low-life characters around to ask. 'Come on, Sean, stop fussing around like an old woman and get your ass in here.'

Sean appeared not to have heard. He seemed more interested in catching glimpses of naked flesh in the bars they were passing.

'Sean!' Nick shouted. 'Come on, will you. You go in one of those places and you'll lose your wallet. You heard what the man said back there. Don't go in one of them places until you've become streetwise. The girls will fleece you. You'll come out broke. Come on, leave it till later.'

'Sorry, Nick, but I can't. I've got to try it out. I'll catch you later. I need to see this.'

'On your own head be it, then,' Nick relented. 'God, Sean, you're a pain at times. Come on, give me half of what's in your wallet. That will cut your losses. You know you'll spend everything you have in your pocket, you always do.'

'You know something, Nick?' Sean asked, as he took out a wad of notes from his wallet. 'I could get to like this place. I feel at home.'

'See you, Sean.' Nick smiled as he watched his friend disappear through a doorway. He caught a glimpse of a line of bikini-clad girls gyrating on stage. He shook his head in despair. He knew Sean well; he'd be penniless before the night was out.

In high expectation, Nick opened the door to The British Bulldog. He felt at ease immediately. The design of the bar resembled a small English pub, there were no go-go girls and the customers looked scruffy. He jostled his way to the bar, ordered a beer and turned to look for somewhere to sit. To his annoyance someone carelessly barged into him.

'Christ's sake!' Nick swore as half his beer shot out the glass and splattered to the ground. He rounded sharply on the customer that had just knocked into him. 'Do you mind, you fucking bozo!'

'Erm, sorry. I'm sorry, I didn't mean to do that.'

Nick glared venomously at the customer. 'What the fuck are you playing at?'

'I, erm, erm. Gee, I'm sorry, can I buy you another?'

'Too bloody right you can, mate.' It was then that he noticed the vague, unfocused look of man's eyes. He sighed and his anger dissipated at the realization that the man was stoned.

'I'm, erm, really sorry. I didn't mean to cause offense.'

Nick changed tactics. 'Never mind, old son. It was just an accident. Look, I've only arrived here today. I need some help, I'd like to talk to you. Can I buy you a drink, instead?'

'Gee, thanks.'

Nick turned back to the bar, waved a note at the bartender and indicated another beer. He returned to his new companion and said, 'My name's Nick by the way. Do you have a few minutes spare? I need a chat about how things work around here.'

'Sure, Nick. Don't see why not. I'm not with anyone. I'm Keith by the way.'

Nick took no time coming to the point. 'Look, Keith, I need work. I've had to leave England in a hurry, if you know what I mean, and I don't intend to return for a long time. Do you know of any work going? I'll do anything, no matter how hard or dirty. Anything at all.'

'Well, not really, Nick. You won't be able to work as a barman or anything like that. The government here won't let foreigners work. Not unless you have special skills, like a doctor or engineer. Even then you need a work permit, which takes ages because of the bureaucracy.'

'But there are lots of blokes here, around this bar, who don't look like tourists. They must work out here to get money to live on. What do they do?'

'Some of them teach English. Others own small businesses.'

'You can own a business, then?'

The Fourth Cart III

'Oh, yeah. But you need a Thai partner to own more than fifty per cent of the business. That can lead to problems. Some of the men here have lost the lot when their partners have sold up in secret and run off with the money. You have to be real careful in this country, Nick. It's not the same as in England.'

'I'm sure,' Nick responded, 'but I don't have enough capital to start a business here. What work do you do, Keith?'

'Erm, well, actually, I don't. I've got some savings I'm living on at the moment.'

'Lucky bugger.'

'There is an American guy I know. He has a bit of a reputation for being, you know, shady. He can supply anything you want, if you know what I mean. He does well out of the Americans.'

'Now that sounds more like it.'

'I, erm, buy stuff from him from time to time. He's a bit fly, but I think he's honest in his dealings. Sometimes I have to pay him in advance but he's never cheated me. He's the sort of person you want to talk to.'

'Can you introduce me?'

'Sure, Nick. He usually comes in around eleven. He takes orders from his customers, sees what people want supplied. That sort of thing. He'll be here soon probably.'

Nick had hope at last. 'Let me buy you another beer, Keith.' Without waiting for a reply, he caught the bartender's eye and indicated two more beers. On turning round he caught Keith toying with a large dark red stone. 'Ruby, is it?'

'Erm, yes. Do you know your gemstones?'

'Nah, just guessing.'

'It comes from Tibet. I used to live there. I used to tutor the Dalai Lama, but we had to flee the country when the Chinese invaded. He got out, but I was captured. I finished up in prison for nearly ten years, but I got this stone when I left.'

Nick was confused. 'Really?' he asked, wondering whether all Tibetan prisoners were given a ruby the size of a plum on finishing their time. He assumed Keith's ramblings were the result of the drugs.

'Yeah, I'm a doctor, you know. I got a PhD from Oxford, I based my thesis on some of the ancient Tibetan religious scrolls the

Dalai Lama allowed me access to. Buddhism is such a fascinating religion. Did you know that the Buddha . . .'

'Hi, Keith. How're you doing?'

Keith stopped speaking to look around at the man who had interrupted him. 'Oh, hi, Mark. Glad you came in. Can I introduce you to Nick, here? He's only just arrived today, and he's looking for work.'

'Great. Hi, Nick. I'm Mark Nolan. What type of work you after?'

'Anything at all.' The look on his face underlined the desperation of his words.

Mark Nolan withdrew a card from his pocket and offered it to Nick. 'I have an apartment not far from here, in Soi Saladaeng. It's about a ten minute walk, turn left at the bottom of this road, cross over and it's the second side road you come to. Come and see me tomorrow afternoon. Two o'clock works best for me. Don't fail, if you're really interested in work, that is.'

'I'll be there, for sure,' Nick replied holding his hand out.

Nick slept fitfully that night. He lay awake brooding over the inevitability of becoming a drug courier. There really wasn't much other work he could have done.

Late morning, he staggered down to the hotel coffee shop to find Sean eating breakfast with a look of guilt on his face he'd seen before.

'You dipstick,' Nick muttered as he approached the table. 'You spent the lot last night, didn't you? Don't lie, I know you too well.'

Sean winced. 'Only half, Nick, you kept the other half, if you remember.'

'Just as well wasn't it, or we wouldn't be able to pay for this food. Jesus, Sean, don't you ever learn? Your brain turns to putty the moment you see a bit of skirt. How are you going to survive here? You'll be dipping your wick every day, getting sozzled, and no doubt buying drinks for every tart in the bar. You'll be broke before the week's finished.'

'I know, Nick. Don't go on about it.'

'You need to learn to keep your trousers on. I take it you brought a tart back here last night. How much did she cost?'

'It was just money for her to get a taxi home, that's all.'

'Bollocks,' Nick retorted. 'No tart's going to sleep with you just for taxi money. You're far too ugly. How much? And don't tell me any porkies.'

'A hundred baht, Nick.'

'A hundred? And is that cheap, expensive, or what?'

'I'm, erm, not sure. It's what she asked for.'

'Oh, dear Christ, Sean. You really do need to wise up. Look, I've managed to find a guy who'll give us work. Nothing much. It's going to involve making deliveries around town. I'll share the work with you, and the money, but you've really got to get streetwise. You're on rations from now on. It's for your own good. You need to be level headed during the day.'

'Whatever you say, Nick.'

'Right, then. Here's a hundred baht. Your task for the day is to find rented accommodation. A small two bedroom flat, perhaps. There must be somewhere cheaper to live than in a hotel. We need to settle down to a normal life here, we're not tourists, we're not going home after a fortnight. We can't afford to live in style. Not yet, anyway. So, off you go. I've got plans to make.'

'Sure, Nick, anything you say.'

And so Nick settled down to a daily routine of being a petty drug courier, picking up supplies in the early afternoon and delivering them to customers around town. Gradually he built up a network, employing drifters he met in bars to act as couriers instead of himself. It meant sharing the money, but it minimized the risk of getting caught. It was a shabby existence. Enough money came his way to survive, but he lived cheaply, spending most of his ill gotten gains on beer and sex.

It was a life, of sorts, and continued for nearly a year before fate took a turn for the worse. The day had started badly, and from the moment he'd entered Mark Nolan's apartment, he could sense the man was in a foul mood.

'Look, Nick,' Mark Nolan spat out the words, 'You've done me proud this last year, why are you giving me grief now? This package is urgent, why won't you take it?'

'I told you already, I haven't got any spare men. I can't do it. I don't have the manpower, alright?'

'But you must do it, Nick. You've never refused before.'

'Well I'm refusing now.'

'You asshole! If you refuse this one, I won't offer you any more.'

'Is that a threat?'

'Yes it damn well is.'

'What?'

'You heard. You do this one, Nick, or else.'

'Or else what?'

'Or else the big guy takes his custom elsewhere, that's what. How much business have you had from me so far, huh? What'll you do without me? Go back home? Come on, Nick. We all know you piss your money away in the evenings. You couldn't scrape enough money together to buy a bus ticket out of the country.'

Nick stopped shouting long enough to consider the consequences of having his only source of income dry up. He conceded the point. 'Okay, okay. I'll have to go myself, though. So don't expect me around for a week.'

Mark Nolan gave Nick a slap on the back. 'Good man. You won't regret it.'

'How much for this trip?'

'Twenty five thousand dollars. All inclusive, pay your own expenses, as usual, but I guess you'll get all of it to yourself this time, no one to cut it with. Good luck is all I can say. It's a hell of a trip to Saigon.'

'Yeah, so I'm told. A few of the lads I've sent before refused to go a second time. They say the journey can get a bit hairy.'

'You'll cope, Nick. You're that type. Always come up smelling of roses, isn't that what you Brits say?'

'Yeah, we do. Right then. Harry's Bar in Saigon it is. Presumably Danny Curtis will be there to receive it?'

'Yep. His unit is flying out tomorrow.'

'Don't suppose he could take the stuff with him?'

'No way, Nick. Not his style. They get checks before they board, you know, ordered by some interfering, do-good, liberal minded wishy-washy Congressional Committee. They would just love to catch a colonel red-handed with fifty Ks of Thai Horse in a bag. Here, don't forget these.' Mark chucked Nick a bunch of keys. 'The old army jeep's just round the corner. Three thousand dollar reimbursement, please, if you don't return it.'

'I won't forget.' Nick cursed under his breath. This was a fool's outing. No one in his right mind would attempt the trip. Not if they knew what perils lay in waiting. He'd heard tales of minefields, snipers, VC patrols, American bombing raids. You name it, everything a war zone could offer, there it was, lying in wait on the road to Saigon.

Chapter Thirteen

'Let's get this straight,' Magee said. 'Earlier this year, Mark Nolan was being interrogated by the American intelligence service in Bangkok. He said under questioning that he saw you strolling through Lumpini Park alongside Khun Sa sometime in the early seventies. Given that you met Nolan on your first night in Bangkok in August 1969, and worked for him from then onwards, he would have known your face well. It's unlikely that he was mistaken about seeing you in the park.'

Nick responded, 'I never denied knowing him.'

Magee reflected on a past conversation he'd had with Nick. 'That's not quite the way I remember things.'

Nick grew angry. 'You knew damn well I didn't want Nittaya to know about those days. I'm not proud of them, Magee. That's why I didn't want to talk about Mark Nolan when you came barging in here, prying into my private life.'

Nittaya gripped her father's hand. 'That's okay, Daddy. It's history. We know it was hard for you to survive. You did what you could. No one's going to hold that against you now.'

Nick pointed towards Magee and muttered to his daughter, 'You should tell that to him.'

Magee scratched his chin and said, 'Let's move on. We've established that you met Keith Gibson on your first night in Bangkok and he introduced you to Mark Nolan. Presumably, Mark was Keith's supplier?'

'So he said. Why, does it matter?'

'Maybe. I'm just trying to put things in place. I'm trying to work out how Khun Sa could have been so close to you without you realizing it, as you insist.'

'I do insist, yes. Very much so. I may have acted as a courier for a year or so, whilst I was down on my luck, but that's a world away from being a drug lord.'

'You're saying you only couriered drugs for a year?'

'Correct.'

'Why. What happened? Something better come along?'

'Yeah. It did, as it happens,' Nick said. 'I met John. He was my lucky charm. He saved me from a living nightmare.'

'I need to hear about that.'

Nick groaned. 'I'd prefer not to talk about, if you don't mind. I still get flashbacks to those times. Ask Nit, they leave me frozen in a stupor. So I don't particularly relish the idea of provoking another bout.'

'Post traumatic shock?' Brigadier Armstrong chipped in.

'I suppose so,' Nick replied.

'I'm told retelling the events is a step forward. It helps get the brain to acknowledge what happened.'

Nick's face crunched up in distaste. 'What? You're a shrink as well?'

'No, not a qualified one,' Brigadier Armstrong said. 'But I was an officer in the Malayan Emergency. I had to deal with many men who suffered what we now know as Posttraumatic Stress Disorder Syndrome.'

Nick crossed his arms and gave the brigadier a piercing look. 'You calling me a nutter?'

'Certainly not. I'm merely suggesting that you might benefit from some psychological therapy.'

Nick sat fuming for a few moments.

'Any chance of a cup of tea?' Brigadier Armstrong asked. 'I really am rather parched.'

Nick Price threw his hands up and said, 'Well excuse me! I'm so sorry, Brigadier. What with you and Magee ripping into my private life, my manners seem to have gone out of the window.'

'I'll see to it,' John Mansell said rising from his chair.

'Thanks, John,' Magee replied. 'But I need your input on how you saved Nick from this nightmare he's mentioned.'

'I'll go,' Paul Mansell said. 'I need to use the bathroom, anyway.'

Nick nodded his appreciation. 'Thanks, Paul. Ask Annie to bring us all some refreshments will you? And let her know it looks like we've got extra guests for lunch.'

Paul replied, 'Will do,' as he left the room.

Nick rubbed his temples. 'You two are making my head hurt. I've forgotten where I was.'

'You were telling us your fond memories of your shabby existence running drugs in Bangkok,' Magee responded. 'But that it only lasted a year.'

'Yeah, that's right. It went well for a year. But that spat with Mark Nolan ruined everything. I should never have done the run to Saigon myself. It was a bloody nightmare, the jeep ran over a landmine and the VC captured and tortured me.' Nick paused for a moment, wiped away a bead of sweat on his forehead, and said, 'Actually, I think John should relate the next part of the story. I wasn't too clear which way was up at that time, thanks to those bastard VC soldiers . . .'

****

Vietnam, July 1970

The helicopter emitted a steady whoop, whoop, whoop noise as it hovered over an open field of long grass reeds. A hundred yards away lay the overturned wreck of an army jeep. The festering neck of a decapitated corpse could be seen swarming with flies. Three other lifeless bodies lay within twenty feet of the wreckage. A survivor, clothed in a blood-stained American Army uniform, sat propped up against the jeep's chassis. He waved in desperation at the helicopter, beckoning it ever nearer.

Sergeant Mike McCoy lowered his field glasses and turned to the helicopter pilot. 'There's one still alive. Looks like he's one of ours.'

'We'd better take a look. Man the guns,' the pilot shouted to the five men seated behind him.

Four American soldiers slung their rifles forward into a firing position and leant out of the open doorways. They were nervous. Was it a trap? Had there been any reports received of a lost jeep? Should they call base first? Were they doing the right thing? Why get involved, why not just put a bullet into the man's skull from the safety of the helicopter?

'Get ready, boys,' Sergeant McCoy shouted over his shoulder. 'We're going in. Not you, John. You stay inside. I can't take responsibility for you wondering around out there. We can't cover you. It's too risky.'

The intended recipient ignored the order. John Mansell was the first man out, jumping before the helicopter had come to rest. 'Shit, John. Come back here, you crazy son of a bitch.' The helicopter rocked slightly, adjusting to the loss of weight.

A smooth skinned, boyishly handsome, blond, nineteen year old English lad ducked as his feet touched the ground. Though dressed in army apparel, he was no soldier. His weapon was the camera, and he worked out of Saigon with Agency News.

Sergeant McCoy ignored the plight of the crazy cameraman and raised his field glasses again as the helicopter settled. 'He's one of ours. He's badly wounded by the look of it. Okay, lads, go in. Make it quick, I'm nervous already.'

The four American soldiers jumped out of the helicopter and headed off on a hundred yard dash through the long grass reeds to their target. John smiled at the ensuing drama. He could capture a perfect shot, with the helicopter in the foreground, the running soldiers wading through thigh length grass in the centre and the wounded man up against the overturned jeep in the background. He stepped backwards, seeking the best angle, his eyes glued to the camera's view finder. On the seventh pace backwards, he disappeared from sight.

As the first American reached the jeep, eight armed VC soldiers sprung from their lair. Caught off guard, the Americans were dead before the hit the ground.

Sergeant McCoy had no more than a second to react to the situation before a ground-launched rocket exploded against the helicopter's window. As the explosive force shattered the glass into his face, he gave vent to an ear piercing scream.

The pilot sat upright, frozen, a two inch shard of glass sticking out of his left eye. A flood of blood gushed down his nostrils, scarcely noticeable against the red sticky mess that had once been his face.

A stray bullet found its mark with the fuel tank. The tank ruptured, turning into a giant flame thrower spraying burning fuel thirty feet in the air. Sergeant McCoy's agonizing screams fell silent as the helicopter exploded in an inferno of mangled metal.

Until the helicopter exploded, John had being lying semi-conscious ten feet down an old VC tunnel, oblivious to what was happening above. The shock wave from the explosion reverberated down the tunnel walls and shook him awake. His head jerked back, he opened his eyes, stuck his hands out and felt his immediate surroundings. Earth. Crumbling earth, all around him. He was trapped underground, buried alive. He wriggled violently and felt panic in the confusion of his dark and unnerving confinement.

As he came to his senses, he stopped struggling to focus his thoughts. He looked upwards. He must have come from that direction, but there was nothing but earth there now. If he tried to claw his way out, he might cause more earth to collapse. He reasoned that tunnels were usually part of a system, so there was likely to be other exits. He realized he had to go down, but shuddered as he pictured himself coming face to face with a twenty foot boa constrictor, with no way to turn and run.

Minutes later, he squirmed his way into an underground chamber in which he could almost stand up. He groped around, fumbling against the walls, until his hand knocked against a bamboo pole. He seized it and explored its shape. Two upright thick poles, small slats binding them together every foot or so. He let out a sigh of relief. Someone up there was looking after him today.

A patch of grass jerked in the field as John wrestled with a trap door. No air. Only smoke. Smoke everywhere, along with a nauseous stench of burning oil. It could only be the helicopter. He froze as he heard the noise of a short burst of rifle fire in the distance. Then another short burst. It was an unsettling sound. No counter fire? Again, isolated, deliberate shots with no resistance. He bit his lip and delicately raised the trap door a few inches.

Even with limited ground level vision, there could be no mistake as to what the VC soldiers were doing. He swore silently. Mike McCoy and his unit had been his best friends these last few months and those bastards were treating them like vermin. What the hell had happened out there?

Voices. Close by. No more than ten feet away. He screwed up his eyes and cursed. Could the VC have counted the number of men in the helicopter? Maybe they hadn't seen him get out. Maybe the tunnel entrance wasn't visible. As long as they didn't stray too far from the wreckage, then they wouldn't see the collapsed tunnel. Hopefully, the helicopter's down-draught would have flattened the grass.

John's knowledge of the Vietnamese language was limited, mainly to coarse names for parts of the human anatomy and bodily functions, but he did know the expression for "Let's go". He heard it now and thanked God for it. He waited an agonizing ten minutes before pushing back the trap door sufficiently to crawl out of his tomb.

From the safety of the grass reeds, he ventured to peer in the direction of the jeep. He watched as the VC soldiers struggled with the man that had been propped up against the jeep. They were kicking him, shouting abuse at him. He watched the scene in a confused state of mind. Why had the man waved at the helicopter? Why hadn't he tried to warn McCoy's unit of the impending danger as they came to his rescue?

As the VC soldiers and their prisoner moved off, he followed them on all fours. Thoughts of revenge crept into his mind. Maybe he could even get a decent photo out of the prisoner's plight. If nothing else, he needed to find a way out of the area.

Twenty minutes later, he slid into a trench for safety as voices came too close for comfort. He peered out from the top of the trench to see a clearing ahead with four wooden huts built on stilts above a pool of black water. The huts looked derelict, but appeared to be home for the VC soldiers who had circled ahead and were now standing on a platform rigged over the water. He checked his possessions; a water canister, a camera, a watch, a few notes in his wallet and a commando knife. Not much for a man stranded in the middle of nowhere. Quite what he was going to do next, he wasn't sure.

As the afternoon passed by, the noise from the huts grew louder. He could hear raucous laughter, shouting and stamping of feet. Every half hour or so, one of the VC soldiers would come out of the hut to urinate over the side of the platform and, every time it occurred, the urinating soldier would scream with laughter. It didn't seem particularly important, but it annoyed him not knowing what was going on. His curiosity got the better of him and he crawled closer to the water's edge for a better view.

The water was stagnant, thick and greasy. It gave off the foulest of smells, a putrefying combination of excrement, oil, rotted water hyacinth and decomposing flesh. He choked back bile as his guts recoiled from the stench, but at least he could now see what the excitement was all about. Beneath the huts, he saw a bamboo cage, immersed in the water, with the prisoner inside.

He shrank back into dense bushes and found some shade to rest in. He removed his camera from around his neck and swigged thirstily from his water flask. As he gulped backed the tepid liquid, he decided he had to help the prisoner, he had to swim to the man's rescue. He screwed his face up in horror at the thought of leeches, snakes and other creepy, crawly things that were bound to live in the water, but he knew he had to try.

A few hours later, both darkness and quietness had fallen. Only the merest gleam of light shone from the distant moon high in the sky. There was a dim light emanating from one of the huts, but no movement and no man-made sound; just the usual noise of a night-time jungle. He rose, but ducked for cover as a groan, loud enough to waken the dead, rumbled through his stomach and echoed all around. He was starving.

He stripped off his clothes, placed them in a neat pile, picked up his knife and sneaked quietly towards the water to test it with his toes. It was so thick it left a scummy film clinging to his foot, but it was, at least, warm. He gripped his knife between his teeth and waded into the water as gently as possible, his nose flinching as obnoxious gases wafted up from the rotting vegetation under his feet. Slime oozed through the gaps between his toes as he sank up to his knees in the putrid silt deposits.

He lowered his torso into the slimy water and swam gently towards the caged man. His progress was smooth and quiet, not even the lightest of sleepers would have been woken, let alone a drunken soldier. Yet with each stroke, a ripple advanced towards the prisoner. The closer he got, the more the cage shook.

'Jesus Christ,' the prisoner gasped, as John reached the cage. 'I thought you were a crocodile.'

John felt for the caged man's right arm and followed it to where it was tied. He cut the bonds, then repeated the action with the other arm. Within seconds the rope securing the cage door was cut and the prisoner was able to ease himself out. He pointed up to the hut and received a nod in response. With a minimum of noise, he hauled himself out of the water on to the platform, and then helped pull the prisoner out.

Both men lay prone for a few seconds listening for any indication that they had been heard. Thankfully, the peaceful sound of snoring continued. John stood up, crept forward and peered into the nearest hut. The soft light of a kerosene lamp hanging from the ceiling cast eerie shadows around the room. In the centre of the floor, the VC soldiers lay sprawled in a drunken state among dozens of whisky bottles and plates of uneaten food.

John knew what had to be done if they were to survive this ordeal, but he had never killed a man before. He looked at the knife lying limply in his hand and wondered if he had the guts to use it. He looked hesitantly at his new companion, standing next to him, and offered him the knife.

'I've a better idea,' the prisoner whispered back.

The prisoner crept forward into the hut and carefully picked up one of the soldier's rifles from the wooden floor. 'I'm dehydrated,' he said. 'You got any piss in you?'

John caught on instantly and nodded. He stood to one side, took aim, and urinated over the sleeping soldiers faces, wildly spraying the jet of yellow liquid around like some unruly child. He burst out laughing whilst doing so; it seemed such an absurd thing to do. Within a split second the soldiers stirred, slapped at whatever it was hitting them in the face and groggily awoke only to be confronted by the weird sight of a naked man pissing on them. They made a grab for their rifles.

'Sweet dreams, you bastards,' the prisoner hissed as he squeezed the trigger.

John had to jump out of the way, hands firmly clenched around his genitals in a desperate attempt at protection. He stood frozen in shock, scarcely able to believe the carnage and destruction being caused by the reckless shooting in such a small enclosed space.

When the shooting stopped, John turned to the prisoner and smiled nervously, acutely aware he was standing naked and vulnerable. 'Hi.'

'Do you always greet people like this?'

'It's been known.'

The prisoner laughed. 'God, you're a welcome sight. I'm really grateful to you. I thought I was going to die down there in that shit.'

'That's okay.'

The two men stared at each other for several more seconds before John became a little embarrassed and put a hand over his genitals. 'I'm John and I'm pleased to meet you.'

'The name's Nick. Nick Price. Glad to meet you too,' Nick said offering his hand.

John griped the hand extended towards him and, unable to think of anything sensible to say, asked 'How long have you been here?'

'Third day now. Three whole days and these fucking pigs didn't give me a thing to eat. Bastards! Look at this lot, there's enough food here to feed an army. Excuse me, but I'll faint if I don't get something inside me.' He dropped to the floor and grabbed a handful of rice from one of the scattered plates.

'I think I'll join you. I haven't eaten a thing since breakfast,' John responded. 'I only had a fry up of bacon, sausage, tomatoes and eggs. I should have had toast and marmalade as well.'

'You bastard!' Nick laughed. 'How am I supposed to enjoy this crap now?'

John and Nick gorged themselves on the remains of the VC soldiers' meal. It was cold, but at least it had hardly been touched. They ate in silence. Each had a hundred questions to ask of each other, but nourishment came first.

After eating his full, John wiped his mouth with the back of his hand, belched and asked, 'Why did you do it? Wave I mean. We thought you were friendly.'

'The bastards had a wire tied around my nuts. They'd jerk it every now and then to remind me to do as I was told. They yanked that wire so much I reckon I'll be singing soprano for the rest of my life. Have you ever had your nuts threatened like that? It makes you real vulnerable to other peoples' suggestions.' Casually, he swung a rifle around and pointed it in a threatening manner at John. He then lowered the barrel of the rifle until the end just touched John's penis, cocked the rifle, prodded John's organ from side to side then jabbed the nozzle into John's scrotum.

John felt queasy. He had never felt so vulnerable in his life. It was even worse than wading into the black water under the huts, or

The Fourth Cart III

evading flying bullets. His mouth dried and he tried to gulp without any spittle. He ventured a nervous laugh, not knowing just how serious his new acquaintance was. He felt quite giddy. Perhaps he shouldn't have freed the man from his cage after all.

'See what I mean? Makes you think, doesn't it?'

'Erm,' John mumbled, unable to think of a suitable response.

'Just teasing,' Nick said removing the rifle and throwing it to one side. 'I reckon you'd have done the same thing as well.'

'I reckon so,' John replied. 'Shit. That's unnerving.'

'Sure is. You should try it with wire.'

'No thanks. That was bad enough.' John sighed with relief. He glanced at his wrist, where his watch would normally have been. 'Come on, let's get out of here. Maybe this lot have got friends nearby.'

'Right. Have you got any clothes, or is that your only suit?'

John sniggered. 'I'm told it fits me well.'

Nick stripped off his soiled clothes and both men playfully took turns ladling water over each other from a large earthenware vat of rainwater. With the disgusting slime washed off, John went off in search of his clothes. He returned to find Nick sitting on top of a wooden box and dressed like a peasant in a sarong and shirt dotted with very prominent, and bloody, bullet holes.

'You should have thought about that before you shot them.'

'These rags will do for now. At least they're not covered in the shit that's down there. Give us a hand with this box, will you?'

'Sorry?'

'My groceries. There's fifty Ks of Thai Horse stashed away in here. I was on my way from Bangkok to Saigon. My armed escorts are lying in the field back there. I'll be a dead man if I lose this.'

'We can't carry that,' John implored. 'It's far too heavy.'

'I'm not intending to. I just want to hide it in case anyone else comes here and finds it. We'll bury it, away from here, out in the jungle perhaps. I'll come back for it later.'

John snorted. 'You'll be lucky.'

'Yep. I feel it in my blood. You seem to be damned lucky. With you as my lucky charm, I'll be back, I'm sure.'

'You're crazy, Nick.' He nevertheless added his weight to the task.

'You don't know the owner. I'm just the courier. If I get back to Bangkok empty handed . . . well, it would have been better if you'd left me down there.'

They hauled the wooden box about a hundred yards away from the hut, slid it into a trench and covered it with branches and dead leaves.

'Right, then,' Nick said slapping John on the back, 'Let's get the hell out of here.'

'Where to?'

'God knows. That way,' Nick said pointing in the direction of the blown-up jeep. 'Let's just follow the track we were heading along.'

'How far have we got to walk?'

'About ten miles, minimum, I reckon. That was about the last thing my driver said before we hit the landmine. He'd done this route before. Villages are pretty scarce on this trail, so I was asking him where we could next find some provisions when BOOM!, the bloody jeep turns over.'

'You'll never make ten miles. I'll be carrying you after five. You're far too weakened.'

'Want a bet?'

'You'll lose. You can hardly stand up now, Nick. God knows what you've picked up from being in that water. You've probably got dysentery, malaria, cholera and every other sodding disease going.'

'So what?'

'How much?' John asked. 'The bet, that is.'

'An evening's supply of beer? Plus entertainment?'

'You're on. C'mon, grab a couple of rifles and ammo belts and let's get the hell out of here.'

Chapter Fourteen

As John paused to finish a cup of tea, Nittaya took advantage of the break to brush away a tear running down her father's cheek.

'That cage,' she said quietly, 'It still haunts you, doesn't it?'

Nick nodded. 'You can have no idea what hell those three days were like for me, Nit. That's what causes my panic attacks, so the doctor says.'

Magee nodded his sympathies. 'I'm sorry this is causing you distress, Nick. I really am. But please bear with it. Now that you've started, you may as well finish. Get it all off your chest.'

Nick sighed deeply. 'You know something, Magee, we haven't even begun to scratch the surface.'

'Do you want John to continue the story or do you want to take over?'

'I'll leave it to John, I wasn't very lucid during this particular escapade.'

Magee looked across at John and nodded.

John put the tea cup down and said, 'Nick struggled through that night much longer than I thought he would. It nearly finished him off though . . .'

****

Road to Saigon, July 1970

John and Nick stuck to the track despite the possibility of further landmines. They made slow progress through the night-time jungle, staggering a mere eight miles in the hours before dawn. Nick slowed the pair down terribly, a severe case of diarrhoea forcing him to squat in agony several times an hour.

As dawn broke, they found themselves resting on top of a small hillock with a bird's eye view of a village of a dozen bamboo huts less than a couple of hundred yards away. There were no signs of life. Nothing moved, yet there were signs that it was still inhabited. Clothes hung over bamboo canes to dry off in the sun, sandals lay outside hut entrances and a rooster had started his morning vocal workout. It was a village in slumber.

'Friendly, you think?'

'Haven't the foggiest idea,' Nick replied. 'We've driven through a few villages like this in the last few days, but we just pointed our weapons and drove like crazy. We never stopped to ask questions.'

'See that?' John asked excitedly. 'Nearest hut on the right. Just to the right of it, there's a lean-to shack. It's got branches for a roof. See what's inside it? It's a jeep isn't it? Or are my eyes deceiving me?'

Nick stared hard in the direction John was pointing and broke into a huge grin. 'I told you there'd be no problem with you around. You ooze good luck, old son. It's an American model I think.'

'Friendly then?'

'No way. Why hide it? Choppers couldn't see it if they flew over, so someone's keeping a trophy.'

'Shall we liberate it?'

'Risky. Might be dogs around, or it could even be booby-trapped. Then there's the problem of petrol, ignition keys, things like that to take care of.'

'What's the alternative?'

'Skirting the village and continuing on foot.'

John considered the prospect of walking for several days, of being captured and even suffering a similar torture as Nick had endured. Then there was Nick's state of health. There was no way Nick could struggle on for much longer, a day at the most perhaps. Nick's body was covered with sweat already, and not just because of physical exertion or the tropical heat. 'You any good with motors?'

Nick broke into a smile. 'One of the reasons I'm here,' he replied cryptically. 'I used to be in the trade until some numbskull called Magee squeezed me out of business.'

'Well I hope you haven't lost your touch. You get delirious in the next ten minutes and you've lost a friend.' He took a firm grip on his rifle and set off down the slope towards the jeep.

They covered the open ground and reached the first hut without incident. They even managed to climb into the jeep without a sign that their presence had been noticed. John clambered into the back and sat, rifle poised, anticipating trouble. Nick pulled down the wires from behind the dashboard and fiddled around with them. Seconds later the engine started to whine. So too did several dogs. The engine refused to catch.

'Shit, Nick. What's wrong?'

'Probably hasn't been used for a while. Give it time.'

'We don't have time.'

Voices rose from inside the nearby hut. Sleepy, confused voices that gained in strength as the realization sunk in that their treasured vehicle was being brought to life. The first man to appear through the hut entrance ducked just in time to miss a blast from John's rifle. He screamed hysterically and ran straight back inside.

'Fuck sake, Nick. Get the fucking thing going, can't you?'

As if responding to command, the engine burst into life. 'Yes!' He thrust the gearstick into reverse and backed into the nearby hut, crashing through the bamboo walls.

John almost toppled out the back. 'For God's sake, Nick, watch out!'

'Hang on, old son.' Nick swung the jeep forward into another hut, scattering the occupants in all directions. He aimed the jeep in the direct path of a peasant running for his life. 'Out the fucking way, you moron,' he screamed. The peasant threw his weapon away and lunged into a ditch.

'You stupid fucking bastard,' John yelled, bouncing everywhere as he tried to clamber over the back seats to the safety of the jeep floor. He finally secured a position and looked up to find Nick smiling, cheering and revelling at the danger they were in. The mood was infectious. He broke into a broad grin. 'Nick, you really are one crazy son of a bitch.'

The jeep screeched away from the village as Nick gunned the accelerator to the floor, forcing John to bounce uncontrollably as they drove along the bumpy tracks.

'You're going the wrong way, Nick. Surely we want to be heading through the village, not this way. We're heading back the way we came, aren't we?'

'Too bloody right we are. I've got my groceries to pick up.'

'What? Are you mad? Come on, Nick, we haven't got time. We've got to get out of this fucking mess.'

'Right again, mate. And I'm in a right fucking mess if I don't get my groceries delivered. Look, the tank's full, there's a spare can in the back by the look of it. We've got nothing else to do, so let's just do it, okay? Anyway, I rescued you, so I get to say where we go.'

'What?' John was incredulous. 'You rescued me? What the fuck do you mean by that? You did nothing of the sort you lying bastard.'

'Says who? I started the jeep and I'm driving it. Right? So, I'm rescuing you. Drinks are on you, old son. I told you I'd win.'

John couldn't believe it. 'Fuck that. Give me the wheel, you cheating bastard.' He tried to climb over the front seats to grab the wheel.

A playful fight started over possession of the steering wheel. Both men giggled and fought like kids, sending the jeep lurching from one side of the track to the other.

'Okay, okay,' Nick conceded. 'Let's call it quits. We'll split the bar bills.'

Two hours later, the box of Thai Horse retrieved, they were back at the outskirts of the village they'd looted from earlier. They sat watching in despair. Unlike earlier, there were now people moving about. They had no choice but to drive through the village centre.

John checked his rifle's action whilst surveying the village below. 'Are you ready for this?'

'It's now or never, I suppose,' Nick replied. He jammed the box of Thai Horse under the back seat.

'They're not going to let us just breeze through. It could get nasty.'

'Let's just pray, then.'

'I'm up for it, let's go.'

'I hope your aim is good,' Nick murmured as he cruised the jeep down the hill. Gripping the steering wheel with one hand, firing in front, he shouted like a lunatic for the villagers to get out the way.

The Fourth Cart III

'Bloody Cockney, no style at all,' John muttered as he sat on the floor, facing backwards. With a rifle in each hand, like some later-day cowboy, he fired at everything that came into view.

Bullets tore into bamboo huts, ricocheted off pots and pans. Dogs yelped, chickens squawked and pigs squealed. Men scattered, mothers pushed their children to the ground and old people stood frozen in horror. The jeep screeched through the village leaving a trail of destruction of worse proportions than a hurricane.

'Yeessss!' Nick screamed in jubilation. 'Saigon, here we come.'

The excitement of their antics soon wore off. Ahead lay a long ride to Saigon. Nick drove, happy to have something to keep his mind off his churning stomach. John dozed in the back.

It wasn't long before Nick's sickness took over. As the jeep veered sharply to the left and screeched to a halt, Nick slumped over the side and vomited up a putrid mixture of digested rice, stew and blood.

'Christ Nick, what's the matter?'

'Fuck knows. I feel so . . .' But he couldn't finish. He gagged as another gullet full of bile came up. 'Christ, this hurts.'

John jumped out the jeep and helped Nick to stagger into the shade of a bush. 'Did you drink any of the water when you were in the cage?'

'Not voluntary, you fucking idiot. I took a few mouthfuls. I couldn't help that. Ahhh! Fucking sweet Jesus!' Nick rolled over on the ground, clutching his stomach.

'Okay. Okay. Look, I'd better get you to hospital. Come on, into the back.'

'No. Not the hospital, I've got to get the Horse to Danny Curtis first. Over at Harry's Place.'

'Sod that Nick, you'll never make it.' John picked up his sick friend from the ground and carried him back to the jeep.

'Please. Please deliver the stuff or I'm finished.'

'You'll be finished anyway at this rate, you jerk, forget the sodding dope for now,'

'Please, John. Colonel Danny Curtis . . . goes to Harry's Bar every morning . . . eleven o'clock . . . coffee and a bun . . . reading newspaper . . .'

'Yeah, yeah,' responded John. 'Whatever you say.'

'Please don't let me down . . .' Nick whispered before passing out.

'Shit, that's all I need,' John muttered.

Chapter Fifteen

'I notice I got the blame for something while you're in the middle of the jungle,' Magee muttered in Nick's direction.

Nick chuckled. 'They were John's own words Magee, not mine.'

Magee frowned at John.

'Artistic license, Magee,' John responded with a huge grin on his face. 'I couldn't resist it. Nick invariably cursed you for his problems. It seemed apt to include the comment.'

Magee looked to his side, caught Melissa's eye, and shook his head in despair. 'So, John, you got him safely to hospital I take it?'

'Yep, eventually,' John continued. 'He was unconscious for eight days if I remember correctly.'

'No lasting damage though?' Magee asked, looking in Nick's direction.

'I wouldn't say that, Magee,' Nick spat back. 'Scarred for life, is how I'd put it. And all thanks to you.'

'So I gather,' Magee sighed. 'Come on then, Nick, tell me about it.'

'Well, actually, thinking about it, it wasn't all bad in hospital. I do remember a nurse who cheered me up . . .'

****

Saigon, July 1970

Nick gradually became aware that he was awake and that someone was rubbing him gently with a wet cloth. He screwed his eyes up and managed to focus on a pretty young Vietnamese nurse who was rather timidly giving him a bed bath. He watched her for several seconds before the girl jumped back, startled.

'Please don't stop,' Nick said quietly. 'It's nice and cooling and I promise I haven't the strength to do anything funny.'

The nurse continued the ablutions. He watched her every movement with an eager eye. She was so young and pretty; so much more innocent than the bar girls that featured so predominantly in his life in Bangkok. If only he had the strength, he would ask for her name. But where was he? And how long had he been here?

To his surprise, the nurse gently massaged his groin, taking care to cover every square inch of his organ. He groaned softly, not from pleasure but from discomfort as the cuts and sores around his groin stung with the absorption of anaesthetic cream. As she performed her duties, she stole the occasional glance into his eyes and smiled cutely. Nick sighed. It was the first time in his life that a girl was massaging him without demanding money, yet there was nothing he could do about it. Nothing seemed to be working down there.

'Please God, make it work again. I promise I'll go to church,' he muttered as he drifted off again into a contended sleep. He dreamt of pleasant thoughts, of having his own home, with his own private nurse in uniform, of receiving bed baths and massages.

'Wake up, you faker.'

'Hmm?' Nick opened his eyes, his dream shattered.

'The doctor said you're alive. No more faking.'

'What do you mean "faking"?' Nick asked, as his eyes began to focus on a set of gleaming white teeth.

'You've been faking death for over a week.'

'Fuck you to,' Nick replied, breaking into a smile. 'Good to see your ugly face.'

'Hey, watch your lip. You should see how the nurses swoon as I walk pass. They can't see enough of me. I've got a present for you, by the way.' He held up a bunch of large bananas.

'Hah, fucking hah.' Nick winced at the thought of his predicament. 'I suppose you think that's funny. Swap places with me and you won't, I can assure you.'

'The doctor says you'll make a full recovery.'

'I damn well hope so. I can't raise a smile at the moment, let alone anything else. I'm wondering whether that wire has finished my sex life for ever.'

'Give it time. I doubt whether anything could stop it functioning as God intended.'

'Christ,' Nick chuckled. 'If God intended for me to use it the way I do, then he must really be a dirty old sod.'

Both men smiled at each other, then averted their eyes. They endured an embarrassing silence for a few seconds, whilst John fidgeted with a newspaper. Neither seemed sure where to start the next conversation.

'So then, John. How's it going? What have you been up to while I've been dozing?'

'Not a lot really. I've just been hanging around at Harry's Bar. Chatting most of the time, that sort of thing.'

'And the jeep? Is it still around?'

'No, sorry. It was impounded. Some bastard army captain stopped me, queried my credentials and decided to repossess it. He threatened to arrest me if I didn't comply.'

'What? But what about my Horse? That was worth a fortune!'

John scratched the back of his head and screwed his eyes up, as though pretending he couldn't remember. 'Umm, let's think.'

Nick stared at the man in horror. 'You telling me it's gone?'

Just as Nick was about to throw a fit, John beamed one of his youthful ear-to-ear grins.

'You bastard,' Nick hissed. 'I nearly had a heart attack. Don't pull my leg, John, I haven't the strength.'

'The jeep wasn't impounded for three days. I took the box to Harry's Bar straight after dropping you off here. It didn't take me long to find your colonel.'

'Thank God for that. I thought for a moment you were going to say the box went with the jeep. Christ, John, promise not to joke about such things, please.'

'It's put some colour back into your cheeks anyway.'

'Fuck you too,' Nick replied, doing his best to grin. 'What about the money for it? Don't tell me you spent it all on whores this week or I'll really get upset.'

'It's under lock and key, at the hotel I'm staying at.'

'All of it?'

'Well, less a few hundred, I suppose, I didn't have much on me and the hospital wanted some money up front.'

'Just a few hundred gone? Blimey, I thought you'd have nicked it all.'

John shrugged his shoulders and replied in a simple, if somewhat innocent, fashion, 'It's yours Nick, not mine. I don't steal from friends.'

Nick took a few moments to compose himself. Honesty was a virtue he rarely came across. 'Half for you, John. Half the profit that is. I've got to pay a three thousand dollar penalty for wrecking the jeep. Reckon you earned it.'

'But I wasn't in on the deal, Nick. It's yours, not mine.'

'Look, John. I wouldn't be here to spend it if it hadn't been for you. There's no way I can thank you enough for that. I owe you my life. This is the least I could do.'

'But . . .'

'No buts. I'm not going to argue. Those Thai guards with me were in for half, I guess you took over from them.'

'So half the profit is how much exactly?'

Nick grinned before replying, 'Well, after I've paid for the jeep, that's twenty two grand between us. Eleven thousand each.'

'Jesus, Nick. That's a fortune. I'm rich!'

'You won't be rich for long if you let it go to your head. Eleven thousand is nothing. You'll piss it up against a wall within a couple of months. Same as me. Do something with it, for Christ sake, open a bank account or something. This could last you a long time. Be conventional for once, eh?'

'Can't say I like the sound of that. You sound just like my father. You're looking as old as him too.'

'Cheeky pig!' Nick grabbed a newspaper and gave John a playful slap with it.

'Okay then, let's invest the money in a legitimate business.'

'Fine. Any ideas?'

'No. None at all. Although running a bar must be easy. Plenty of customers in Bangkok. How about it?'

'Just so long as there are no go-go girls. They bore me to death. And working girls, none of them please, it'll break my heart and wallet to be surrounded by them all the time.'

'It's a deal. We'll open a drinking den, then. Lucy's Tiger Den.'

'What?'

'The name of our bar; Lucy's Tiger Den.'

'Who the fuck is Lucy?'
'No idea.'
'Where the hell did you conjure up the name from then?'
'I've a good imagination, that's all.'
'Okay, you dolt. Lucy's Tiger Den it is. But it sounds like a cheap clip joint to me.'
'Should get the punters in then.'
'Yeah, but won't they be disappointed?'
'Probably, but at least they won't get fleeced by some tart.'
'For some reason, I think I'm going to regret this, but okay John, let's do it. Lucy's Tiger Den it is. Fifty-fifty.'

Chapter Sixteen

'Lucy's Tiger Den,' Nittaya whispered. 'That's where the name came from? From a hospital bedside?'

'It was indeed, Nit.'

'I thought the bar's origins would be more romantic than that.'

'They were, Nit, much more, but it's a story in itself and I don't think Magee has come here to hear about how I met your mother.'

'Actually, Nick,' Magee intervened as he poured himself a second cup of tea. 'I need to know everything, including everything your wife. Nothing is not relevant at this stage, I'm afraid. I need to hear it all, I need to get everything in perspective.'

'Very well, in that case you need to know how that incident with the VC changed me completely. I wasn't the same afterwards. I suppose you'd say it traumatized me.'

'A leopard never changes its spots,' Magee muttered.

'That's where you're wrong Magee. I changed totally. It hit me really hard on the return trip from Saigon . . .'

****

South China Sea, August 1970

Nick and John were relaxing in deckchairs, gazing at the red sunset, as the rusty old cargo ship gently bobbed up and down on the South China Sea.

'This is the life, isn't it,' Nick said. He sipped at a cool can of beer and continued, 'It doesn't get better than this. Not in my experience, anyway.'

'Mmm,' replied John, half asleep. 'Don't you just love the way the sun's light shimmers across the surface of the sea at this time of day? It's so beautiful. I've taken some exceptional shots during the last few months living out this way, especially on the beach, early evening, with branches of palm trees draping down in the foreground. I'm trying to sell them for postcard material, but I'm not having much luck so far.'

They were the only passengers on the cargo ship. Two hundred and fifty dollars each for the trip from Saigon to Bangkok, paid straight to the captain. Captain's perks, accepting paying passengers for the half dozen berths on board. Bring your own booze, pay for your meals as you go.

'How did you get into it, John? Photography, that is? You being rather young and all.'

'Well, it was a hobby of mine in my early teens. Then I started seeing Tim Page's shots cropping up in magazines back in London. For a kid brought up in suburbia, Arnos Grove that is, Page's work was so intensely dramatic.'

'But how did you make the leap from Arnos Grove to Bangkok. That's not your typical career path is it?'

'No, but then I doubt yours is either.' John fell silent for a few moments before continuing, 'To be honest, Nick, my father threw me out of home. He told me never to come back. I was just eighteen. Any idea how hard that is?'

'Actually, John, yes, I know precisely how that feels. I was sixteen when it happened to me. I'd lived with relations since I was a kid. They couldn't cope with me any more, just told me to go. They didn't care where.'

'Shit, really? What a bummer. I don't think I could have handled it any earlier.'

'You survive. You have to. You have no choice.'

'Yeah, I know. I went to an uncle. I was in a terrible state at the time. He let me stay a few months, didn't tell my father. Dad would have been really pissed off with his brother if he'd known I was hiding out at his home. We thought it better to let my father stew a little, hoping he would change his mind, soften up a bit. We got word back from my father that he'd struck me out of his life. Forever. Full stop. Didn't want my name mentioned again, ever.'

'Did you get on well with him, beforehand that is?'

'Yeah, I did. That's what's so sad. Ignorant bigot, got his eyes closed to the world.'

'You're lucky. I never had any love when I was young.'

The two men stared at the disappearing sun in an attempt to avert each other's moist eyes. The ball of red fire was almost completely over the horizon. It seemed symbolic, as if setting on their past lives, bringing an unhappy era to a close.

'My uncle's a man of the world,' John continued, having brushed away a tear. 'He told me I would find happiness out here. He also paid for my airplane fare, and subbed me for a six month stay. He'd never been to Bangkok but, boy, did he know his onions.'

'Onions?' Nick interrupted. 'You came here for onions?'

John sniggered. 'You know what I mean. Sex. Whatever you want you can find it in Bangkok, right?'

'Never done it with an onion, though.'

'Fuck you too. Anyway, I owe that man a lot. He writes every month, keeps an eye on me. I'll repay him one day, I hope.'

'You're lucky that you've got someone in the family who does care. Me, I have no one. None of them give a shit. They're all glad I'm somewhere else.'

John popped another can of beer. The alcohol helped the flow of words. 'Bangkok turned out to be the ideal choice of location, being near the action in Vietnam, that is. It gave me a good chance to meet people who'd been caught up in the war. It brought me closer to Page's work. It's amazing how he managed to capture the thrills, horrors and suffering all at the same time. It filled my mind with totally idiotic ideas about war. If Vietnam had made it for Tim Page, then why not for me?'

'So?'

'So I got a job, as a war photographer. Well, not so much a job really. I only get paid if the Agency manages to sell one of my photos. I've done reasonably well so far, but my boss is a real asshole and, by god, the work is so bloody dangerous. I'm not sure I want to continue with it for much longer. Without meeting you, and getting this money, I reckon I wouldn't have lasted any more than a few months. You have to get right up close to the action for a good shot, a bit too close for my liking.'

'Well, you'll just have to find something new to photograph, won't you? More sunsets, maybe? Or maybe nudes,' Nick added with a smirk. 'Now there's a thought, John, how about the nude magazine market?'

'Mmm. Sounds good doesn't it. Maybe as a side-line to the bar.'

A light abruptly came on behind them, interrupting their conversation. Two of the Chinese crew walked across the deck, one carrying a tray piled high with prepared food dishes whilst the other carried an old banana box. Nick and John handed over five dollars each as the tray was placed on the box, serving as a table. They smiled their thanks, neither speaking a word of each other's language.

'Can't beat the service, can you? Even if it is a bit pricey. Wow!' said Nick as he took the lid off one of the dishes. 'Look at the size of that fish. I take it back.'

'They obviously know you need feeding up. Doctor's orders if you remember. You've got to put on, what was it, two stone?'

'Something like that. Won't be hard either, with meals like this. Jesus, I don't think I can take five days of food like this.'

'You're under doctor's orders to take life easy for a few months, Nick, not just the five days of this trip.'

'Yeah, all right, all right, don't harp on about it.'

They ate in silence, an uncomfortable silence, for a couple of minutes. Eventually John could bear the tension no more. 'Do you want to talk about it?'

'About what?'

'About what's pissing you off? What the hell did I say to offend you just now?'

Nick remained silent a few seconds, gathering his thoughts, wondering whether to be honest. 'Back in London, I used to play the hard man. Since I was a kid, certainly for as long as I can remember, I've always been aggressive. I used to beat my classmates up in the playground for their pocket money. When I left school at sixteen I went into the protection racket. I thought I was "The Man", you know what I mean? I reckoned I could intimidate anyone into handing over their cash. I thought it okay at the time, socially acceptable even. Guess I was angry with the world, trying to get my own back; for my mother dying when I was young; for my aunt and uncle being bad adoptive parents, that sort of thing. I'm sure some shrink would be able to explain away those days.'

'We have that much in common, Nick. The need of a psychologist, that is. I guess both our lives have been screwed up.'

'Yeah, I suppose you're right. Thing is, John, that incident with the VC has had a serious effect on me. I've been scared shitless ever since. I keep waking up in the middle of the night in a deep sweat. I keep reliving those moments of being tied to the jeep with a wire around my nuts. You know, in that cesspit of a cage, under the huts, I nearly lost it. I cried so many times I couldn't count them. I even prayed for a quick death. You know something else? The worst part was that I was only there for three days. Just three days. I cracked up in just three shitting days. I can't fathom that, John. Me, Nick Price, the hard man of the East End of London, not even surviving a mildly hellish ordeal for three days. How in God's name do some people survive years of conditions worse than that?'

'You saying you're not as tough as you thought you were?'

'Yeah, that's the truth of it, John. I can't handle it anymore. I just want an easy life from now on. No more Mr Tough Guy, no more violence, no more experiences like I've had over the last year. Those doctor's orders you just mentioned, I intend to carry them out for more than just a few months. I want to change my life. I'm suffering too badly right now. I'm really not as tough as I used to pretend.'

'A bar seems like quiet work.'

'I want a better life than just bar work, John.'

'It's a start.'

'Yeah, sure is. But I'm so fucking scared I just want to build a fortress and lock myself up inside, in comfort, and keep the rest of the world at a distance. Does that seem odd to you? Weak, from my point of view?'

'Sounds sensible to me. You've got skeletons in your past. You're just acknowledging them. Sounds like good therapy.'

Nick winced. 'Therapy? Christ, John. You don't think I need therapy do you? I'm not a nutter am I?'

'No, Nick, you're not a nutter. You're just suffering from trauma. It will pass.'

'You think so? God, I hope you're right.'

'Look on the bright side. We've got a pile of money. It will keep us going for months, years maybe, until we land The Big One. Then we can retire in style.'

Nick grunted. 'The Big One? Huh! Not you as well, John, I hear those words so often in Bangkok. Everyone is chasing The Big One, some scam or other that will net them millions.'

'It's just a dream. We all need our dreams. You just told me your dream; you'll need money to build your fortress.'

'Yeah, that's true enough. A few million would come in handy, I'll say.'

'And just where would you build this fortress?'

'In the countryside, away from London. Nice big house, with a high wall, barbed wire, security guards, dogs, landmines, that sort of thing.'

'Well, you've got that planned out, so we just need some real money, right?'

'Yep. Just got to work on that.'

'Nothing too hard, then,' John teased. 'We've got a few days to think it through, shouldn't be too difficult.'

The two men sipped their beers for a few minutes contemplating The Big One.

'John?'

'Yeah?'

'Do us a favour.'

'Sure, Nick.'

'Forget everything I just told you. Don't tell anyone, will you? They'll think I'm a dickhead.'

John didn't speak his answer. Instead he looked Nick squarely in the eyes, and gave an almost imperceptible, but sincerely earnest, shake of his head.

Chapter Seventeen

'This is getting too lovey-dovey for me,' Magee sneered.

'Up yours, Magee,' Nick spat back. 'You wanted the truth, you're getting it. Warts and all.'

'Okay, okay. Let's try to move on. So we've established you two formed a close bond at a young age. It explains a lot about your relationship, but can we get back to the main plot please?'

'Sure, Magee,' Nick said sharply. 'If you'll just tell me what that is. You still haven't told me what it is you expect from this history lesson.'

Magee squirmed. He waved his hand in a dismissive gesture. 'Just get on with it. So, your boat trip is over, you arrive back in Bangkok, I assume. Where to next?'

Nick closed his eyes, choked back a tear and said, 'That's when John introduced me to Maliwan.'

Magee caught himself from making an unnecessary comment. 'Do you want John to do this?'

'No, Magee. This has got to come from me, for Nittaya's sake.' He caught John's eyes. 'Do you mind? Talking about Jook, that is?'

John shook his head. 'It's history for me, Nick. Sad. Unbelievably sad, but I learnt to live with it a long time ago.'

Magee frowned and glanced across at Brigadier Armstrong who had noticeably perked up.

'Tell me about Jook please,' said Brigadier Armstrong. 'After what happened in Bangkok earlier this year, you'll understand I need you to be very clear on that subject.'

Nick brushed a hand across his mouth. 'Well, it was the thought of returning to my sad existence with Sean in Bangkok. I just couldn't face it. I wanted something else. Just a change for a while, I suppose, until my body recovered.' He gripped his daughter's hand hard. 'It was fate, Nit. Meeting John led me to your mother . . .'

****

Bangkok, August 1970

'Where will you go now, Nick?' John asked as his feet touched the quayside jetty in Bangkok's port of Klong Toey.

'I don't know,' Nick responded.

'Do you have accommodation?'

'Not really. I just flit around amongst cheap lodgings. Anyway, I lost everything I owned when that bloody jeep blew up. I suppose I'll have to start again and look around for some new digs. What about you?'

'I rent a house on the outskirts of the city. You're welcome to stay. It's nothing special, but it serves a purpose. There's a spare bedroom and it's yours if you want it whilst you're still recuperating.'

'Great. Thanks, I'll help out with . . .'

'Just a second, Nick. There's one condition to my offer. Before you accept it, I want you to see the house first. You see, I've got a problem, but I can't explain it at the moment.'

Nick was puzzled. 'I don't understand. What sort of problem could stop me accepting a room? All I need is a bed, John. I'm not after some posh hotel with silk bed sheets for Christ sake. Honestly, if you have a spare mattress on the floor, I'll take it.'

'Please, Nick. It's not that easy. Just wait until you see it, okay? I don't want to talk about it right now. You'll just have to wait and see for yourself, and I won't be the slightest bit offended if you decline the offer.'

Nick let the matter rest. 'Lead the way, then, I'll keep my mouth shut.'

'We'll take a river bus. It doesn't take long, and the scenery is spectacular. My home's about five miles down the Chao Phraya river. It's in a small village called Mahahwong. Do you know it?'

'Never heard of it. Couldn't say it either, never have been good with the local lingo.'

For the price of one baht each, the two men boarded a ferry boat and sat in quiet solitude whilst the journey progressed. The city was soon left behind. The scenery changed from semi-industrial to fruit plantations, speckled by the odd wooden hut, children playing in the river, mothers washing their wares in the waters. Nick's spirits rose. If the village they were heading for was like this, he would love it. It would be just what the doctor had ordered; fresh air, rest and privacy to recover. No more the madness of the city, with its sleaze and incessant presence of the American soldiers on leave. He felt a wonderful sense of serenity.

'This is our stop,' John said as the boat gently touched a pontoon.

They disembarked. Nick remained silent whilst they walked the last three hundred yards towards a group of wooden houses each set six feet high off the ground on stilts.

At the top of the stairs to his house, John took his shoes off and gently pushed open the door. 'Jook? Where are you, Jook? I'm home.'

The most beautiful girl Nick had ever seen in his life appeared out of one of the rooms. She smiled gleefully at John, then wai'd him respectfully.

'Maliwan, this is my friend Nick,' John said in slow belaboured English. Then turning to Nick, he said, 'Nick, this is Maliwan.'

But Nick hadn't heard. He was gawking at the girl. He was flabbergasted. Never before had he seen such stunning looks, even for a Thai girl, of which he'd seen thousands. And such a gleaming smile, her beauty radiated and filled the room. Such warmth in her eyes, such long flowing, silky hair. If it was possible to fall in love at first sight, Nick had done so. He was in a trance.

'Nick?'

'Erm, sorry, John. Did you say something?'

'This is Maliwan, Nick.'

'Maliwan. Right. I'm pleased to meet you, Maliwan,' Nick said advancing with his hand held out. Maliwan ignored the hand and performed a wai instead. 'Dear God, John, you never told me that you had such a stunningly beautiful girlfriend.'

'I haven't . . .' But John didn't finish his sentence. A shriek of joy came from another room accompanied by the unmistakable sound of running feet. Another equally beautiful Thai, bearing a striking resemblance to Maliwan, appeared. 'Nick, this is Jook. He's Maliwan's brother.'

'Um, I can see the family likeness, but . . .' Nick paused, not knowing how to verbalize his thoughts.

Jook, dressed in shorts and T-shirt, as slender and almost as feminine as his sister, jumped up and threw his arms around John, hugging him tightly.

'Jook takes care of everything for me. Maliwan lives here as well. They're actually twins, eighteen years old now, but orphaned since they were about eight. They were brought up by their grandmother who lives about a hundred yards down the track. I've known Jook for about six months now.'

Nick followed John, who still had Jook wrapped around his torso, into the kitchen. He remained quiet, trying to suss out the situation. John managed to wrench Jook off, filled a kettle with water and put it on a stove. The silence between the two men was awkward. John passed a couple of minutes busying himself with the teapot. Nick remained silent until the tea was brought into the main living area. Jook plonked himself down on John's knees and put an arm around his lover's neck. The two Englishmen stared at each other, a little awkwardly.

The moment to talk had arrived. The situation was obvious, although there was always room for doubt in such cases. Nick decided to be frank about it. 'I take it that Jook is the problem you were referring to earlier.'

'Yes.'

'He keeps you warm at night, I take it?'

'Yes.'

'How long has he been with you?'

'Since the first day I met him, six months ago. I saw him walking around a shop in Bangkok one day, couldn't keep my eyes off of him. One look into those big black eyes and I just fell in love on the spot. I followed him around the shop until he realized I was gawking at him. Fortunately, he responded, smiled back. I rented this house so that we had our privacy but still be near his grandmother and his old friends. The neighbours are very relaxed about it all. They love having a farang in the area. Gives them some status I suppose, something to gossip about.'

'I see.' Nick watched how Jook was leaning against John, hugging him as though frightened he would disappear again. So feminine, so beautiful, just like a girl, he thought. How weird, he could almost fancy the boy, lady-boy that is, himself. He'd seen a few around the bars, but none as pretty as Jook. 'He's obviously missed you.'

'Yes. That's the main reason I'm happy to give up the Agency job in Saigon. Jook had just got to the stage of being used to me being around when I ran out of money and had to take the job. I didn't want to go away and leave him. It broke my heart being away from him. And his, I expect. I managed to get back for two brief visits in the last three months, but it wasn't for very long. Now I've got some cash, hopefully we can be together again.'

'I take it that at this point most people throw up and walk out on you?'

'You got it.'

Nick broke into a smile and said, 'You know, John,' 'I never had you down as a shirt-lifting nancy boy.'

'Thanks a bunch.'

'It must be a difficult life though.'

'Sure is. When we're out together, the locals don't seem to mind, but the international community don't approve. Guess they think I'm some sort of deprived pervert.'

'John, look, I don't understand something. He looks almost like a girl, his mannerisms are like a girl, he's as pretty as a girl, so why not have a girl? Surely it's madness to take him out with you, isn't it? You're asking for snide remarks if you walk into a bar, or shop, arm in arm.'

'I know,' John sighed. 'But it's the way I'm made. Always have been.'

'Ah! That was your problem in England wasn't it? What happened? Caught in the act?'

'Exactly that, yes. My parents came home early one Sunday afternoon from visiting relations. I never did find out why they returned so early that day. I was only eighteen, but had a younger friend, Tommy, who was sex crazy. We were forever meeting up in the school bogs for a quick wank between classes or we would find somewhere to go after school. Every Sunday was the same, he would come over to my place whilst my folks were away and we'd spend the afternoon in bed rutting away until we were exhausted. Tommy loved it, couldn't get enough.'

'Don't tell me . . .'

The Fourth Cart III

'Yeah, you guessed it. That particular afternoon we had the record player on loud, so neither of us heard my parents come back. I guess they came upstairs to tell me to turn the music down. Anyway, there we were on top of the bed. Tommy was on his back with his ankles behind his ears. I was grinding away in ecstasy and I suddenly heard a scream. I looked up to see my mother at the bedroom door looking horrified. Do you know what I thought at the time? The only thing I could think of to say was, Oh God, not now, Mum. I'm . . . just . . . COMING! AHHH!'

Nick howled with laughter. He could appreciate the humour of the situation. He wouldn't have stopped either.

'By the time I'd come, my father had joined my mother at the doorway. Both of them stared at the scene in utter horror. Talk about no privacy. There was no "Oh, excuse me, I'll come back later". So I thought, well, if you want a show I'll give you one. I'd been wanking Tommy while screwing him so I continued doing so. Tommy grunted in relief as a great jet of spunk shot out onto his chest. Well, we were enjoying it, so why stop?'

'So you got your marching orders then?'

'Yep. My father shouted at me for hours, then he grabbed his wallet, emptied it, and threw all the cash at me. Told me to get out and never come back. Ever. He said as far as he was concerned I was dead.'

'That's a bit dramatic, isn't it?'

'Well, my father misinterpreted something. You see I've got this kid brother, Paul. He's only three years old. Four, now, I suppose. Paul idolized me. I was far more of a father figure to him than Dad ever was. To tell you the truth, I think Dad was jealous of our relationship. Paul always followed me around like a little lost lamb. Whatever I was doing, Paul wanted to do it as well. Whatever Mum wanted Paul to do, he wouldn't do it until he saw me do it first,' John paused for a while and choked back a tear.

'That sounds perfectly normal to me.'

'Yeah, but there're two things Dad got totally wrong. Firstly, bath-time. Paul always wanted to bathe with me, he hated anyone else washing him. Secondly, Paul invariably woke up early in the morning and used to sneak into my bed. If Mum couldn't find Paul first thing, she would never worry, she knew he would be snuggled up to me, asleep. Well, Dad accused me of abusing Paul. He accused me of getting cheap kicks from bathing and touching Paul. That was sick, really sick. Okay, I admit I like boys, feminine boys, especially these Thai lady-boys, but not until they get well past puberty, for Christ's sake. And certainly not my own kid brother. There was never anything but brotherly love between Paul and myself. The thought of molesting Paul disgusted me. Anyone caught fiddling with him would have had me to answer to. I'd have murdered any pervert that went anywhere near Paul. Anyway, Paul came off badly. I was told never to see him again, never to contact him in anyway or Dad would inform the police about me screwing Tommy, who was only seventeen. Dad said that he would give evidence against me, that I'd interfered with Paul.'

'That's pretty harsh, especially from your own father,' Nick muttered. 'What a bastard.'

'Bastard isn't the right word. He destroyed my life. Paul's as well I expect. I don't think I'll ever forgive him for chucking me out. Mind you, I doubt whether he'll ever forgive me for being a "sexual deviant", as he called me.'

'What happened to Paul?'

'My last memories of home were of Paul being restrained by my father at the front door. Paul was screaming his head off as I left home. He must have realized that I wasn't coming back. Dad insisted that I said goodbye from a considerable distance and not to even give Paul one last hug. I don't think I'll ever forget that scene, it killed something inside me.'

There was a mournful silence for a while. It seemed appropriate in the circumstances.

'So now you know what my bad habits are. Your tea is finished. Do you want to go now?'

'Actually, John. I was just thinking.'

'What about?'

'You see, I have a problem with women. I just can't get enough sex and I'm always falling out with my friends because I want to screw their girlfriends. I usually succeed and it's left me with very few close friends. I just can't help it. I see a friend with a pretty girl and I get jealous. I'm not happy until I've screwed her and that usually means a fight with my friend. I suppose it's something to do with always trying to prove myself better than the next man. I don't know,'

Nick paused on reflection of the number of fights he'd had with friends. 'It's just something I can't control.'

'That sounds as anti-social as my own bad habit.'

'Quite. It made me think, though. At least we'll never argue over some dumb broad, or lady-boy for that matter.'

John's face broke into the broadest grin ever. 'You mean, you'll stay?'

'Yes please.'

'But . . . but you called me a shirt-lifting nancy boy. I assumed you didn't approve.'

Nick guffawed. 'You big girl's blouse. I wasn't being serious.'

'But what of my lifestyle. Other lady-boys come round here, friends of Jook, that is. We often get carried away and have, erm, fun together.'

Nick was incredulous. 'You mean Jook lets you have sex with his friends? Isn't he jealous?'

'No, I don't think so. He usually encourages his friends to get it off with me,' John paused, smiled, then added tongue in cheek, 'I suppose it's because I'm so young and handsome, they can't resist my movie-star looks.'

'You old tart. You bloody lucky old tart. Never have I met a girl who'd do that. You jammy bugger!'

'I guess my lifestyle has compensations. I don't know how many conquests you've had this last year, but I've had around a hundred.'

'A hundred,' Nick spluttered. 'In one year? Dear God, John, you really are a tart. I've had about ten, I'm too mean to pay much.'

'Now there's another benefit, I don't pay.'

'You get it free?' Nick asked in pained astonishment.

'Teenage lady-boys tend to give it away by the bucket-load. It's the hormones, I suppose, they just can't get enough sex at that age.'

'Stop,' Nick said, putting his hands to his ears. 'This is too much. I don't want to hear any more. You're making me jealous. I don't get teenagers for free, that's just not fair.'

'Then there are the sauna houses. There are hundreds there some nights, they all give it away free.'

'What?'

'You don't know about the sauna houses? It's where the local gay men go for mutual sex. Many straight men go as well, for sex with the lady-boys, because it's easier and cheaper than with a mistress.'

'Enough,' Nick hollered, laughing. 'You're starting to piss me off now. Sex costs a fortune for straight men, this isn't right.'

'You could always change.'

'Me? Turn into a woofter?' Nick asked in disbelief. 'I don't think so.' He then added seriously, 'You wouldn't try to change me would you?'

'That's impossible, Nick. It's the way you're born. Don't worry, it's not catching. But you'll have to get used to a few young screaming queens around at times. They may make eyes at you, egg you on a bit. Flirt outrageously with you, even. You'll just have to get used to it, no need to get angry with them. They'll only be playing.'

'Hmm. I guess I'll give it a try. Just don't try to pass any of them off as the real thing.'

'I won't. But that reminds me, Nick. I saw the way you were looking at Mal when we came in.'

'Mal? Oh, you mean . . .'

'Yes, I mean the way your eyes were out on stalks, and your tongue hanging out. I thought you told me in hospital that your . . . private parts . . . weren't functioning properly.'

'Umm, well, thinking about it, I guess I've got some feeling coming back after all.'

'Because of Mal?'

Nick thought carefully for a while. 'Look, John. Mal is the most beautiful girl I've ever seen. Would you be upset if I tried to, you know, make something of it?'

John smiled warmly at his new housemate. 'She's no bar girl, Nick. She's very young and extremely innocent. She's a village girl, not a city girl. You can't just bulldoze your way in and expect to get your wicked way with her. It may take weeks, months even, of hard work.'

'That's okay. I don't reckon I'll be functioning on all fours for a while anyway.'

'Take it slowly then. Treat her with kid gloves. Just remember she's a human being, not a lump of flesh like the girls on display in Patpong.'

'You're sounding like a father speaking.'

'Yeah, I guess I do. And you're just a no-good bit of rough, young man, so don't go getting ideas above your head.'

They both chuckled. Within an hour of arriving at John's house, Nick felt as much at home as he had done anywhere else in his life. The four-way relationship seemed perfect. They could all be friends and live in peace with each other. Neither party was a threat to the other.

A month went by quickly, during which much attention was focused on the subject of Lucy's Tiger Den. Eventually, they found themselves surveying the insides of a run down, recently closed shop on Silom Road. It was packed ceiling high with old boxes and products covered in dust. It had been a Chinese family emporium, typically trying to cater for every possible customer need.

'So what do you think?'

'I suppose it's got potential for a bar. It's certainly big enough.'

John, Jook and Maliwan looked expectantly at Nick, waiting for a sign of approval as though he was the senior partner, the one who would ultimately give the nod.

'Yeah. Okay, folks. It's just about close enough to Patpong to get some of their passing trade. The rent is reasonable. It fronts Silom Road, handy for all the shops and restaurants. There's a two bedroom apartment upstairs as well, that could come in use. Yeah. I like it. Let's do it.'

'Then I hereby name this bar Lucy's Tiger Den,' said John euphorically.

'You still haven't told me who Lucy is,' Nick said shaking his head. 'And what the hell is this tiger den stuff all about?'

'Blowed if I know, as I keep telling you. It's just intuition, something inside me says we'll be blessed with good luck if we use that name.'

'Well, if you insist, but I'm not keen on taking advice from someone who hears voices in his head.'

Nick received a gentle swat on his arm from John in retribution.

'The owner says if we sign up the lease today, we've still got a week to wait before we can move in. They'll take that long to clear this rubbish. So, how about a week on the beach? It may be the last opportunity we get for a long time.'

'Just the four of us?'

'We can rent a bungalow down in Pattaya. Well, more of a beach shack really.'

'I've always wanted to go there,' Nick sighed 'I keep hearing the Americans talk about the place, just never got around to it. Yeah, why not, it sounds fun.'

'I know this beautiful spot, Dongtan Beach, it's along Jomthein Beach just outside Pattaya. There's never more than about three or four jeeps up there, you have to take your own picnic, but it's wonderfully calm, peaceful, private.'

'Hmm. What are we waiting for? It sounds ideal. What about services? I've heard it's still a bit basic down there.'

'Yeah, but that's the charm of it. Cool breezes from the sea instead of air conditioning, no electricity. It's fun, really.'

'And the sleeping arrangements?'

'There are a few shacks I know that have three or more bedrooms, three should do us.'

'Yeah, sure, I thought so.'

Jook caught Nick's eye and returned a wicked smile.

They set off early the next morning, in a jeep, and made good progress along country roads, some of which were mere dirt tracks, arriving in Pattaya well before lunchtime. Determined to make the most of their stay, they literally threw their bags onto the bungalow floor and set off immediately for Dongtan Beach.

'Dear God, John, this is paradise,' Nick uttered in near bewilderment as he walked bare-footed, splashing in the warm waters that gently broke onto the sandy shoreline. 'And it's all to ourselves, there's no one else for miles. I had no idea it was so beautiful down here, I just thought it was all bars and brothels.'

'And that didn't appeal to you?'

'Well, no, actually it didn't. There's only so much you can take of that. But this, John, I could take a lot of this.'

'Let's spread out over there, under the shade of those trees. Let's eat, I'm starving.'

Jook and Maliwan set up camp in a shady area, two blankets between the four of them, several hampers of pre-prepared food and dozens of bottles of soft drinks. To a series of wolf whistles, all four stripped off to reveal scanty, newly purchased swim suits. They scoffed their way through a lunch of mildly warm rice dishes. After eating, Jook stretched out for a nap, and John settled himself down with a notepad.

'I thought you were going to rest? What's that you've got?'

The Fourth Cart III

'It's something that's been bugging me for months. I want to write a book. Need to write, actually. I need to express myself on paper, I suppose I've got a lot of anger inside me, because of my father and losing my kid brother. I think this is going to help.'

'Seriously?'

'Yep. Seriously. It's a perfect place to start; quiet, peaceful, fresh air, exotic scenery, a really romantic location.'

'Romance,' Nick huffed. 'Thanks for reminding me, you've ruined my day now.'

As if on cue, John moved his arm slightly to nudge Jook. He caught Jook's eyes and silently mouthed something. Jook nodded and said something quietly to Maliwan who, on hearing it, giggled and slapped her brother on the arm.

Nick was amused. 'What was that about?'

'No idea, why don't you just relax. Turn over on to your front and doze.'

'Good idea. I'll catch a few minutes sleep.'

Before Nick had shut his eyes, though, Maliwan had eased herself nearer to him. She poured a little coconut oil on to his back and shoulders and started to gently massage it into his skin. Within a minute, she repositioned herself more comfortably, sitting astride him and for a quarter of an hour proceeded to give him the most tender, sensual, relaxing massage he'd ever experienced.

Having worked her delicate, agile fingers all over Nick's head, neck, back and legs, she whispered in his ear to turnover. Nick did so, reluctantly. He had felt stirrings in places that hadn't worked for weeks.

Maliwan sat astride his stomach and continued her massage, working her hands down his chest and stomach region. Nick reached for a towel, and draped it over his crutch in the vain hope that it would hide his bulging modesty.

'Don't be a dickhead, Nick,' John said quietly. 'You don't need to hide that thing from us. Quite frankly, my dear, you're not my type. Jook's seen you in the shower at home several times, he says you're not his cup of tea either. Too rough, I think he said. But on the other hand, I think Maliwan might well be interested in inspecting the goods.'

'You're having me on.'

'Nope.'

Rather embarrassed, but with his heart pounding, Nick removed the towel. Maliwan smiled as she slid down to Nick's knees and ran her nimble fingers down his thighs, her massage turning into more of a caress.

'Dear God, I don't think I can take much more of this. I had no idea she was so talented.'

'They both learned massage at school, in the temple, at Wat Mahahwong.'

'They teach this at a temple?'

John laughed. 'Jook has taught her some special techniques, but she learned the basics of traditional Thai massage at school, so the kids can relieve their parents of tension after a hard day's work.'

'Well I'm certainly going to be relieved of a lot of tension if she carries on like this much longer.'

'Save it for later.'

'You think so?'

'You should see the smile on her face. She's certainly impressed. You'll be bursting out of those trunks in a second.'

'I know, but it's incredibly uncomfortable. I've got a few hairs caught up under my foreskin, the tension is pulling them out. I'm too shy to do anything about it though.'

John guffawed. 'God you're a romantic, aren't you.'

'You think she'll think I'm being too quick off the mark if I adjust myself? It's getting quite painful, there must be a whole handful of hair caught up.'

'Nick, please. You're giving me just a little too much information. Look, sort yourself out, neither of us two are going anywhere near that filthy thing of yours.'

'It's not filthy. I clean it regularly.'

'That's not what I meant. It's been in some disgusting places, by all accounts.'

'Huh! Hark who's talking,' Nick responded grinning as he put his hand down his trunks to sort himself out. He couldn't help noticing a grin appearing on Maliwan's angelic young face. Maybe not so angelic, he contemplated. 'What's the time?'

'About two-thirty.'

'Not time to go yet then?'

'Go? Why, Nick? I thought you were enjoying yourself?'

'I am.'

'Then why?'

'Maybe I'll enjoy myself even more back in the bungalow. Who knows? Maliwan seems to be in exceptionally good spirits today. It looks as though it might be my lucky day.'

'Don't push your luck, you old tart. Let her lead. She's still only eighteen, Nick. I'm not sure if she's done anything before, with a man that is.'

'She's doing well so far.'

'That's because Jook has been teaching her this last week or so.'

Nick was astonished. 'This is planned?'

'You'd better believe it, old son. Haven't you noticed the way the two of them have been giggling away in their rooms recently?'

'Yeah, but there's nothing new about that.'

'Well, they've been talking about nothing but sex, how big you are, how to do it, does it hurt, you know, kid's questions like that. Jook's stolen a few looks at you in the shower in order to report back to her.'

'Good old Jook,' Nick mused. 'It must have worked. Funny that, never would have thought I'd be grateful for a lady-boy to eye me up naked. It's a queer world out here. Sorry, I didn't mean anything by that.'

'It's called a pun, you dope. But you're right, it really is a queer place to be. Thankfully.'

After the most gorgeous afternoon Nick had ever spent on a beach, he drifted back to the bungalow in an odd mood. 'You know something, John, I'm actually nervous about this. What if it doesn't work out? I'd be mortified; you know how much I fancy her.'

'Nick, just take it easy. Let her lead. Don't jump her, and don't force yourself on her. Let her take complete control.'

'Right. This is going to be a new experience. God, I'm shitting myself. What if it doesn't work? I can't remember the last time it functioned properly.'

'For god's sake, Nick. Get in your bedroom and have a shower. We'll sort out the details for you.'

'Right. Thanks, John. You're a real mate, you know that?'

'Get out of here.'

Nick busied himself in his room, unpacking, moving toiletries around and generally fidgeting like a nervous teenager, before heading for the shower. He had to wash himself three times before being satisfied that his armpits didn't pong. As he withdrew from the shower room, towel loosely draped around him, Maliwan entered the room with nothing more than a bath towel wrapped around her torso. Nick found himself putting his hand on the back of a chair to steady himself. He felt quite faint.

Maliwan moved closer, and reached out for his towel. She pulled it aside and let it drop to the floor. Nick stood frozen, as Maliwan put her delicate young fingers around his penis, squeezing him slightly. The effect was immediate, he swelled in response.

Maliwan let her own towel drop to the floor, and twirled around slowly, giving Nick a full view of her firm young slender body. He swallowed hard as she reached for his hand to lead him to the bed. His mouth dried up. She gently pushed him back on to the mattress, and sat astride him, as she had done so on the beach. He couldn't resist her youthful body any more, slowly raised his hands, caressed her firm petite breasts, then slid his hands down her sides to her impossibly slender stomach. Never had he felt such smooth skin, never before had he held such innocence in his hands.

Maliwan leant over, kissed him lightly, then gradually ran her tongue along his lips. She gently slid her tongue into his mouth and sighed as she engaged in her first ever passionate kiss. He ran his fingers down her back, over her buttocks, and between her thighs. She grunted and shivered involuntary, as he ran his fingers over her moist patch. She sat up, in apparent surprise at the sensations she was feeling. She smiled down at Nick, placed a hand on his penis and inserted the tip into herself. She shuddered in pleasure, and looked at him in astonishment.

Nick resisted the urge to thrust into her. Instead he forced himself to lay calm as Maliwan took time to slowly ease herself down on him. She rocked in slow motion, up and down, until he was all in. She took a few seconds to gaze in wonder down at her small patch of pubic hair, locked together with him. She smiled in admiration, and started to rise up and down, rhythmically, giving them both pleasures beyond belief.

Maliwan came first, her legs involuntarily shuddered as spasms raced through her body. Nick lay staring up at her in bewilderment, a sense of warmth teeming through his body, as he too reached his climax. He couldn't understand what had happened, what was happening, she swung her legs backwards and nestled her face on top of his chest. She remained there, calm, his manhood still pulsating inside her. He lay there content, caressing her back, realizing he'd never had sex like it before, ever. Then it dawned on him, he finally understood that he'd not just had sex, but, instead, had made love. For that's what Nick was feeling. Love, for the first time he could ever remember in his life.

John and Jook were preparing the evening meal when Nick finally emerged from his room. He grabbed a can of beer and sat down on the bungalow's veranda, looking out over Jomthein Beach in the moonlight. 'You know something, John, I don't think I ever want to leave this place.'

John nodded. 'You were a long time in there. I take it Maliwan meets with your approval.'

'John, I'm a changed man. I can't get over what happened just now. I've never known a girl like her. Not just her stunning looks, but her personality. She's so, so, oh I don't know, I can't find the words.'

'Do I detect love?'

'I would have scoffed at that word until a few weeks ago, but yeah, you know something, I think it may be love. Shit, I can't believe I said that. I didn't think guys felt like that.'

'Why not?'

'Well, not tough guys anyway. Not real men. It makes me sound like a pansy to talk of love.'

'Nick, you're only just twenty years old. You've got a lot to learn in life. Love is what makes the world go around. You've had none in your life so far, it's about time you had a bit.'

'Yeah. Yeah, maybe you're right,' Nick sighed contentedly. 'Jesus, I feel so different inside. I never knew you could feel such a way for someone else. Do you think she loves me too?'

'Nick, she's fancied you since the moment she first saw you, she just never let on to you. Jook told me that. Now she's given herself to you, freely, of her own accord. I reckon you've got a match made in heaven. Don't lose that, it's what makes life worthwhile; it's what life is all about. You're a lucky man, not everyone gets to experience it.'

'God, I hope she stays with me.'

'She will. I'm sure. You're a businessman now, you've got a bar to run. You've got status. She couldn't do better, she couldn't want for more. Really. You'll see, she'll settle down with you. You'll be making babies next.'

'Babies? Me? Christ, John, that sounds heavy.'

'Fatherhood will do you good, Nick. You wait and see.'

'I'm not sure I could handle it.'

'Sure you can. It's only natural. The responsibility will do you good. Besides, you need to create a family around you. You never had one before. It's what's missing in your life.'

The week passed in similar fashion. The two pairs of lovers spent their time frolicking on the beach, cavorting in the sea and romping around on their beach mats like the kids they were. By the end of the week, Maliwan had conceived her first child.

Chapter Eighteen

'I think that may be just a touch too much information for my needs,' Magee said. He looked over at Nittaya, wondering how the girl was coping with such revelations from her father.

'No holds barred, Magee,' Nick replied. 'That's the way you wanted it, isn't it?'

'Umm, yes, but there has to be limits, Nick.'

Nittaya caught Magee's eye. 'You don't have to worry about me, Chief Inspector. I'm not at all embarrassed. I thought that was a lovely story, it's the first time Daddy has ever talked about loving my mother like that.'

'Well,' Magee said blowing through his reddened cheeks. 'If you're sure.'

'Yes, thank you, Chief Inspector,' Nittaya responded. 'I'm quite sure. You see, Daddy has never opened up like this, I know nothing about that part of his life, about his daily life with my mother.'

Nick brushed a few strands of loose hair away from his daughter's face. 'I fell in love with your mother on that beach, Nit. We visited it whenever we could, whenever we could get someone to run the bar whilst we were away.'

Nittaya smiled sweetly at her father. 'I have no recollection of it at all.'

'You couldn't have. Our last visit was just after Christmas in nineteen seventy-two. You were only four months old. We thought it best to get away from Bangkok for the New Year celebrations. Dongtan Beach was far more peaceful . . .'

****

Dongtan Beach, Thailand
New Year's Day 1973

Walking bare-foot along the shore of Dongtan Beach, hand in hand with Maliwan, his beloved wife, was one of those enjoyments Nick knew he'd treasure for the rest of his days. He had walked a mile along the near-deserted beach, doing no more than any other young man would do on holiday. Frolicking in the warm water with a beautiful Thai girl, marvelling at the sun's rays shimmering on the calm turquoise blue sea, stealing as many kisses as he could.

He spotted John leaning back against one of the hundreds of Hoo Kwang trees lining the top of the beach, and gave a wave in his direction. With a heavy sigh he said, 'Come on, Mal, I suppose we'd better get back to the kids.'

Nick and Maliwan ambled back to the little camp they'd set up earlier that day. On the ground lay a couple of raffia mats, on which lay two hampers of food, a cooler box, a baby sound asleep, a toddler fiddling with a bamboo cane and Jook watching over his young charges.

As Maliwan knelt to tend her baby, Nick plunged a hand into the cooler box, rummaged amongst the melting ice and dug out a can of beer. He looked over to his mate leaning against the tree and called out, 'Fancy a beer, John?'

John looked at his watch and replied, 'Not right now, thanks. I want a quick dip first. I've been sitting here far too long doing bugger all, I need to stretch my legs. And I'm getting writer's block.' He walked over to one of the raffia mats, chucked a notebook and pen down and said, 'Hey, Jook, coming for a swim?'

John moved a short distance away with Jook, muttered something into his ear, then raced the lad for the water's edge, play-fighting along the way, wrestling him to the ground, tumbling head over heels in the hot sand. With a whoop of laughter, he hoisted Jook into the air and hurled him into the water.

Nick sat down on a mat, pulled the ring on the beer can, took a sip, and watched the childlike antics of his best mate playing in the water with a touch of envy. At times he felt old, much older than the twenty-two years asserted by his birth certificate. His very bones seemed to ache at times. But then that wasn't surprising, not with the scrapes he'd been in. Yet the path he'd taken had had its compensations, for without the bitter past experiences he wouldn't now be a father of two and married to the most beautiful woman in the world.

He looked over at his wife who was squatting a few feet away, cradling her baby as it fed, and said, 'Everything okay, Mal?'

'Everything fine, Nick. You enjoy beer. Never mind me.' Maliwan's appreciation for sarcasm had come on well since her marriage to a caustic Londoner.

Nick beamed from ear to ear, raised his beer can and responded, 'You're the one who wanted another baby.'

The bony remains of a chicken leg narrowly missed his head. He watched it land a few yards away in the sand. 'That's okay, Mal, I wasn't after chicken anyway.'

Maliwan appeared to have misinterpreted her husband's remark. 'You hungry?'

Nick looked lovingly at his baby daughter before replying, 'Maybe.'

'What you like?'

'I'd like what Nittaya's having, please, once she's finished.'

It took Maliwan a few moments to catch his meaning. 'You crazy man,' she replied. The look on her innocent face was nevertheless anything but reproachful.

Nick edged closer to his wife. Somsuk waddled over, dropped the bamboo cane in his father's lap and babbled a few incomprehensible words. Nick picked it up, inserted his fingers either side of a split in the wood and wrenched it open to reveal a four inch long tube of sticky rice mixed with red beans. He handed the cane back to his son, ruffling the boy's black hair in affection. Somsuk thanked his father in a confused mixture of Thai and English words and promptly fell into a sitting position.

For a few moments Nick sat watching his son scooping out the sweet sticky dessert, stuffing it into his mouth with apparent glee. Once the boy appeared satiated, Nick turned to his wife and said, 'Mal?'

Maliwan looked up.

'Would you like a third one? A third kid that is?'

Maliwan looked away coyly, her eyes drifting back down at the baby. 'Maybe.'

A grin appeared on Nick's face. 'Can we start trying?'

Another coy look. 'Maybe.'

'Tonight?'

Maliwan returned a sheepish smile.

Nick lay back, a look of content on his face. Never had he imagined he'd find such happiness. He had truly found heaven on earth.

With the warmth of the sun filtering through the leaves overhanging their camp, Nick drifted off to a peaceful sleep.

Half an hour later his snooze ended with a prod to his chest and a boisterous voice proclaiming, 'Oi! Where's my beer? You haven't drunk it, have you?'

Nick opened his eyes to find John's handsome set of white teeth gleaming down at him. 'They're in the blue bag, you dipstick. The cooler box over there. Chuck me one too, please.'

'It's getting on for six,' John said. 'We'd better head back to the bungalow soon.'

'Why? What's the rush?'

'Oh, nothing. Just my usual urges coming on strong.'

Nick tutted. 'You're a tart, mate. As I've told you many a time.'

'And we'd better phone Lucy's, make sure Todd has everything under control for tonight.'

Nick snorted. 'Bugger the bar. Last thing on my mind is Lucy's bloody Tiger Den. It can burn to the ground, for all I care. All I want in life is here with me right now.'

John grunted. 'You know you're getting soppy in your old age, mate.'

'Marriage has made me happier than I could ever imagine.'

John stuck two fingers in his mouth and made a vomiting gesture. 'I thought you weren't happy? Well, in one direction anyway.'

'Well, yes, maybe. She hasn't let me anywhere near her for four months, not since her labour pains began. But it can wait. Not for too long though, I hope, I don't think I can cope much longer without, well, without you-know-what.'

'Your right hand getting sore, is it?'

'Too bloody right it is! You know something, I found myself thinking about asking that young tart you brought in last Wednesday afternoon to help me out. That's how desperate I'm getting.'

John guffawed. 'I've told you already, Mal really doesn't mind if you go with lady-boys.'

Nick shrugged. 'Trouble is, mate, what if it's catching? What if I enjoy it a bit too much? Then what, where would it end?'

'It would end right afterwards you numbskull. You're straight. Gratification with a lady-boy would be very short-lived. Anyway, from what Jook has just told me, tonight is likely to be your lucky night. Just take it easy though, no rough stuff. Be gentle with her.'

'Gentle? That's easier said than done. You should know that. You're never gentle. Your bedroom walls shake so much some afternoons when you're entertaining Jook's friends I worry your bed's going to collapse through the floor into the bar. God knows what effect that sight would have on our regulars. Doesn't bear thinking about.'

John sniggered. 'Come on, drink your beer. It should help relax you.'

Nick and John sat for ten minutes, beers in hand, watching the sun go down, watching over their loved ones. Eventually, John broke the intimate silence. 'I may have mentioned this before, but I don't think I'll ever tire of this beach. It's truly paradise here.'

Nick took a moment to respond. 'Yeah, I guess it is.'

'We just need a large pile of cash to set us up in life. Just one big job will do it, set us free. Land us The Big One, Nick; then we can stay here on this beach forever.'

'I'll drink to that,' Nick said raising his can. 'To The Big One. Whatever, and wherever, it is.'

John raised his can too. 'Some day, Nick, we'll get there. I know it in my bones. We'll be rich beyond our imagination. We'll be the happiest men alive.'

Chapter Nineteen

Nittaya wiped away a tear. 'Thank you, Daddy. That was lovely. You've never talked about us as a family unit like that, about how you talked with Mum.'

Nick wiped away a tear of his own. 'She was fun. She had a terrific sense of humour. She must have done, to put up with me.'

Magee checked his watch and coughed to get everyone's attention. 'I think we've covered that ground sufficiently. Perhaps we could start moving towards the main crux of this account? Keith Gibson and his story of Tibet?'

Nick sighed. 'You mean the fourth bloody cart? You know something, Magee, I got sick to death of that story. I never did believe it.'

'So how did it fit in?'

'It was Keith's party piece. It was all he ever talked about when he was stoned. It was what started our trouble, Keith mouthing off to every stranger that came into the bar . . .'

****

Bangkok, January 1973

'Not again, Keith, for crying out loud!'

Despite the din of the Beach Boys Surfin' USA blaring out of a juke box in the corner of the bar, Nick had still made out the words Dali Lama in Keith's conversation. He approached Keith and said, 'How many times have I got to tell you, nobody wants to hear your stupid sodding story. You're boring my customers to death.'

'Sorry, Nick,' Keith Gibson mumbled apologetically.

The Fourth Cart III

'I do apologize for my friend here,' Nick said to a large well-built young lad who had been stifling yawns for the last ten minutes. 'He gets carried away, thinks he's back in Shangri La or wherever it was he reckons he came from.'

'That's okay, it was quite interesting. Quite a tale really, this Fourth Cart business.'

'Oh God, not the Fourth Cart again. You know mate, I've heard that tale being told so many times I can't bear to listen to it any more. It really grates on me. Keith here thinks it was him with the Dalai Lama, but I've known countless other people tell the same story, only each time it's a bit different, more exaggerated, more treasure involved, more mystery. Honestly mate, don't bother with it. Do you really think it likely there's a fortune sitting out there waiting to be dug up? It's just a Patpong bar story. An urban myth.'

The customer didn't look convinced. 'Still,' he said, 'it does stir up the imagination. It certainly conjures up some fanciful ideas about liberating it, becoming a millionaire. I could do with earning a few bob myself. This year-off I'm having travelling the world is costing me far more than I expected.'

'Well, you've chosen the right bar if you're looking for work. We get all sorts in here, if you know what I mean. If you'll do anything, and I mean anything, then I'll pass the word around. What's your name, son?'

'Geoff. Geoffrey Rees Smith.' The customer offered his hand.

'I'm Nick. And my partner behind the bar over there, the blond one, is John. We've run this place for two years now, been around longer than that as well. Anything you want, we can usually find it, or at least arrange it.'

'Right, thanks. I'm certainly interested in any work opportunities. So is my mate, Des, over there by the Juke box.'

'Well, a big strong boy like you shouldn't have any trouble. There's always work available for someone with muscle. You work out in the gym?'

'I used to. We left university last summer. Oxford, that is. I won a Blue in my last rugby season. Number eight in the scrum, I was. I used to train really hard, hence the bulk I'm carrying.'

'Well, Geoff, hang around, I'm sure something will turn up soon.'

'Thanks, Nick.'

'You're welcome, Geoff. And as for you, Keith, make yourself useful for Christ's sake. Go and collect the empty glasses or something.'

'Sure, Nick.'

'And turn that fucking racket down, Todd,' Nick screamed across the room. 'I can't hear myself think.'

'I hear you, Nick. Sorry, I just love this song,' Todd Conners replied.

As Nick headed back to the bar, Geoff turned to Keith and asked, 'Is he always this crabby?'

'Nah. He's usually far worse.'

'Worse? Why do you put up with that?'

'He's a good man really, Geoff. You should see him with his wife and two young kids. He's another character completely with his family around. He adores them, worships the ground Maliwan walks on. You wouldn't expect that of someone who has a bark like that, would you?'

'No, indeed,' Geoff responded. 'But can he deliver?'

'Sure can. He's the boss around here. He can arrange anything. He's got some pretty heavy contacts.'

'Hmm. He sounds interesting indeed.'

On reaching the bar, Nick leant heavily on a stool and lowered his head in exasperation. 'Sweet Jesus, thank God for that,' he sighed as the bar's noise level became a little more bearable.

John stopped polishing beer glasses and frowned at his friend, 'What's got your goat tonight, you've been snapping at everyone. Still not getting enough?'

'Nah. No trouble there,' Nick sighed.

'Are you sure? I saw you giving one of Jook's younger friends the eye-over yesterday.'

'That little tart? Christ, John, I was just shocked, that's all. I've never known such a mincing queen, and so young as well. I was just stunned by the way he minced through the bar and up the stairs, waggling his butt at all the customers.'

John had a glint in his eye. 'Hmm. He did have a cute little butt, didn't he?'

'You didn't did you? You had him? He only looked about twelve. You old tart.'

'He was of legal age, I checked his ID card. Young, but dear god he knew what he wanted.'

Nick eyed his friend, and shook his head slowly. 'One day, you'll pay dearly for all the sex you have. It will burn you up, dry you out. Your good looks will desert you.'

'Beg to differ there, old boy. I'm getting on already, twenty-three this year, and getting more handsome every day.'

'Trollop,' was all Nick could think of in response. He loved his friend, his best mate, and loved the way he wasn't quite as other men were.

'So, as I said, what's hacked you off today? I heard you biting poor Keith's ear off. He doesn't deserve it, even if he is a bit barmy. He's just stoned.'

'Sorry. Guess I'm just a bit pissed off. It's this bar life, it's getting a bit stale, that's all. We seem to be wasting our life away. As you say, you're going to be twenty-three this year. So am I. We've both been over here for more than three years now. What have we made of ourselves?'

'Blimey, Nick. You are in a state. Take a rest. Go over and have a drink with Ronnie. He always seems to manage to cheer you up. Jook and I can manage on the bar.'

'Yeah, good idea. Thanks. Sorry, I'm not feeling at my best. I had another bad night last night.'

'The jeep again?'

'Yeah. Same fucking nightmare. I'm sitting there, waving at the helicopter, and as you lot jump out, it's me pulling the fucking trigger. Jesus, John, I don't get it. It's been what, more than two years, now? And I still wake up in a sweat about it. Won't it ever go away?'

'Give it time, Nick. Traumas take a hell of a long time to get over.'

'Yeah. Time. That's one thing we've got plenty of. Thanks,' he said as John passed him over a beer. 'Fifty years in this shithole of a city I reckon.'

Nick kicked his heels as he dragged across the bar floor, the usual strut gone from his step. He slouched over Ronnie Nelson's table and the two of them started putting the world to rights.

Life had continued much the same for Nick and his bar-flies, day after day, month after month, for the two and a half years of owning and running Lucy's Tiger Den. March the ninth, nineteen seventy-three was no different, but from then on life would never be the same again.

'Okay, chaps. Listen up,' Nick shouted to all and sundry in the bar that evening. 'For those of you who don't know what planet you're on, tomorrow is March the tenth, and that means it's the twenty-first birthday of Maliwan and Jook.'

'Both?' asked someone from the back of the room.

'They're twins, you dolt,' Nick retorted.

'Well I never.'

'Thank you, thank you,' Nick shouted over the ensuing din of laughter. 'Calm down. Now then, we're going to have a huge party tomorrow evening. There'll be free food along with a couple of crates of beer. I, for one, am going to get thoroughly pissed. You're all invited provided you get pissed with me and join in the fun.'

The bar burst out into a spontaneous round of applause and whistles. As he turned back to the bar, Nick took Geoffrey Rees Smith to one side.

'Look, Geoff,' he said firmly, 'I know you don't like Jook, but it will be his birthday party as well, not just Maliwan's, so please, don't piss him off. Okay? Just try to tolerate his presence for one night. No taunting and no calling him "Gook". He knows it's derogatory, he knows you're being disrespectful to him, he isn't stupid.'

'Yeah, okay Nick,' Geoff grunted in response. 'I promise.'

'Oh, and one other thing Geoff, try and relax at the party. Cut out the power games bollocks, please. This is my bar, I'm the boss. I'm the one who gives you work. I want to enjoy myself tomorrow. I really can't be dealing with the bollocks you've been giving me recently. Okay?'

Geoff nodded.

But Nick wasn't so sure of Geoff's response. He suspected there'd be a showdown one day. Trouble had been brewing in the air since the man had walked into his bar.

The birthday celebrations started early. By seven in the evening dozens of plates of cold meats, crudities, sandwiches and crisps had been prepared and left scattered around the bar. Customers were greeted at the door by Maliwan and Jook, together, and were given a fresh orchid flower in honour of the auspicious occasion. In return, many of the regular customers offered gifts to the twins.

'Happy birthday, son,' Geoffrey Rees Smith said with a false smile as he accepted a flower from Jook. 'You too Maliwan. This is for the pair of you,' he said handing over a gift-wrapped present. 'I'm afraid I couldn't cut it in half.'

Maliwan let her brother take it. Jook beamed in delight and ripped at the paper like an excited kid. His mouth dropped wide open as he unzipped a leather case and found himself staring at a superb camera.

'Thank you, Khun Geoff.'

'You're welcome,' Geoffrey Rees Smith responded forcing another smile. He patted Jook's shoulder and held out a paper bag. 'Here're a couple of rolls of film as well.'

Jook ran to the bar to show off his new toy to John, and to have the film fitted. John's professional eyes nearly popped out when he saw it. He'd never seen such an expensive camera, let alone possessed one. Surely Geoff of all people wouldn't have purchased it; he always gave the impression he detested lady-boys.

One by one, Nick's entourage of misfits drifted into the bar, accepting flowers, handing over small gifts to the twins and heading straight for the free buffet. By nine o'clock the party was in full swing and the twins were in heaven. Jook preened himself endlessly; Maliwan enjoyed fending off flirtatious comments. Between them they had a huge pile of presents, and every farang did their best to entertain with silly capers and inharmonious singing.

A surprise birthday cake, lit up by twenty-one candles, was wheeled in from the kitchen. Moments later, the bar door opened and a tall imposing man entered during the rendition of "Happy Birthday". Nick clocked the new customer immediately. There was something odd about his presence. He stood out a mile from the motley band of party revellers. Something about the man worried him. He had strong Germanic facial features, a few greyish strands of hair, perhaps a little over fifty years of age, and was dressed smartly in a suit. No one wore a suit in Lucy's Tiger Den. The seedy drinking den just wasn't the sort of place an elegant man would stumble into. As the man meandered over to the bar and sat on a stool, Nick moved closer to keep an eye on him.

The well-dressed customer ordered a whisky and water, and covertly surveyed the characters around the bar. Nick's hackles rose, he and his mates were being sussed out. He smelt trouble in the air.

It wasn't long before the well-dressed man's eyes fell on Keith Gibson. His facial expression relaxed as though relieved to locate his mark. He casually moved towards the far end of the bar, near to the toilets, and ordered another whisky.

Ten minutes later, Keith excused himself apologetically as he stumbled through the mass of legs surrounding a table of partying men. As he came out from the toilet, the well-dressed man caught his attention.

'Gutten tag, Herr Doctor. May I have a word?'

'Excuse me?'

'It is Doctor Gibson, is it not?'

'Erm, yes. Yes it is,' Keith replied in a vague, far away air. 'Sorry. Nobody calls me by that title. Umm, I don't seem to be able to place you. Do we know each other?'

'No, Herr Doctor. We have not met. Not exactly, but I feel we have. I have read your thesis, thoroughly.'

'Really? You're the first person I've met who has.'

'It was most enlightening. I've always thought that Tibet is such a fascinating country. Such a tragic history though. I was there, myself, just last year, doing a little research. I was even allowed to visit the Potala Palace. And I've met both Heinrich Harrer and Peter Aufschnaiter.'

'You know them? They're two of my biggest heroes.'

'I wouldn't say I know them. I briefly met them, years ago. My research has taken me a lifetime already it seems. I was able to pull a few strings, get short interviews. Just a few minutes with each man about their adventures in Tibet.'

'You know something, Seven years in Tibet gave me tremendous inspiration when I was at university. It was one of the reasons that made me want to go there in the first place.'

'But I thought your inspiration would have come from your grandfather. After all, it was that connection that helped you obtain a visa was it not? I would have imagined that your grandfather would have told you fascinating tales when you were young, no?'

'How . . .?' Keith stuttered, 'How on earth do you know about my grandfather?'

'As I just told you, I've undergone what seems like a lifetime of research. It never ends. You have no idea what a privilege it is to finally meet you.'

'To meet me? Why is that a privilege?'

'Oh come now, Herr Doctor. Do not be so modest. You were a legend in your own right in Tibet. Especially because of what you did on the day the palace fell.'

Keith gripped the bar as if to steady himself. 'I . . . I . . . Look, I'm sorry, but how do you know about that part of my life? I didn't write about such things.'

'No, maybe not,' the well-dressed man responded, 'but others have talked of you. Tenzin, for instance,' he added tantalizingly.

'You've spoken of me with Tenzin?'

'Of course. Research, Herr Doctor.'

'Are you writing a book?'

'Maybe. I should, I suppose, I certainly know enough. Tibet does have an enthralling history. Does it not?'

'I loved that country with a passion,' Keith responded as though a long dormant fire within him had being rekindled. 'I still do. Please tell me more about your research.'

'Of course, Herr Doctor. But let me introduce myself first. My name is Hans Schmidt. Please call me Hans, after all we are of a kindred spirit.'

'Then please call me Keith. I'm not used to formality, and we tend to operate on a first name basis here. Some people don't like their real names being used at all.'

'As you wish. Well, Keith, I hope I'm not disturbing your evening, but may I buy you a beer? I would be honoured if you would join me for a drink.'

'Sure. That's very kind of you, Hans. Thanks.' Keith sat down on a stool next to Hans and gestured for another bottle. Nick took the order, it gave him an opportunity to loiter close by.

'Well, I think a toast to Tibet is in order,' Hans said holding up his beer in salutation.

'Cheers, Hans. To Tibet.'

'You must have many fond memories of Tibet, Keith. I would love to hear about your time there. It would help my research.'

'Well, I'd love to, but it's not a good idea around here. Nick shouts at me if I mention anything to do with Tibet. He says I bore his customers and they never come back.'

'Nick?' Hans pondered for a moment. 'Ah, you mean the co-owner of this bar? Nick Price?'

'Yes. That's right. You know Nick?'

'Only by reputation. Who does not know of Nick Price in Bangkok? Look, do not worry. If Mr Price gets upset, then I will say I started the conversation. And I promise I will not be bored by anything you say. Please Keith, do me the honour of telling me of your memories.'

Keith frowned. 'You want to hear my memories? Most people don't, they just tell me to shut up after a couple of minutes.'

'Oh, come on, Keith. I am a fellow worshipper of Tibet. Your memories will be fascinating, I'm sure. Honestly, I have nothing to do tonight and I would love to be reminded of Tibet. Everything you can remember. I mean it.'

'Well, okay. If you insist,' Keith replied and started his usual tale.

For thirty minutes Keith talked of his exploits in Tibet. He missed little out; from the days he had gone to Tibet as a student to the last day in the Potala Palace before it fell to the Chinese. It was a story Keith had told so often that it flowed out of his mouth effortlessly. Hans Schmidt listened politely, occasionally prompting Keith with the odd remark, and appeared genuinely interested in Keith's academic works. Only twice did Hans stifle a yawn.

'. . . and this is that very ruby. I've always kept it as a memento,' Keith concluded his tale, and withdrew the gem from a leather pouch tied around his neck. The action was the dramatic climax to his story. He had always ended his story like that, trying to impress his audience with the largest ruby imaginable. Everyone else in the bar had seen the gem so often they'd long since tired of it.

Hans' eyes almost popped out of their sockets. 'May I see it? Closer, please,' Hans said softly. He held it in his hands, stroked it, caressed it and held it up to the light. 'It is beautiful, Keith. The most beautiful ruby I have ever seen.'

Keith shrugged his shoulders. 'When I show it, most people just laugh and say it must be glass.'

Hans frowned, removed an eyepiece from his pocket and subjected the ruby to a closer, professional inspection.

Standing behind the bar, Nick didn't miss a trick. 'Shit,' he mumbled under his breath and put his beer glass down.

Hans smiled, turned to Keith, and said, 'I'll give you one thousand dollars for it.'

The Fourth Cart III

'No! No thank you, Hans. It's not for sale. I couldn't possibly depart with it. It's part of what I am now.'

'Fifteen hundred dollars then. Cash. Right now. I have the money in my pocket.'

'Thanks again, but . . .'

'Two thousand dollars. My final offer. Come now, you look as though you could do with a bit of money. It could be months before I'm back in Bangkok, it might be your last chance.'

Nick came within a few feet of Keith and studied the German. Two thousand dollars? Now? Just like that? Without a proper look in daylight? It had to be genuine then. And if it was genuine, then what about the rest of Keith's story? Hadn't Keith said that there were hundreds of gems like this?

'It's not for sale,' Nick said in a tone that spelt an end to the expected deal. He took the stone back from the German.

Hans stared hard into Nick's cold eyes. 'The story is true then?'

'What story would that be?' Nick asked.

'The Fourth Cart, of course.'

Nick moaned, 'Not the bloody Fourth Cart again.'

'Mr Gibson likes to talk doesn't he? You know, the story of the Fourth Cart came to me more than ten years ago. But it was not told to me by Mr Gibson. I heard it from a Tibetan monk. He said it was a legend in his own country, said it inspired the locals in their resistance against Chinese occupation. It was a story that has intrigued me ever since. It has taken a long time to put the pieces together, a long time for Mr Gibson's location to be revealed. Still, I have had many people working on the problem. They pass on interesting information, for a price. Finally, I have had the honour of meeting Mr Gibson, and he has just kindly confirmed what I thought.'

'And what would that be?'

'The truth of what happened to the Potala treasures hours before the palace fell to the Chinese. It's one of the big mysteries in my profession.'

'It's just a story isn't it? There were no treasures there. It's just bollocks.'

'Oh no. Definitely not, Herr Price. You see, I have confirmation from other sources that there was immense wealth stored in the palace. Much gold and silver was taken out in nineteen fifty when the

Dalai Lama first tried to flee the country, but many jewels, especially those set within religious artifacts, were still there right up until the end. They were taken away on the last day. Four carts full. Three carts were recaptured by the Chinese Army, but the fourth cart got away. Mr Gibson was driving that fourth cart. It disappeared, to the frustration of the Chinese. Only Mr Gibson knows what happened to it.'

'Keith was driving the cart? What the hell was he doing there? Why was he involved? Why didn't this Dalai Lama bloke take the stuff himself?' A thousand other questions flashed through Nick's mind.

'I suggest you listen to Mr Gibson. It's his story, not mine.'

'We've heard it too many times already.'

'Well, I suggest you listen again.' Hans looked around the cheap tacky bar and chuckled aloud, 'Oh, but of course, Herr Price, you have never believed the story have you?'

Nick's face dropped. Why had he never listened properly? It had been well over three years since he had first bumped into Keith. Three whole years. Three years in which he had been searching for the Big One, the great scheme that could earn him a fortune. And it was here all the time? 'You're not going to tell anyone else about this are you?'

'Certainly not,' Hans replied. 'I have no intention of telling a soul.'

'Good.' Nick locked eyes with Hans.

'Of course, if the story is really true and you are able to, how can I say, liberate the jewels, then you'll need to find a market. Do you know about jewels, Mr Price? Can you spot a fake? What if you are told a jewel is a worthless fake? Would you know if you were being cheated?'

Nick bit his lip hard. The man was good. He had sussed out the situation well. He was confident, but not arrogant. He weighed up the possibilities of getting ripped off.

'My card,' Hans said, offering it to Nick. 'I have an office here in Bangkok as well as in Amsterdam. I have a legitimate business buying and selling gems. I have a license to export jewels out of this country. No one will raise questions if I transport and sell jewels, no matter what quantity. But I think if you tried to sell a large quantity of gems, it would be presumed . . . well, I don't mean to be rude, Herr Price,

The Fourth Cart III

but you do not look the type of man who would come across jewels legitimately. I doubt whether you would get more than, say, ten per cent of the value you could get in a respectable European auction house. I also think that you would bring the attention of the authorities on to yourself. Do you not agree?'

Nick stood, riveted, as the truth of that statement dawned upon him. He continued to stare, unblinking, into the German's eyes and replied, 'How much?'

'Mr Gibson says there are thousands of these rubies?'

'Yes,' Nick nodded.

'Then we are talking about several million dollars of merchandise. My commission would be twenty per cent of gross sales value.'

'Ten per cent,' Nick countered.

'Fifteen per cent,' Hans replied.

'Ten per cent. You won't be doing any of the hard work.'

'Twelve and a half per cent, plus my expenses. No less.'

'Twelve and a half per cent of what we get left with after the auction house commission, plus all your traveling expenses. I'll want to see receipts, so keep a decent set of books. I don't care what you put through your official books.'

Hans turned to Keith Gibson and asked, 'How many thousands of jewels were in the Fourth Cart, Mr Gibson? Can you be specific? No exaggeration, please.'

'I never had time to count,' Keith replied. 'There were all types, diamonds, emeralds, rubies, sapphires. A thousand perhaps? No, that's on the light side. Maybe two or three thousand, I'm not sure, the cart was full of other stuff, ornaments, gold bars and the like. There were about hundred or so shoulder sacks which we'd used to put everything in, but most went into the other carts. I suppose we had fifteen or twenty of those sacks, a few hundred jewels in each I should think. But none were as big as this one, most were less than half its size.'

Nick was flabbergasted. 'Mr Schmidt . . .'

'Hans, please.'

'Hans, just now, you offered Keith two thousand dollars for his ruby. How much would that fetch in a proper auction room. Tell me the truth, please.'

Hans smiled weakly. 'You will appreciate that I could not offer top price, not here in the bar. I would need to see it in the daylight.'

'How much?'

Hans squirmed. 'I only offered what I was carrying.'

'I understand that. How much?'

'I believe that particular ruby would fetch in excess of eight thousand dollars under the right conditions at auction in Amsterdam.'

'Eight grand,' Nick whistled, 'And you offered two. Jesus, is that your usual mark up?'

'I am a businessman, Herr Price. It is in my nature to seek a profit. However, I am also a man of my word. You will not find anything wrong with my books, or my calculation of twelve and a half per cent commission. I will not be offended if you check my operations with a fine tooth comb as I believe you say in England.'

Nick let a smile be shown. He was already dreaming of counting the money. There could be five million dollars or more if what Keith was saying was true.

'They must all come through me, Herr Price. And remember that any leak of information could cause ripples in the market. Please do not try to find alternative outlets because rumours would start, other parties would get jealous. They would start interfering, trying to get in on the action.'

'I understand. The fewer who know, the better.'

'Good,' Hans nodded. 'I will be able to pass them through auction in large quantities, perhaps a couple of hundred at a time, but it will take months. I cannot place several thousand on the market in one go. It would disrupt the market.'

'How long then?'

'Maybe a year. Yes, a year is safer. It is better you understand that now. I would not want you to be disappointed later.'

'Okay, agreed.' Nick held out his hand to cement the new partnership. He smiled warmly when Hans shook it firmly. 'Now, if you don't mind, Mr Schmidt, my friends and I have some business to discuss.'

Hans rose from the stool, pulled his wallet from his pocket and placed a few notes on the counter. 'It has been a pleasure, gentlemen. I look forward to hearing from you. I like your style Mr Price. I am surprised you didn't fare better in Limehouse.'

The Fourth Cart III

Nick looked at Hans quizzically. 'Limehouse?'

'I had you checked out Herr Price. There is still a contract out on your life. Five hundred pounds, I believe. A rather small amount, don't you think. An insult really. I would have expected you to be worth more.'

'Have you been spying on me?'

'No. Just research, Herr Price. I am a careful man. I have to be, in my profession. I wanted all the facts before I came in here. I needed to know who I was dealing with.'

Nick broke into a broad grin. 'I would have settled for twenty per cent.'

'And I would have settled for less than ten per cent,' Hans rebutted. 'Please contact me if you are successful. I look forward to doing business in the near future. Goodbye, Herr Price, Herr Doctor.'

Nick bade farewell to Hans Schmidt, who courteously nodded to the two men before turning to leave. He stood in contemplation for a few moments as the German walked out the bar, then turned, faced Keith and shook his head in disbelief. 'I really don't know what to make of this, old son. We all thought this Fourth Cart crap was just some bad trip you've had.'

'Nick, I've never lied to you,' Keith protested. 'Well, exaggerated a bit, maybe, but I really was there, in Tibet.'

'This is really heavy shit, Keith,' Nick muttered under his breath. 'Come on, let's sit down, in the corner over there with Ronnie and Todd. I need to give this some serious thinking, but it's going to take better brains than mine to sort it out.'

Nick steered Keith across the floor, motioning a few of the regulars to join him. 'John, get Keith another beer will you, and join us. We're having a conference.'

'Coming up,' John said as he was returning to the bar with a handful of empties.

'Right, Keith,' Nick said as a group huddled around a table, 'Tell us about The Fourth Cart.'

'What? But . . .' Keith stuttered. 'You banned me from talking about it.'

'Well, that's changed. Tonight I really do want to hear it. So does everyone else. You got that everyone? Keith is going to tell us about

The Fourth Cart. This time no one interrupts, and I mean no one, for any reason at all. Got it?'

'Yeah, if you say so,' came the response from a handful of slightly bemused regulars, along with a few moans.

'Okay, Keith, take it away.'

'From the beginning? From when I was at university?'

'Nah, We'll be here all night,' Nick exclaimed. 'Just the necessary bits. What were you doing in Tibet, for a start?'

'I was, erm, I was researching my doctoral thesis.'

Geoffrey Rees Smith was impressed. 'You're a doctor?'

'Yeah, I got my PhD at Oxford.'

'Which college? I was at Balliol.'

'For fuck sake Geoff,' rebuked Nick. 'This is going to be hard enough as it is, don't prolong it.'

'Sorry, Nick.'

'Right, Keith, back to where we were before being interrupted. You were studying, right, in Tibet?'

'Yeah. I managed to get a visa because of some old family connections.'

'And you met this Dalai Lama bloke?'

'Er, yeah. I stayed at the Potala Palace for a few years. I got to know him quite well.'

'So who is this guy?'

'He's the God-king of Tibet,' Geoff put in. 'He's the country's spiritual leader as well as being the head of government.'

'This is Keith's story, Geoff.'

'I happen to know something about him, that's all,' Geoff said. 'The Chinese eventually took over Tibet in nineteen fifty-nine, and he fled the country. He's been in exile in India ever since. He wants his country back; the Chinese want to keep it.'

Nick stared daggers at Geoff.

'Sorry,' Geoff said shrugging his shoulders, 'but I thought you'd prefer a sober summary.'

Nick turned his attention back to Keith. 'What is this business with jewels? Why were you involved?'

'On the last day, before the Chinese Army invaded the palace, we were instructed to gather up all the gold, silver, jewels and precious artifacts we could find . . .'

'. . . and put them into four carts?' Nick asked. 'That's what Hans said wasn't it?'

'Who the hell is Hans?' John asked.

'Huh? Oh, sorry, John, I haven't told you yet. He was the German guy in a suit in the corner earlier. I'll get on to him later. Point is though, he confirmed Keith's story. It's true, so he says, he's researched it, spoke to someone who knows the inside story, apparently.'

'Shit,' John swore. Most of the others sighed in disbelief.

'Yeah, three carts got recaptured, ain't that right Keith?'

'I'm not sure, Nick. I wasn't with them, I was in another cart.'

'Exactly. This is the good part, John, Keith was the driver on another cart, cart number four. Hence the story of the fourth cart. And Hans said this fourth cart got clean away, disappeared into thin air.'

John looked puzzled. 'But you said Keith was the driver. It couldn't have disappeared, or if it did then Keith must know what happened to it.'

'You're catching on, old son.'

Everyone turned to stare at Keith. They saw only blank, vacant eyes. 'Umm, sorry? Did someone ask a question?'

'Keith, you dipstick, what happened to the cart you were driving? The fourth cart?'

'We drove it to a small town called Shekar. It was a village really, just one temple and a few scattered huts.'

'And?' Nick butted in. 'What about the treasures?'

'We took the crates up the mountain, to the old castle. We had planned to hide the crates if the Chinese Army got too close.'

'Hide them?' Geoff asked. 'You hid the treasures? Where?'

'In the tunnels beneath the castle.'

'But are they still there?'

'Er, well, they were in nineteen sixty-eight.'

'Nineteen sixty-eight? Geoff, I thought you just said this Dalai Lama bloke fled Tibet in nineteen fifty-nine?'

'I did. He did.'

'Keith old son. Have you got your dates right?'

'Sure, Nick. We buried them in nineteen fifty-nine. I was then arrested and put in prison. I didn't get out until nineteen sixty-eight.

That's when I last saw them. I was forced up the mountain by Lieutenant Tchen, he wanted to steal them, I think.'

'Lieutenant Tch . . . what? Who the hell is he?'

'Lieutenant Tchen. He found me in prison. He knew I knew where the treasures were. He tortured me to get the information, then took me to Shekar to locate them.'

'You mean someone else has got there already?'

'Well yes, no. I mean, he didn't reach the top of the mountain. He, erm, had an accident on the way up.'

'So he didn't find them? But you said that was the last time you saw them.'

'Yeah, that's true. After Lieutenant Tchen's accident, I went on, to the tunnel. I had nothing, you see. I'd been in prison for nine years. I thought it would be alright if I took a small bag of jewels or coins. Just enough to get me to India, so I could tell the Dalai Lama where we'd hidden them.'

'And they were there then, in nineteen sixty-eight?'

'Yeah.'

'But you took some. How much?'

'Just a small pouch full. And my ruby of course. This one,' Keith said touching the leather pouch around his neck.

Nick coughed. 'Hans says that it's worth eight thousand dollars. He offered Keith two thousand on the spot.'

Nine pairs of eyes stared, spellbound by the ruby shimmering in the dim bar light. There was a sudden unnatural quietness to the bar. The normally incessantly blaring juke box had ceased its noise long ago.

Geoff could bear the silence no more. 'So the jewels were still there five years ago. How many others know about this tunnel?'

'I'm the only one who knows where they actually are,' Keith responded. 'The others with me, well, they didn't survive.'

'You're the only one?'

'Umm, well, I did tell the Dalai Lama where they were buried, but he didn't seem to be interested.'

'So you're the only one who knows,' Geoff repeated.

'Keith. No exaggeration now, please. Just how many jewels are there buried in that tunnel? You said two or three thousand to Hans earlier, but how many are there like this one?'

'Well, they're not all this size, obviously. Some are only half the size.'

Nick chuckled at the word "only". It seemed such an inappropriate description for a jewel the size of a plum.

'How many, Keith?' most of the others prompted in unison.

'Well, I took just a leather pouch out of one of the shoulder bags that had been collected by the monks. There were just under a hundred diamonds inside, along with some gold coins and trinkets. I sold the diamonds for one hundred and twenty five thousand dollars when I first arrived here.'

Nick thought he must have misheard. 'You what?'

'Where do you think my money comes from, Nick? You know I don't work. I never seem to be able to raise the energy for it. It went straight into the bank, I live on the interest.'

Nick was shocked. He'd noticed Keith always seemed to have an ample supply of money for a joint, or a beer, but he had never questioned where the money had come from. It made sense now. He sighed deeply. Why, oh why, had he never listened before? 'And you say there were twenty shoulder bags?'

'That only makes two thousand diamonds, Keith,' Geoff put in.

'Right,' Nick countered quickly. 'So which is it, Keith, two thousand or more?'

'Umm, I really don't know, Nick. I guess it's easier to go by the number of bags. But they didn't all contain diamonds. There were other stones as well. And a lot of gold, that wasn't put into the bags. We put the gold straight into the crates. But, yeah, I reckon that there must be twenty bags of at least one hundred stones.'

'So we're looking at, what, two million dollars?' Geoff whistled.

'That's not counting the gold though, is it?' John interjected.

Nick sighed again. 'Christ Almighty, I just don't believe this.' He lowered his voice and spoke gently as if to a child, 'Keith, would you be able to find this tunnel again?'

'No problem, Nick. It's still fresh in my mind.'

'Would you though? If we all went together, would you show us where it was?'

Keith looked around at nine pairs of eyes firmly fixed on him and screwed his eyes up in confusion. 'Well, Nick, they're not really mine, are they? They still belong to the Dalai Lama.'

'You said he didn't seem interested in them.'

'Yeah, but . . .'

'Keith,' Geoff butted in, 'the Dalai Lama has managed to survive this last fourteen years without these treasures. He receives a lot of charitable contributions doesn't he? He gets donations from wealthy people because he has nothing, right? If it was announced that the Dalai Lama had suddenly acquired considerable wealth, that his palace jewels had turned up, well, who knows what would happen? Maybe the rest of the world would stop donating to his cause. No one gives charity to a rich man, do they? People only give money to the poor. You could be doing the Dalai Lama a terrible disservice by handing over jewels and gold to him. People get very emotive about wealth.'

'Gee, I hadn't thought of that.'

Des McAlister, Geoff's buddy, picked up the argument. 'That's right, Keith. Who gives aid to someone who doesn't need it? If you're wealthy, you don't get alms. If you're poor, then people will help you. If you're rich, then you're expected to give to the poor. These jewels could literally ruin the Dalai Lama. He must get millions each year in donations and you'd be threatening that income if you suddenly turned up with several crates of diamonds and gold. It's like winning the football pools, you lose all your friends and family overnight because everyone wants a little piece of your good fortune.'

'Well, if you put it like that.'

'Keith,' Geoff said, continuing the challenge, 'there's nothing to stop you, or us for that matter, giving small amounts . . . now and then . . . to the Dalai Lama, pretending it's just a charitable donation. That way the Dalai Lama gets his money back from his jewels, yet doesn't know it. We could all give him a share of any income we receive. What do you say lads, let's give half of our annual income to the Dalai Lama.'

'A sort of tithe on our income? Like in medieval days, tithing income to the church,' Des clarified. 'Sounds fair to me.'

'Right then, Keith,' Nick took up the suggestion. 'We all promise to give half of our annual income to the Dalai Lama. What can be fairer than that?'

Everyone nodded and promised faithfully to tithe their income as Geoff had suggested. At that moment, they'd promise anything just to get Keith to say "Yes".

'Well, in that case,' Keith said smiling. 'Okay, Nick, I'll show you where it is.'

With that, a roar of cheers went up, fresh beer cans were opened and the atmosphere in the bar changed to euphoria. They were all going to be rich. Rich beyond their wildest dreams. Life was suddenly wonderful and they were going to celebrate it in style.

Nick and John exchanged glances. This was it. "The Big One" had arrived. They were finally going to break free from their low-life existence. The two friends held each other's stares for a full minute, smiling at each other. At long last they were going to make it. They would go to Tibet, bring the jewels back, sell them through Hans and clear a million dollars each. This was it.

'Come on lads,' Nick shouted. 'It's not midnight yet. It's still Maliwan and Jook's birthday, so let's have another round. On the house!'

The euphoria of the occasion was redirected, away from thoughts of treasure, towards Maliwan and Jook and their birthday party. The group sang. They drank. They laughed. They played childish games and struck up pretend kick boxing matches. The twins were in ecstasy, never before the focal point of such celebrations. As the chimes of midnight struck, Jook grabbed his camera.

'Photo, photo!' Jook shrieked and waved at the others to form a circle in front of the bar. Ten rather drunk, shabbily dressed young men huddled in two rows in front of Jook.

'Come on, Mal, get your sexy little ass over here,' Nick shouted to his beloved wife.

With a giggling Maliwan nestled next to Nick, each man clutching a beer can, they all shouted "Cheers!" in unison as Jook pressed the button and a bright flash of light blinded them all as it bounced off the wall mirrors. Jook's camera caught the mood of the moment. Greed. Sheer, unadulterated greed.

Chapter Twenty

'Just a second, Nick,' Magee said, interrupting Nick's narration. He pulled out from his briefcase a copy of a photograph he'd been given by Keith Gibson's mother. 'Let's get this straight. It was definitely Jook that took the photograph? This photograph?'

'Yes he did. Does it matter?'

'As it happens, yes it does.'

'Care to explain?'

Magee mulled over in his mind the significance of the photograph that had been critical to his serial murder case. 'Nope. Not at this stage, Nick. It would only divert your thoughts, but I'd like to hear more about it.'

'Shall I continue then?'

'Sorry, yes, please do. Presumably we're about to hear about how you got so rich.'

'So rich, and yet so poor,' Nick responded.

'Do you want me to take over?' John asked.

Nick bit his lip and said, 'Thanks, John. I'll keep it going for now. But jump in if you think I've forgotten anything.'

'Will do.'

'Where were we up to?'

'The morning after the party,' John said. 'You had one hell of a hangover, if I recall correctly.'

'Me? Never! Must have been something I ate . . .'

****

Lucy's Tiger Den, March 11th 1973

The Fourth Cart III

'Christ, what a mess,' Nick cursed as he staggered downstairs into the bar holding a cold wet towel to his throbbing head. 'Oi! Do you have to make such a noise?'

John stopped throwing empty beer bottles into a wooden crate, looked up and laughed at his best friend's plight. 'Serves you damned well right. I think we beat the record last night. Pity most of it was for free though.'

'Stop whining you pillock. It hurts my head even more. What time is it?'

'Eleven thirty. And we're late opening.'

'Never mind opening time. There're more important things to worry about. Was I dreaming last night, or did I really sit through all that fourth cart bullshit and actually believe it?'

'You believed it. We all did.'

Nick groaned. 'Sod it. That's what I thought you'd say. I must have been fucking mad.'

'But, Nick,' John replied with an impish grin, 'you had it all planned out last night. Remember?'

Nick screwed up his forehead and stared hard into John's eyes. 'I remember some bullshit about raiding a sodding mountain top castle in Tibet, but have you any idea how idiotic that sounds in the cold light of the morning. We must have been fucking crazy thinking about such things. It's fucking impossible.'

'Sorry, Nick. It's too late to back out. We're all counting on you. This is The Big One, remember, you can't let us down. You've got to start thinking how to do it.'

Nick sighed deeply. 'Fuck, that's what I thought. I'm going back to bed. See you tonight, maybe. I'll think about it tomorrow.' He turned, bumped into the wall and tripped up the first three stairs. 'Bollocks,' he shouted at no one in particular.

Keith Gibson breezed into Lucy's Tiger Den at six o'clock in the evening, on the dot, sat down on a bar stool and stared at a photograph lying discarded near him. He picked it up and examined it closely.

'My God. Talk about ugly bastards. Did we really look like this last night?'

John looked at Keith in his army fatigues and smirked. 'Sure did. Same every night, haven't you noticed? Keep it if you like. Jook's had about twenty copies run off, enough for one each plus a few to pin up behind the bar or to throw darts at.'

'Thanks. I'll send it to my mother. That will cheer her up. She'll think I'm mixing with a bunch of mercenaries.'

'How charming, she must love you.'

'Would you mind writing everyone's names on the back, I'm not sure of some of them.'

'Sure.' He picked up a pen from the counter. 'Let's see now, top left we have Todd. Mike and Robert in the middle alongside your good self and Ronnie. Down the bottom we have Des with his friend, the big man, Jeff. Then Nick's old friend from London, Sean. Lastly, the two most beautiful people in the world, myself and Mal. Then good old Nick himself. There, done. Don't put it back on the bar, the ink will smudge. I've just had that problem with one I've done for Jook.'

'Don't worry I won't.'

'What's that you got?'

Keith turned to see Todd Connors standing behind him. 'Just looking at the evidence of how hammered we got last night.'

Todd looked over the photo. 'Jesus! That would give my mother a fright!'

'That's exactly what I was thinking. Want one?'

'Yeah, might as well.'

Nick and Maliwan wandered downstairs shortly afterwards. Nick drifted over to his usual table whilst Maliwan disappeared behind the bar to join John and Jook.

'Come over here, Todd,' Nick shouted from the other end of the bar. 'Grab your beer and get your ass over here. We've got things to talk about. The others will be here soon.' Nick swung a couple of tables end to end. 'We'd better start making plans.'

Over the course of the next hour, the two tables got piled high with beer bottles as the intimate gang from the night before gathered and discussed tactics.

'Can you take over here for a while, Mal?' John asked. 'Nick wants me over there with the others.'

'Okay. Jook and I manage.'

John grabbed a beer bottle and joined the others. 'Okay, we're all here. Just the ten of us. No one else needs to be involved.'

'Except Hans,' Nick stated.

'Yeah,' said Geoff, 'just who is this Hans bloke?'

'Hans,' Nick responded as though talking to a child, 'is the bloke who's going to sell everything for us. He's legit. He's got a license to export gemstones from here and has a business in Amsterdam. He'll get us top whack for the stuff. He's on twelve and a half per cent commission, but I don't want to hear any complaints, he's worth more than that to us.'

Geoff scoffed. 'How do you know he's trustworthy?'

'I don't for sure. Let's just say intuition. I'll shadow his every move in Amsterdam, and we won't be giving him all the gear at once. It will take a year or so to pass it off onto the market. I'll be dealing with that end, don't you worry about that.'

'Huh,' replied Geoff.

'Anyway, that's all in the future. First, we've got to sort out the mechanics of the operation. Okay, lads? Right, thinking caps on. First of all, let's get one thing straight, I'm in charge of this operation, along with John.'

'I thought as much,' Geoff mumbled.

'Look Geoff, we're going to need to buy a lot of things, and John and I are the only ones with the readies. You idle buggers just piss all your money away. Do you want to fund this trip Geoff? It will probably cost five grand, in dollars, not baht. You got that sort of dosh?'

Geoff squirmed, shrugged his shoulders and responded 'Yeah, well, whatever. But does that mean you'll be taking the lion's share of the bounty?'

'No, Geoff, it does not,' Nick snapped. 'This time, everything brought back will be split equally. Everyone who goes in will get a fair share. Got that? Equal shares, no cheating, no one gets more than the other.'

'What if we don't all come back?' Geoff asked.

That was a good idea, Nick thought, maybe they could leave Geoff in Tibet. He shrugged his shoulders. 'Any thoughts on the matter? Yes, Sean?'

'You go out, you come back, you get an equal share. If you don't come back, you get nothing. We can't be expected to chase up on distant relations to hand over a share of money. It would look suspicious. Someone might ask questions, it might make it difficult for the rest of us.'

'Fair comment. Let's take a vote. All those in favour?' Nick looked around. 'Carried. Fine. Next on the agenda; transport. We need a plane. Over to you Ronnie.'

Ronnie Nelson, an English qualified pilot, seconded to the Royal Thai Air Force and working with the Mapping Organization of the Ministry of Defence, personally knew just about every plane in the country. 'I suppose we could borrow the Prince 3A again,' he suggested. 'As long as we pay the usual backhanders, there should be no problem.'

'What about re-fuelling stops?' Nick asked.

'The Prince 3A has a range of nearly nine hundred miles, so the manual says. We'll leave from Chiang Mai, it's quieter up there. First stop Bhutan, we should just about be able to make that trip non-stop, if the wind's in the right direction. Then Kathmandu. It's about another three hundred miles, or so, to Shekar. Keith said the valley floor is pretty flat, so we should be able to land close to the town. There should be just enough fuel to last the round trip from Kathmandu into Tibet and out again.'

Nick nodded his head, 'Sounds okay.'

'One plane may not be enough, though,' Ronnie continued. 'Sorry to talk technical stuff, but the all-up weight of the Prince 3A is eleven thousand pounds, the tare weight is fractionally over eight thousand pounds so that only leaves three thousand pounds for the carrying load. There're ten of us at an average of, say, twelve stone each. We must have a combined weight of sixteen hundred pounds. We won't have too much capacity for provisions. We might have difficulty getting off the ground.'

Nick thought of the expense of the extra backhanders involved, plus fuel. 'We'll travel light. We'll only be there for one day anyway, I should think. We'll each carry enough food and water for two days only, plus an M16 rifle, ammunition, a few personal things such as cigarettes. A thick jacket, but no spare clothes.'

'Okay, if you say so,' Ronnie responded shrugging his shoulders. 'It's your call.'

'When can you get it organized?'

'Two weeks at least,' Ronnie replied.

Nick mentally counted off the days. 'So, let's say, the fourth of April?'

'Fine,' Ronnie nodded.

'Nick, just a second,' Des McAllister interjected. 'What are you planning with the plane? Do you really think you can just fly into Tibet, unnoticed?'

Nick shrugged and turned to Ronnie for help.

'Low level flight in. We'll chart a route down a pass and keep below the mountain tops.'

'What about radar?'

'We'll be too low.'

'In that case they could see us clearly.'

'Who?'

'I don't know. Border guards? Army? Anyone on the ground?'

'Visual sightings won't matter.'

'They'll matter if they order up a welcoming committee of jet fighters,' Des countered.

'It wouldn't happen,' Ronnie replied in a matter of fact tone. 'Not if we fly early in the morning. At dawn, preferably.'

'Why?' Nick asked.

'You obviously don't know the Chinese. They're extraordinarily bureaucratic. The observation stations at the borders will be slow in responding. Believe me. If any soldier on the ground spots us, he'll have to notify his station boss who in turn reports it to his regional boss. It takes ages for the message to reach Headquarters in Beijing. The Army HQ will then have to notify the Air Force who will then request further details from the Army. The Air Force won't be able to see us on radar and will probably dismiss the sighting. Anyway, at such an early hour, it's likely that the high ranking general, or whoever, with the required authority to determine the appropriate action is fast asleep. Would you want to wake up a slumbering general? Especially without radar confirmation? The general would be pretty pissed off if it was a false alarm, or not important. It's not as though a small plane makes an invasion force. The general's staff will convince themselves there would be a perfectly good reason for the plane. It's a dangerous thing to wake a sleeping general. It wouldn't be worth the hassle.'

'You're relying on bureaucratic inefficiency?' Des muttered quietly. 'God help us. I just hope you're right.'

'So it's a low level flight in at dawn. Surprise attack on this Shekar town, we simply march through and bluff it out. We hike up the mountain, dig the crates up and carry them down again. Load up the plane and a low level flight out. We'll be in and out within a few hours? It's a nice clean job. It will be a picnic. Any questions? Yes, Des?'

'What about the M16 rifles. I'm not shooting anyone.'

Geoff snorted in indignation. 'We don't expect you to shoot anyone, Des. We know you're a fucking pacifist. Shooting people in the pursuit of wealth just wouldn't sit with your socialist beliefs, would it?'

Nick frowned in Geoff's direction. There was an art to verbal persuasion. Abusive comments didn't help. 'Don't worry, Des. We'll be dressed like soldiers, wearing dark glasses and carrying M16 rifles. We'll look like mercenaries. We'll be looking so fucking mean, no one will dare come near us. You won't need to shoot anyone, okay? The rifles are just for show. Anyway, I doubt anyone will have a gun where we're going; no one will be shooting at us, so we won't have to shoot at them. What do you reckon, Keith?'

'Shekar's only a small town, Nick. It's extremely unlikely that anyone there would possess a gun of any description.'

'Right, there you go, Des. Any other points?'

Everyone shook their heads.

'Right then, lads. That's it, then. We'll all move up to Chiang Mai in the first few days of April. Check in at the Rose Hotel. Everyone know it? I reckon you've all been there before. Good. We'll meet up there on the second of April. That will leave one spare day, for last minute problems. Make your own way up there. Go alone or in pairs, don't go in a crowd or you'll attract attention. Try to be inconspicuous for a change, dress up as a tourist or something. Geoff, you help John load up the supplies here and then drive up in the van. We'll need it there to bring the stuff back.'

Chapter Twenty-One

'Can I stop you there please,' Magee interrupted.

'If you must,' Nick shot back.

Magee turned his attention to John Mansell. 'You say you wrote everyone's names on the back of one of the copies of this photograph for Jook?'

'I did, yes.'

'Surnames as well as Christian names?'

'Just Christian names. I'm not sure I knew everyone's surnames. Anyway, even if I did, we weren't in the sort of environment you'd use them. Why?'

'Well, last year, I was convinced this photograph was the killer's death list. I was wondering how someone could have remembered all the names after twenty years. Having a copy of this photograph would have been a good start.'

'Even with just Christian names on it? I can't see how anyone would remember after twenty years.'

'Maybe the killer didn't wait so long to establish the death list. Maybe the killer compiled the list back in nineteen seventy-three. Surely, if anyone was determined enough, they could have asked at the hotels or apartment blocks where you lived? The photograph would have jogged memories and, if the killer had asked back then, receptionists would have easily remembered the faces and paperwork would have been available to yield surnames.'

John looked horrified. 'Bollocks!' he responded.

Magee let the matter sink in with the others before resuming. 'There was just the ten of you involved?'

'Yeah, that's right?' Nick replied. 'Why?'

Magee scratched the back of his head. 'It's just, well, I assumed you'd include Jook and Maliwan in this caper.'

Nick looked over at John and sighed deeply. 'That's what I hoped initially.'

'But?'

Nick looked at his daughter and shook his head slowly. 'You've got no idea how stubborn Mal could be. As stubborn as you, Nit. Maybe more.'

'So she did go?'

'I tried to stop her,' Nick said, choking back a tear. 'God knows I tried hard enough, but she wouldn't take no for an answer . . .'

****

Bangkok, 1st April 1973

'No way, Mal. For the hundredth time, no. You are not coming with us.'

'But Jook is going,' Maliwan persisted. 'John says he can go, why not me?'

'Because he's a man, Mal.'

'No he's not.'

'You know what I mean. This trip is going to be tough, Mal, it could get dangerous. I want you to look after Somsuk and Nittaya. They need their mother.'

'Ay will look after them,' Maliwan said, referring to her maid. 'She has looked after them before. The babies will be okay with her.'

'No, Mal.'

'Yes, Nick.'

'No.'

'Yes.'

'John. Help me out here, will you?'

'Sorry, mate. I'm not fighting Mal. She beat me up last time I tried.'

'Thanks a bunch, you big girl's blouse,' Nick replied, smiling as he recalled the occasion Maliwan had pummelled John with fists after losing her first ever game of Monopoly. 'Oh, for goodness sake, Mal, okay. As long as it will keep you quiet.'

The Fourth Cart III

'Eeee! Thank you, Khun Nick,' Maliwan screamed throwing her arms around her husband.

'Yeah, yeah, I know, I'm the world's greatest husband.' His eyes lifted to catch John's, 'Thanks for your support, schmuck.'

'You're welcome. Schmuck yourself. You're the one who's always getting bullied into submission by your wife. Me, I would put my foot down about such things.'

'Bollocks,' Nick snorted in laughter. 'I've seen you kowtow to Jook's demands, he's got more lip than this one, any day.'

'At least Jook's useful for getting the provisions together. What's Mal going to do? Flash her innocent eyes and wiggle her jugs until someone puts a bag of diamonds in her hand?'

'Yeah. That's why she's determined to go, I'm sure. Doesn't miss a trick this one. She's not going to pass the opportunity of grabbing a few stones, I bet.'

'I hope she hasn't spread the word about. We don't want any publicity. You know what will happen if her friends find out; they'll all want a share.'

'Nah. Don't worry, she won't jabber. It's some of our lot you've got to worry about. They're the ones with loose mouths. I saw that creep Martin Shorrocks at lunchtime today. God he makes my skin crawl, he's, so, so . . .'

'Reptilian?'

'Yeah, that's a good word. Reptilian. Just like a lizard, he slid into the bar, then slithered from one customer to another, asking questions for his paper, I suppose. I reckon he might know something already. We'd better keep our eyes on him. It would be just his style to grass on us.'

'I'll deal with him,' John responded. 'I've got a few things on him I can use.'

'Really? Like what? Not boys, surely?'

'Yeah, I'm afraid so. Very young ones too, pre-puberty even, it's disgusting. He would lose his job at the Bangkok Post if it was found out. I'll give him a reminder next time I see him.'

'You do that,' Nick replied. His mind drifted onto more serious matters. 'We've got to make this work, John. In the last two weeks, we've used up nearly all our savings buying provisions and paying backhanders. I didn't figure on having to fork out quite so much to lift the army kits from the stores at Ubonratchadanee. I reckoned on our man there doing it for free. Still, Keith said we'd need windproof down jackets, so that's what we've got. I just hope they're not wasted.'

'Tibet's cold Nick, there will be snow and ice up the mountain we're going to.'

'So why the sunglasses, lip salve and sun cream?'

'Something to do with the rarefied atmosphere, I think. You know, people who go skiing in Switzerland in winter come back with suntans.'

'Really? I don't mix with such toffs. Christ, John, I'm shitting myself about this trip. I lie awake at night, thinking it through, realizing we must be stark raving bonkers to attempt it. You really think it will work out?'

'Sounds like a touch of the old Vietnam jungle blues there.'

'Too bloody right. I can just see this trip going tits up, running out of fuel, crashing into some mountainside, marooned for weeks, beaten up by some horde of barbarian tribesman. You listened to some of Keith's stories about local customs there?'

'I try not to.'

'They're barbaric. He said they butcher dead people, cut all the meat and bones up, then leave them out on the mountainside for the vultures to feast on. They put criminals in sacks and beat them to death. Cut limbs off for stealing. It ain't normal, they're worse than the VC.'

'We'll be alright. We'll be in and out within the day. Two days tops, depending on the climb. Keith says it takes five hours going up the mountain, three down, if we fly early in the morning, we might be out in the evening.'

'I just hope you're right, old son, I've got bad feelings in my bones.'

'Are you having second thoughts?'

'Nah. No way. I'm going. This is going to make or break us. It's just that I've had enough of life in Bangkok. It's been nothing but war, dirt, pain, stress, corruption, petty scams and boredom for the last few years. It's become too much of a routine way of life for me. I guess I want out, to go back home. I miss England I suppose. All this sex, drugs and booze scene has grown wearisome. I've got the best wife in the world, two smashing kids. I want something better for them.'

'You want to go back?'

'Yeah, sorry, I guess I do. I don't mean anything by it. You're my best mate. Always will be. But, well, you know, things change, time moves on.'

'That's okay, Nick, you don't have to explain. We had some good times together. We will again, I'm sure. A break will do you good. Anyway, if this mad scheme works out, you'll need to be within easy traveling distance of Amsterdam.'

'No hard feelings?'

'None at all, mate.'

'You know something,' Nick said wiping away a tear from the corner of his eye, 'Sometimes I feel like hugging you. Does that mean I'm turning into a shirt-lifter as well?'

'Hah! You? I don't think so, not for one minute,' John laughed then added, 'I feel the same way about this place sometimes. Let's just pray this caper works out so we can escape from it all.'

'I do, John, believe me. I'm praying hard for this one.'

At four o'clock in the morning of the fourth of April, nineteen seventy-three, Nick and his motley gang of nine other Englishmen, along with Jook and Maliwan, stood beside their kit shivering, not with cold but with nerves in anticipation of the task ahead. Parked in a hanger nearby sat the Princess 3A plane, fully loaded with fuel.

'Have you all checked you've got your uniforms and weapons packed?'

They all nodded their agreement.

'Fine. We have enough food and water for five days. If we get our act together, we won't need more than three. We should reach Kathmandu today, one day in Tibet and one day to get back. Anyone want to back out? If you do, then now's your last chance, so speak up or keep your mouth shut.'

Nick saw most of his men shaking their heads. 'Des? What about you? No last minute change of heart? Once we get inside the plane there's no going back, you know that.'

'I'll be fine, Nick. Honest.'

'Right then, let's get going,' Nick turned to Mal and lifted her up into the airplane. 'Pass your kit up to Jook and Mal, they'll stash it away in the back.'

Jook and Mal made themselves useful loading provisions, and the men squeezed into the plane as best they could. There weren't ten seats, but there was sufficient floor space to stretch out. It wasn't going to be a particularly comfortable flight.

The dawn light was barely breaking through the darkness as the Princess 3A took off from Chiang Mai and headed north-west for Bhutan, their first refuelling stage. The flight passed relatively smoothly, refuelling went without a hitch, and Ronnie Nelson touched down in Kathmandu early evening that same day. By seven o'clock in the evening the team had checked into a cheap hotel, near the airstrip.

Long before dawn, Nick was up and ready, dressed in American Army kit. So was Maliwan. The sight caused Nick to snigger.

'Why you laugh at me? This not look good?'

'I'm not laughing at you, Mal. It's just … it's just your name tag. I think John's having a bit of fun, that's all.'

'Someone call me?' John asked as his head appeared around the hotel room door.

'Yes! You explain to her why I'm laughing at her name tag. You put it there, not me.'

John chuckled. 'It suits you, Mal. It means you're beautiful. Really. Don't listen to him.' And with that, he disappeared quickly.

Mal gave her husband a look of disapproval.

'Come on, Mal. You look great. Real sexy. We need to get going.'

In the hotel's reception, Nick found everyone assembled waiting to go.

'Put all your civvies in these suitcases lads, and any identification papers. I've arranged to leave the cases here at the hotel. We don't want the excess weight, and we don't want to accidentally drop anything that will give us away.'

Des McAlistair asked, 'Don't you think carrying passports could be a good idea?'

'No, Des, I don't.'

'We might need to have to prove we're English.'

'Yeah? To who?' Nick demanded. 'Don't be so negative, Des. You'll jinx us from the outset.'

'Well, don't say I didn't warn you.'

'Yeah, yeah,' Nick mumbled. 'Come on, let's get on with it.'

By five in the morning they were airborne again. Shortly thereafter, the crucial moment arrived. They were flying into Tibetan airspace. There was no stopping them now, there was no turning back.

'This is it lads. We're here. It's going to be a pushover.' Nick's words did nothing to ease the tension.

Ronnie Nelson's flying skills were second to none, keeping the plane so low to the ground the wheels nearly touched. With a desperation he'd never experienced before, he stayed within the comfort zone of mountain passes, rarely rising except to hug the contours of the odd snow-capped peak.

'Shit,' Ronnie shouted aloud to no one in particular.

Nick stuck his head into the cockpit. 'What's up, Ron?'

'We just flew over some sort of military building. I could see some guards.'

'Military? You sure?'

'Quite sure, Nick. I was close enough to see their uniforms.'

'They spotted us?'

'Couldn't miss us. I saw two ducking out the way.'

'Bugger. What about our markings? Could they identify us?'

'Unlikely.'

'If they called up base, how long would we have?'

'Who knows. If we stay within the mountain passes we may not get picked up by anyone else. Maybe they'll forget us, especially if no one else confirms a sighting.'

'Just keep low, then, huh?'

'I can't get any lower, Nick, not without crashing. Relax, I'm sure it will be okay.'

Nick nodded his satisfaction, sat back and stared out of the window. How long, he wondered. How long before they'd be shot down?

A half hour passed. A nerve wracking thirty minutes of stomach churning agony. 'Shit,' Nick finally spat out, as a jet appeared from behind. 'That's all we fucking well need.'

The jet screamed past, shaking the Princess 3A in its wake. Ronnie's mouth dropped open. 'What shall we do, Nick?'

'Let's turn and get the fuck out of here,' Des screamed.

'You stupid bastard,' Geoff screamed at his friend. 'We haven't a fucking chance against a jet.'

'Maybe we can bluff it out,' Nick cut in. 'Tell them we were heading for Vietnam and got lost.'

'Heading for Vietnam? From where, for Christ sake?'

'Tell them we had navigation problems after leaving Kathmandu,' Geoff piped up. 'Compass has gone haywire.'

'Better still, smash the bloody thing. Stand back,' Nick shouted aiming his rifle at the control board. He pulled the trigger and sprayed the controls.

'Jesus, Nick,' Ronnie screamed as shards of glass sprayed everywhere.

Nick just laughed. 'We'll just say we had an accident. Someone got lightheaded and accidentally pulled a trigger.'

'Now we really are fucked up, Nick. I can't navigate at all now.'

Nick shrugged. It had seemed a good idea at the time. No good crying over spilt milk. 'What's done is done. Use the sun, like the old days.'

'Old days? What the fuck do you know about the old days?'

'Live with it, Ron. Anyway, it's back,' Nick said gesturing to the jet fighter which had looped the loop and had come up slowly alongside them. The pilot signalled to follow him.

Fifteen minutes later the pilot indicated they were to land at a small military airstrip on the outskirts of a city. As the Princess 3A came into land, Nick looked out the window, horrified to see the airstrip surrounded by army jeeps.

'Keep calm everyone. They seem to have a welcome party for us, but just stick to our story that we're American soldiers on a routine flight. We'll be back up in the air in a few hours, escorted out the country, then we can try again by foot some other day.'

'You're some optimist,' Geoff grunted.

'Trust me,' Nick said firmly, as they came in to land.

A hundred rifles were cocked as the plane door opened. Nick stood still for a few seconds, sizing up the situation. 'Okay, lads. Let's ease out nice and slowly. No sudden movements.'

A nervous squad of Chinese soldiers edged towards the plane, waived their rifles, shouted and pointed upwards into the air.

'They want us to raise our hands, Nick,' Keith whimpered.

Nick was astonished. 'You speak Chinese? You never told us that.'

'Mandarin. Fluently.'

The Fourth Cart III

'Right, don't speak any Chinese to them. And don't let them know you understand what they're saying. Just translate for me quietly and try not to let them suspect it.'

'Okay.'

'Right, lads,' Nick said firmly. 'Hands up high, and no arguing.'

The group of twelve were crudely and roughly searched and relieved of their weapons which were held high by the Chinese soldiers like trophies of war.

As an officer stepped out of a jeep and approached them, Nick gave a respectful salute. 'Sorry about this, sir. We're rather lost,' he said in a passable American accent.

The officer inspected the plane and ran his fingers over a captured rifle. He approached Nick, frowned and then asked a series of questions.

Nick shrugged his shoulders implying a total lack of comprehension.

A dozen soldiers came up behind, formed a circle and not so gently prodded them forward.

'Where are we going?' Nick asked Keith quietly.

'This is Shigatse. We're going to be marched to the town prison. It's about three miles or so away.'

'There's no prison here? It's a military base isn't it?'

'I'm not sure,' Keith replied. 'Anyway, this is the base commander and he says we're not his problem.'

'Not his problem? Then whose?'

'Dunno, Nick. It wasn't clear.'

An hour later the shabby group, looking like mercenaries, halted outside a huge pair of wooden prison gates. Slowly the gates creaked open, and the group of twelve were urged through, prodded like cattle.

The gates slammed shut. The sound resonated harshly through their skulls. They were whisked through a courtyard, into a depressing concrete building and through to the cells. A cell door was opened and they were pushed inside. As the cell door was slammed shut, Keith sank to his knees.

'That went well,' Nick muttered as he took stock of the dingy cell. 'A nice clean execution of a beautifully constructed plan. My ass. How the fuck did we land in here? And where the hell is here anyway?'

It was Keith who responded, fighting back the tears. 'It's my old cell.'

'You've been here before?'

'For nine years,' Keith sobbed.

'Shit. Nine years in this cell?'

Keith wiped his sleeve across his eyes. 'You never did listen to my stories, did you Nick. If you don't believe me, you'll find my initials scratched into the stonework. Over there, to the bottom left of the window.'

Nick squeezed passed the others to take a look. 'Sorry, Keith, I really didn't know. Did you get out much, or were you locked up all the time.'

'We were forced to work on building new roads for the Chinese. Smashing up rocks, shifting earth, back-breaking stuff like that. It was cheap to use prisoners.'

'Nine years hard labour?'

'I only survived five years.' Keith snuffled. 'The food is appalling here. That and the work weakened me too much. I collapsed on site one day, just a bag of bones, they dragged me back here to die, but I managed to hang on. At least I was left alone during the daytime.'

'Shit. So what do you reckon we'll get?'

'I . . . I . . . have no idea Nick,' Keith answered, sobbing again.

'We've done nothing,' Des interjected. 'The Embassy will get us out.'

'There's no Embassy here, Des,' Keith replied.

'Then we'll make protestations,' Des responded in a panic. 'We'll get our case heard by the Embassy in Beijing. We'll be out in a day or so, won't we?'

'I damn well hope so,' Nick muttered as he leant against a wall and sank to the floor. 'I'm not keen on confined spaces.'

A week passed. Seven days, crammed together in the foulest conditions, with no one able to eat more than a spoonful of the slops served at mealtimes. When news of their fate came, it wasn't what Nick wanted to hear.

'Illegal entry? Illegal transportation of weapons? Illegal flight? Mercenaries? Us?' Nick spluttered, exasperated as the charges against them were read out by the prison warden, standing in the middle of the cell, and translated into pigeon English by an aide.

'Nick, calm down,' John hissed, 'You'll make it worse.'

'How the fuck can this get worse? We've been in this shit hole for a week already. We've had no communication from the outside world. And now we're being charged. Jesus Christ, I don't believe this.'

'Leave it Nick, don't create a scene now. We need to think this one through.'

The prison warden left, the cell door clunking behind him. Everyone voiced expressions of astonishment, anger, incredulity. Geoff was the first one to put a cohesive sentence together. 'Keith, you know Chinese culture and customs better than us. In your opinion, what do you think they'll do with us?'

'They're building a case against us. All these "illegal" activities they mentioned; it can mean only one thing.'

Everyone fell silent, staring at Keith, waiting for a conclusion. It didn't seem to be forthcoming.

'Well?' Geoff asked.

'I'd rather not say. I can't say really. If we were Chinese, then what we've been accused of would probably result in the death penalty.'

'What?'

'The Chinese courts like to set an example to their people. A bullet in the back of the head is a quick and cheap punishment. It keeps prison numbers down. It serves as a warning to others. The prisoner's family even gets a bill for the bullet used.'

'But we're English,' Des protested.

'Yeah,' Todd butted in, 'but none of us can prove that. We didn't bring our passports, did we Nick?'

'Yeah, yeah, alright, no need to harp on about that.'

'And they know we're not Americans,' Todd continued, 'we don't have dog tags. They may have been useful, Nick.'

'You want a smack, Todd,' Nick blurted out angrily. 'Your comments aren't helpful. We need some positive ideas to get us out of here. Can't you think of an escape plan, or something, rather than harping on about the mistakes you reckon I made.'

Todd crawled off into a corner to sulk alone.

'Ronnie, any thoughts? Mike? Sean?' Nick received nothing but a shake of the head. 'Geoff, do you think you could take on the guards?'

'As a last resort, Nick, I'd give it a go. I'll go down fighting, if that's what you mean, but even if we do overcome the guards, where would we go? How the hell do we get out of the country? We can't take on the whole fucking Chinese army.'

'John? You've usually got a good idea. Why are you being so quiet? Come on, share it with us.'

'I've been thinking. Well, trying to think I should say. There's something I've overheard Keith say in the past. It's nagging me, but I can't think clearly with all this bollocks going on in the room. Something about his life here. Something that's important.'

'Like what?'

'That's the problem, I don't know. I've only ever half listened to Keith's tales, but there's a part of his story of his time in this country that keeps trying to surface in my mind.'

'Any clue?'

John shook his head and turned to Keith. 'Do you know anyone that could help us? Someone who could get us out? Someone high ranking, with authority to get us off the hook?'

'Erm, no, sorry John,' Keith mumbled. 'Everyone I knew either left in nineteen fifty-nine, or would have been murdered if they'd stayed on. The only high ranking officials I knew were in the Dalai Lama's government, and they're in exile now, there's no way the Chinese would speak with them, let alone listen.'

'No Chinese officials?'

'None at all, we didn't mix with them. We tried to keep out of their way.'

'Keith,' John spoke quietly, 'there's something you must do for us. You must tell us your story again. But this time, no exaggerations, no half-truths, don't make up anything, you don't need to try to impress us. You need to relive your time in Tibet. Tell us every detail of your life here.'

Everyone in the room groaned. 'Must we?' Nick asked.

'Sorry, Nick, but yes, we must. Must, that is, if we want to get out alive.'

'Okay, lads, let's give this a go. Keith, sit back against the wall. Make yourself comfortable, this could take a while. No one interrupts, okay?'

'Here we go again,' Geoff muttered.

'That's exactly the problem, Geoff,' John said testily. 'Last time, we didn't let Keith speak. We kept interrupting him. Especially you, Geoff. Maybe if we had let him talk, we wouldn't be in this mess.'

'Yeah,' Nick chuckled. 'Blame yourself, not me, Mr Big Mouth.'

'Alright, alright,' Geoff replied. 'I won't interrupt.'

'Right Keith, take it away.'

'From the beginning?'

'Sounds like a good place to start.'

'What, from when I was at university?'

'If that's where it starts, then yes, fine.'

'It will take a couple of hours, more maybe.'

'Keith, in case you hadn't noticed, we're not going anywhere.'

'Right. Sure.'

'Everyone pay attention,' Nick said loudly. 'Take note of what Keith says. Geoff, Des, you're university educated, you've got better brains than us, you should be able to pick up on things faster than us.'

'Ready?' Keith asked nervously.

'Take it away, old son.'

Chapter Twenty-Two

'I'm sorry, Magee, if you want to know what happened to Keith in Tibet, I guess your luck just run out. I certainly can't remember much of what he said. Can you, John?'

John Mansell shook his head. 'No, sorry, Magee, me neither. He was too verbose.'

Magee smiled in response.

Nick frowned quizzically. 'Is Keith's story important, Magee?'

'Yes it is, Nick. It's an integral part of your own life at that time. It's the reason why you went on this mad venture in the first place.'

Nittaya chose to spoke. 'I'd certainly like to know what Keith did, Daddy. Don't you remember anything?'

'No. Not really.'

'But you will hear it, Nittaya, don't worry about that,' Magee replied. He rummaged through his briefcase and extracted a manuscript. 'Keith had been putting his memories down on paper. I think you'll find this covers his time from university through to the end of his days in Tibet.'

'Good god, Magee,' Nick spat out, 'Where the hell did you get that from?'

'His mother. She let me borrow it.'

Nick's face screwed up. 'This visit of yours has been well planned, hasn't it, Magee. Too well planned for my liking. What other little surprises have you got up your sleeve, may I ask?'

Magee briefly caught Brigadier Armstrong's eye. The action was not lost on Nick. 'Shit, Magee, something's going on here, isn't it?'

'Certainly not,' Magee protested. 'Now then, there are aspects of Keith's story that the Brigadier needs to take fully into his consideration. However, we can't be sure what Keith has written is fact or fiction. So, may I suggest that Melissa reads it out aloud, and then you and John butt in if anything sounds out of kilter?'

'Fine by me,' Nick said. 'Though I want lunch first, it's past one o'clock. I imagine Annie's laid out a cold buffet in the dining room.'

'Thank you, Mr Price,' Brigadier Armstrong said. 'And if I may, I wouldn't mind a short guided tour of your humble abode. I could do with stretching my legs and getting a breath of fresh air.'

'Would you mind if someone else took you around?' Nick replied. 'My legs still give my pain. They're not fully healed yet.'

'Yes, of course. I do apologize, I'd forgotten. You're off the crutches, I see.'

'I'm getting there. I can't stand up unsupported for too long.'

'I'll take him,' Paul Mansell said. 'You want to come, Melissa? Magee?'

'Please,' Melissa replied.

'Not for me, thanks,' Magee responded. 'I know the house well.'

Nick Price gave Magee an odd look. 'You do? How?'

'Years ago,' Magee replied. 'The previous owners, who ran this place as a school, bought the house in Lewes I grew up in. They used to invite me in for drinks after the summer fetes they held here. They had the rooms above where we sit at the moment as a self-contained flat.'

Nick Price gave Magee another odd look. 'That's creepy. That's my bedroom suite. I'm not sure I wanted to know that.'

Magee grinned. 'That will add to your nightmares, won't it?'

'It will. I may need to swap rooms. C'mon, let's go and grab a sandwich.'

After lunch, they settled back in the sitting room and Magee passed the manuscript to Melissa. 'In your own time, if you will, Melissa.'

Melissa took the manuscript and heaved a sigh. 'Well, at least I'll feel included.'

'Believe me, Melissa,' Magee said quietly, 'You are.'

Melissa turned to the first page of the manuscript. 'Here goes then. It's titled The Fourth Cart, by Keith Gibson . . . '

Chapter Twenty-Three

One hour later, Melissa reached the end of the last page of Keith Gibson's tale. She closed the manuscript respectfully, and handed it back to Magee.

'And all this really happened?' asked Brigadier Armstrong.

'I'd say it's difficult to know where reality mixes with fiction,' Magee responded. 'What do you reckon, Nick?'

Nick shrugged. 'All I can comment on is the bit about the treasure. There seems no point making the rest up, just to fit around that.'

'So we're to accept this as true then?' Brigadier Armstrong muttered. 'I find that hard to believe. There are no records of any foreigner that close to the Dalai Lama after Heinrich Harrier left.'

'Well, for what it's worth, Brigadier, I can tell you that what happened to us next seemed to confirm it.'

'This, I can't wait to hear,' Magee said with a smile on his face. 'Come on then, Nick, let's hear what happened next.'

'It was John who worked it out. Worked out how we were to get out of that shit-hole of a prison . . .'

****

Shigatse Prison 12th April 1973

The cell was hushed. Jook and Maliwan had fallen asleep long ago, the others squatted, heads resting on their knees. Keith had finally ceased talking, it had taken him three hours to retell everything he could possibly remember about his former life in Tibet.

John jerked his head up. 'That's it. That's the answer.'

'What? What is?'

'The Chinese officer. We can use him to get us out of this mess.'

'You mean Lieutenant Tchen?' Keith asked. 'But he's dead. Or at least I assume he is after falling over that precipice.'

'Not him, the other one.'

'The other one? There was only one of him.'

'His boss, Colonel Sin, or something.'

'Colonel Tsim? But I don't know him.'

'Maybe not,' John persisted, 'but you know about him.'

'Sorry, John,' Nick interjected. 'But you've lost me as well. Would you mind, for the benefit of us thickos, explaining what the hell you're on about.'

'Right. Listen up. Keith said Lieutenant Tchen's boss, Colonel thingy, was obsessed with the fourth cart.'

'Tsim. Colonel Tsim,' Keith corrected.

'What of it, John?'

'Well, you said Lieutenant Tchen's career had been blighted, that he'd deliberately been held down, without promotion, by his boss, this colonel.'

'Yep.'

'And that the only way Lieutenant Tchen was ever going to redeem himself in the eyes of Colonel Tsim was to locate the treasures of the fourth cart. Hence his search for you.'

'Yep, again, I'm with you.'

'But when Lieutenant Tchen had the opportunity to redeem himself, when he had you in his clutches, he acted alone. He went solo.'

'Correct.'

'Sorry, John,' Nick interrupted. 'But I don't see where this is leading.'

'Dear god,' John muttered, 'do I have to spell it out?'

'Yes, please,' Nick said without a trace of sarcasm.

'Colonel Tsim wants the treasures of the Fourth Cart for himself. He's obviously not going to share them with Chairman Mao or anyone else. Lieutenant Tchen didn't tell Colonel Tsim that he'd found you, Keith. If he had, then Colonel Tsim would have been alongside you going up that mountain. Agreed?'

'It certainly seems likely,' Keith said.

'So, this Colonel Tsim is sitting somewhere behind a desk, really pissed off that he hasn't found the fourth cart yet. Worse, his lieutenant has disappeared. Maybe the body was never found? Anyway, maybe he thinks that his lieutenant found the treasure and fled to a new life overseas. Whatever, I bet there's one mighty pissed off colonel out there, desperate for information on his lieutenant and, more importantly, the fourth cart.'

Nick was still confused. 'So how does this help us?'

'We contact this colonel, tell him we're here and need his help to get us out. In exchange, we tell him where the treasure is.'

'I'm not sure about that,' Nick grumbled. 'He'd get the treasure, and he'd probably have us executed.'

'So we do a deal, Nick. He gets us out the country, we cut him a share.'

'And just how do we guarantee he'll get us out?'

'Hmm,' John muttered, 'I haven't quite worked that one out, yet.'

'Boys,' Sean butted in.

'Pardon?'

'Boys. That's how we get his cooperation,' Sean continued. 'Keith mentioned a conversation he had with Lieutenant Tchen, that Colonel Tsim dreamt of idling away his time on a beach being entertained by boys. It sounded as though the man wanted to escape, to run off to paradise somewhere. Sorry, John, but it made me think of your own life. Maybe we could tempt this colonel bloke to flee the country with us, to Bangkok. We could guarantee him a good time there, he could have as many boys as he liked.'

'Homosexuality is illegal in China,' Keith said. 'If he does like boys, life must be very difficult for him. It would be hard for him to have any sort of sex life. He would risk being exposed, dishonoured, locked up, shot even. I imagine he would leap at the chance of escaping.'

Nick looked at John agog. 'John, you old bugger, I think you've just found the key.'

'But how do we contact him?' Des McAlister asked. 'How the hell can we track him down? We're in prison, in case you've forgotten. We don't have a telephone.'

'No, that's true,' Nick replied, 'but I bet the warden does.'

'And just how the hell do we get him to lend it to us?' Des continued.

'Keith old son, I assume you still have that ruby around your neck?'

'Erm, yes of course, Nick, why?'

'Would you mind exchanging it for a telephone call?'

'I, erm, guess not, Nick. It's no good to me dead.'

'Right then, Keith, we need to prepare a script for you. We'll only have one shot at this, so you need to be word perfect. I just hope your Tibetan is up to it.'

Two hours later, two hours of role play and rehearsal of the right words to say, Nick reckoned Keith was up to scratch.

'Right then, are you ready, Keith?' Nick asked. 'Are you up to this?'

'Don't fret, Nick. I can do it. I haven't been so sober for years.'

'Here's a hundred dollars, Keith. It might come in handy, but it's all we have so don't give it away all at once. We might need some spare money later.'

'It's okay, Nick. I can do this.'

'Call the guard then.'

Keith took a deep breath and banged hard on the cell door to attract the guard's attention. 'Open up. I need to see the warden.'

The guard appeared with a look of astonishment on his face. 'I can't do that,' the guard replied.

'Of course you can,' Keith retorted. 'Go and tell the warden I need to see him urgently. Tell him I have money and that I wish to buy something. Go now.'

Ten minutes later there was a loud clanking of keys against the door, which then opened slowly. 'The warden will see you.'

The wary guard took Keith and Nick straight to the warden's office. He gestured them to enter.

The warden looked up from his desk. 'What is this nonsense about wishing to buy something from me?'

'I would like to make a telephone call, sir.'

'Really? To whom?'

'Colonel Tsim, he was based in Lhasa in the nineteen fifties, maybe until the late nineteen sixties.'

'And you wish to speak to him because of what exactly?'

'A private matter.'

'I see. And you know his number?'

'No.'

'Do you know where he is?'

'No.'

'His base? His unit? The city he lives in?'

'No.'

'Then how do you propose contacting him?'

'I am hoping you will be able to do that. With your status, sir, you should be able to make the connection.'

'But why would I want to do this task for you?'

Keith turned towards the guard, and looked back at the warden before speaking. 'May I talk to you in private, sir?'

The warden appeared to think the matter over, in silence, for a few seconds. 'Leave us,' he said to the guard.

Nick gave Keith an encouraging nod.

'This task would take a lot of my time,' the warden said. 'I would have to pull a few strings, questions will no doubt be asked. Your presence is causing a lot of embarrassment in Beijing. I am not sure how my interference would be received.'

'I understand, sir. That is why I propose to compensate you for any inconvenience suffered.'

'And how much compensation do you propose?'

On hearing this request, Keith undid his top shirt bottom, pulled out the leather pouch and extracted the giant ruby stone. 'This ruby has been valued at eight thousand American dollars.'

The warden's eyes bulged so much Keith thought they would burst. 'May I see it? Closer please.'

'The phone call first, please, sir.'

The warden licked his lips. 'How do I know it is genuine?'

'Do you not recognize me, sir?'

'Recognize you? No. Should I?'

'I was here, as a prisoner, for nine years. You came here in May nineteen sixty-eight. At your inaugural inspection of the prisoners, you asked my name. I gave you my English name rather than the false Tibetan name you had on my record. Shortly afterwards, a Lieutenant Tchen came here and took me away.'

The warden looked pensive, as though he was trying to recall the event. 'That was you?'

'Yes, sir.'

'But you were just a bag of bones. I thought you'd be dead within a few days.'

'Yes, sir. But the point I want to make is that I know what life is like here. I know what hell it is to be imprisoned here, to be forced to work on building roads, to eat lousy food, to sleep on the floor.'

'We are not a hotel.'

'Yes, sir. That is exactly my point. I am under no illusions as to my fate here. I could not endure another custodial sentence here, or at any other prison for that matter.'

'Then . . . ?'

'I am expecting Colonel Tsim to arrange freedom for myself and my friends. I am sure that he can clear up any misunderstanding about our presence here.'

'Really? That would be a remarkable feat.'

'Yes, sir. It would, but I think he will do it. And my point is that I am trading this ruby for my freedom. After the phone call, I will give it to you. I am sure you will then have it authenticated. I am in no doubt that you will have me executed, slowly and painfully, if it turned out to be a fake.'

'You are indeed correct there. Your death would be excruciatingly painful, as would be that of all your friends.' The warden sat back in his chair as if to contemplate the situation. He studied Keith's face for nigh on a full minute before responding, 'Very well. Take a seat. Now, just how do you expect me to get this Colonel Tsim to talk to you?'

'I have a message for him, sir. Please tell him I know what happened to Lieutenant Tchen. And give him my name, sir. It's imperative that you give him my English name. If you'll give me a piece of paper, sir, I'll write it down.'

It took the warden five phone calls, and a total of twenty minutes to trace the location of Colonel Tsim. Now based in Beijing, now General Tsim. The warden's forehead broke out in a sweat as he commanded a subaltern to connect him to the general immediately, on urgent business.

'Who is this?' General Tsim demanded.

'This is the warden of the city prison in Shigatse speaking. I have a prisoner who wishes to talk to you.'

'A prisoner? I don't take telephone calls from prisoners. What the hell are you playing at?'

'He says he knows what happened to your junior officer, Lieutenant Tchen.'

There was a silence on the end of the phone.

'General? General? Are you still there?'

'What is the name of this prisoner?'

'It is English, General. My spoken English is not good, but I know the characters. I will spell the name out, sir.'

Seconds later, General Tsim blurted out, 'Keith Gibson! You have Keith Gibson in your prison?'

'Yes, sir. He is sitting in front of my desk as we speak.'

'Why is he there?'

The warden went into some depth to explain Keith's presence. In fact, it took the warden ten minutes to relay all the information he knew. Ten sticky minutes. Finally the general requested the warden to hand the phone over to Keith.

'Mr Gibson, it is a pleasure to finally talk to you. I believe you have something I want. Do you know the location of the treasures of the Fourth Cart?'

'Yes, sir. I do,' Keith replied in fluent Mandarin.

'Four years ago, Lieutenant Tchen disappeared. Did he find those treasures?'

'No, sir, he did not get that far.'

'So he did not flee to another country? I imagined that he might have done so.'

'No, sir, he made me tell him . . . the location . . .' Keith said cautiously. 'I took him there, but he met with an accident. He died before completing his mission.'

'I see,' General Tsim said. 'Then the treasures are untouched?'

'Yes, sir.'

'And you are the only one who knows where they are?'

'Correct, sir.'

'And you are now facing execution?'

Keith was shocked. 'Execution?'

'That is the word in Beijing. The sentence has been discussed, if not yet made public.'

'I see.'

'I assume you want to trade? The location of the Fourth Cart treasures for your life?'

'And my friends, sir, all twelve of us. We want to get out of the country, we want to go back to our homes in Bangkok.'

'Bangkok?' General Tsim asked surprised. 'I thought you were English?'

'We all live in Thailand, sir. It is a paradise there, as you may know. Warm seas, beautiful beaches, light brown skinned nubile teenage bodies to keep us amused. Oil massages, exotic dances. With money, you can live like a king there, sir. I recommend you go there for a long holiday sometime, I'm sure you'll enjoy it. It's the sort of country you fall in love with and want to stay forever.'

The phone fell silent for a while. 'Mr Gibson, am I right in thinking that you came back to Tibet to retrieve the treasures of the Fourth Cart?'

'Yes, sir.'

'Then your freedom will cost you dearly. Are you prepared for that?'

'We are, sir.'

'Then I will say goodbye. There is much to be done. Please hand the phone back to the warden.'

Keith handed the phone over, as requested. The warden listened for a minute before saying, 'Yes, of course, General,' and put the phone down. He stared across his desk at Keith, a less than friendly appearance on his face. He held out his hand, palm up, in expectation.

Keith passed over the ruby. 'Thank you for your assistance, sir.'

'You seem to have friends in high places,' the warden said with a touch of bitterness. 'Apparently, I have to look after you. The general was most insistent that I keep you in good spirits and feed you well. He said he will be visiting here shortly, and will be most upset if your health is not good. I can't pretend I am happy with that arrangement; you are a prisoner, not my guest.'

'I apologize for any inconvenience, sir.'

The warden looked down at the paper on which Keith had written his name. 'What is it about you, Mr Gibson? Four years ago you were released from here under the orders of some flunkey from Beijing waving papers at me. Now, a general, no less, is coming here to visit you. I assume he too will wave papers at me, insisting I release you. What the hell is so special about you?'

'I'm sorry, sir, I don't know.'

The warden frowned as if in irritation. 'You are dismissed. The guard will take you back to your cell. Oh, before you go, if you and your friends want decent food you'd better give me some money. We have a very low budget here, as you know.'

'Thank you, sir,' Keith said turning out fifty dollars from his pocket. As he rose, he caught Nick's eye and smiled.

Chapter Twenty-Four

'Just a moment, Nick, you're just guessing what Keith said to the warden aren't you? He must have spoken Tibetan or Chinese, surely? I asked you to stick to the facts, why are you embellishing the story?'

Nick snorted. 'Why? I'll tell you why, Magee. Because that bastard of a warden turned on us, that's why. And I want you to understand just what an asshole he was.'

Magee's forehead creased as he digested the information. 'You mean you're just putting the stick in?'

'If you like, yeah. I'm just setting the scene, so you understand what happened later.'

'It's relevant?'

'It certainly is.'

'Okay, Nick. I take it we're nearly there now?'

Nick sighed, gripped his daughter's hand and said, 'Yeah, crunch time, Magee, here we go . . .'

****

Shigatse Prison 26th April 1973

The cell door burst open so suddenly and unexpectedly that everyone bolted, startled. Slowly, at a deliberate pace, the short, chubby yet authoritative figure of General Tsim stepped into the room. The prisoners stood up, sharply, out of respect, for they knew instantly who the man must be.

The general purposefully studied the faces in the cell. Keith steeped forward and nodded his head.

'Mr Gibson,' General Tsim said. 'We meet at last.'

'Yes, sir,' Keith replied in his politest Mandarin.

'My colleagues thought you were some sort of preliminary invasion force. They thought you were testing for weak points in our defences. Looking around at the state of your friends, I find that very hard to credit. Still, your sentence will still be execution.'

'But sir,' Keith protested, 'we have not been tried yet.'

'No, but the advantage of a predetermined outcome is that it saves the court's time,' General Tsim said with a hint of a smile.

The panic showed clearly on Keith's face. His eyes bulged, he'd gone white, his jaw had dropped. It seemed to please the general. 'I . . . I . . .' Keith stuttered, unable to form a sentence.

'I want to get this very clear from the start, Mr Gibson. You and your friends face the death penalty. You will be shot if you do not cooperate with me. Please communicate this to everyone in the room.'

Keith translated the general's words precisely. The threat worked, that was quite clear from the audible sighs from all corners of the room.

'Good. We understand each other,' General Tsim said in passable English. 'We will talk in English, I do not want the guards to understand what we say. But slowly please, my English is not perfect. Now, who is the leader here?'

'Nick is,' Keith responded, as Nick stepped forward. 'This is Nick Price, we follow him.'

'Everyone stand still please,' General Tsim ordered. He proceeded to inspect the prisoners. He stopped in front of Jook, looking quizzically at his appearance, and seemingly comparing him to Maliwan. 'Is this a boy or girl?'

John took control of the conversation. 'Maliwan is a girl. Jook is Maliwan's brother, and is what we call a lady-boy. He is physically a boy, but he acts like a girl. His skin is smooth like a girl, his figure is feminine like a girl, but physically he is a boy.'

General Tsim held his hand up to caress Jook's tender face. Jook did not flinch, but merely batted his eyelids and acted coyly.

'Are there many of these lady-boys in Bangkok?'

'Yes, sir,' John replied, 'Many. I know a hundred or more. All friends of Jook.'

'Really?' General Tsim murmured under his breath. 'How astonishing.'

'You must visit Bangkok, sir,' John continued, 'I would be happy to be your guide.'

The general looked kindly at John. 'Yes. Yes, that would be welcome. But first, I believe we have some business to conclude.'

'As you wish, sir.'

'Mr Price. Do you have any idea of the value of the treasures that were in the Fourth Cart?'

'We believe there's something like five million dollars there,' Nick replied courteously.

The general looked directly into Nick's eyes. 'Five million dollars? That is a lot of money. How were you going to split it?'

'Equal shares amongst us.'

'I want half. Agreed?'

Nick bit his lip in an attempt to keep his cool. Realizing that at this stage it was purely academic anyway, he decided he had nothing to lose except his life. 'Agreed,' he responded, 'but what do we get in return for that?'

'Safe passage out of the country,' General Tsim replied.

'How do we know that, sir?'

'I will come with you.'

'With us? Back to Bangkok?'

'Yes, I think so. It is time for me to relax and enjoy life. I would prefer to do so in the decadent West. Bangkok seems a good place to start.'

'It is indeed, sir.'

General Tsim turned to Keith. 'Are the treasures near here, Mr Gibson?'

Keith looked to Nick and received a curt nod. It was noticed by the general.

'Shekar,' Keith replied. 'We buried it at the top of the mountain. In the basement of the old castle.'

The general sighed. 'If only I'd known that earlier, life would have been so different.'

'We will need transport, sir,' Nick interjected.

'Of course,' General Tsim replied. 'I have arranged for the use of a truck from the army base here.'

'And more men, sir,' Keith interjected.

'There are ten of you, is that not enough?'

'No, sir,' Keith responded. 'When we climbed that mountain in nineteen fifty-nine, we carried eight crates with us, very heavy crates. We had two yaks, along with two strong young monks, per crate. If you intend to bring the crates down, we will need at least the same amount of men and yaks. We'll also need ropes.'

'Hmm,' General Tsim pondered. 'I was not aware that the task would be such trouble. Never mind, we will have to find those resources when we get there. Come, let us go. Now.'

'Now?' Nick spluttered.

'Yes, now. I have papers with me. You are to be released into my custody. The warden knows this. I have ten of my most trusted men with me. They will act as guards and will help with carrying the treasure.'

Without further ado, though slightly bemused by the ease and rapidity of it all, the twelve prisoners filed out the cell behind General Tsim and his ten guards, all of whom were sporting AK47s. Within minutes they were on their way to Shekar.

They drove all through the night. It was still early morning when Keith sluggishly opened his eyes and peered out the back of the truck at the scenery passing by. None of it was familiar, but then the village he'd known had expanded fast since he'd last visited. As the truck groaned to a halt he popped his head out and looked to the front. There, unmistakably, way up in the distance, were the ruins of the old castle. This was it.

The general disembarked, came round to the back of the truck and barked a few orders at the guards who politely nodded.

'What's happening, Keith?' Nick asked.

'The general's going off to find the head man, whoever's in charge around here. Only the Chinese get such status positions now. He will commandeer some men, yaks, food, water and such like. It won't take him long, I'm sure. No one is going to defy him.'

'And us?'

'We can stretch our legs, but we mustn't stray out of sight of the guards. His orders were made simple for them to understand; shoot if we try anything on.'

'How nice,' Nick responded. 'Okay, guys, get your asses out of the truck. Let's take it easy.'

Thirty minutes later the general reappeared smiling, his guards burdened with the weight of several sacks. 'Come, eat. We make picnic. Is that what you say?'

Nick smiled in response. This was turning out to be a doddle. The food was shared out into greedily awaiting hands.

'We leave in twenty minutes,' General Tsim stated. 'There will be yaks and men to go with us, as you requested, Mr Gibson. The men will carry more food and water for us.'

Nick was impressed. 'You have this well organized, sir.'

'Better organized than yourself, Mr Price, if I may say so.'

Nick chortled in spite of himself. 'Yes, indeed, sir. Much better organized. I should have contacted you earlier, it would have saved us a lot of aggravation.'

The general nodded. 'It is strange, Mr Price, what life throws at us. I have dreamt of being here, about to find the treasures of the Fourth Cart, for many years. But never did I think it would happen like this, with such ease. I always had this nightmare that other soldiers, higher ranking, would be with me, would take it away from me. I see more trust in your eyes than I do with my own people.'

Nick studied the general's face intently. There was nothing but sincerity being expressed. 'Thank you, sir.'

'We have a long day ahead of us, Mr Price. Eat. You need energy. It is a long climb up that mountain.'

Within the hour, Nick was learning the hard way just how right the general was. Walking up a mountain was by no means easy in Tibet, especially for those who had been confined to a prison cell for three weeks. The refined air and the low level of oxygen hampered progress severely. For the ten Englishmen, their lungs strained, desperate for air from the simple effort of putting one foot in front of the next.

The group walked in silence to conserve energy. Keith took the lead, alongside General Tsim, followed by two guards. Behind them came sixteen yaks cajoled by their owners and ten local men hired for the day. Behind them were four more guards, followed by Nick and the rest of his entourage, with four more guards bringing up the rear. The pace was set by the slowness of the yaks.

Four hours into the climb John paused to catch Nick's attention. 'Did you see that? Down in the valley.'

'What?' asked Nick who, like most of the others, could barely focus on anything except the next piece of ground in front of his feet.

'Something was glinting. It was moving, but caught the sun. It looked like a plane.'

'Really? So what?'

'There's no airstrip down there.'

'So?'

'It was coming in to land, I'm sure of it. It was low, it had to be landing.'

'John, old son, this trek is hell for me. I'm busting my guts. Sorry, but I don't give a damn.'

For the next half hour, John turned round frequently, as if unable to forget what he'd seen, as if something was amiss.

Eventually the train of men came to a halt. Nick came up level with the front. 'What's going on Keith?'

'We've got to take this path off to the left. The yaks won't be able to make it though, it's far too narrow for them. They'll have to stay here.'

'How far from here?'

'About fifteen minutes, this path curves around the mountain to a tunnel entrance. It's a bit treacherous at times, so watch out.'

'How do we get the treasure back here?'

'We'll have to carry the crates by hand.'

'Is that what you did originally?'

'No, we were able to get the yaks up to the castle.' Keith pointed to the ruins further up. 'From there we only had to carry the crates for a few minutes down into the castle basement.'

Nick sighed. 'I'm not sure I'm up to carrying anything. There's no sodding air up here.'

Ten minutes later the group came to another junction. Keith halted, staring ahead, lost in thought.

'Is something wrong, Mr Gibson?' General Tsim asked.

'I was just thinking of Lieutenant Tchen. He slipped on the loose stones on this path and went over the ledge down there,' Keith replied in a low voice. 'As he fell, he pleaded for help. I just stood and watched as he went over the edge, screaming.'

General Tsim nodded. 'I assume he tortured you, back in prison. That's how he got you to come here, am I correct?'

'Yes, sir,' Keith replied. 'He burnt me, countless times, with a cigarette. I'd never known such pain.'

'Do not worry about him, Mr Gibson. He got what was coming to him. He did some pretty barbaric things in his life, especially to the local inhabitants. I am not proud of what he did under my command. I certainly did not sanction what he did.'

'But he was following your orders, wasn't he?'

'Yes, indeed, regrettably. But he took pleasure in the pain he inflicted on people. His father was a high ranking Party official. I don't think his father liked him, certainly no one else did. He was a most unpleasant man. His father put pressure on someone in the army to accept him, and he was sent as far away as possible, where he could do no harm, or so they thought anyway.'

'Still, he was a human being. He didn't deserve to die that way.'

'On the contrary, Mr Gibson, I think he did. He murdered many people in his career. Innocent people, of course, many monks as well. He would often lose control of his temper, lose touch with his humanity. He may not have deserved to die, but he certainly did not deserve to live. He lost his right to a civilized life, long ago.'

'Thank you, sir. I have to tell the truth, though. I knew this path was dangerous. I deliberately led him along it, hoping he would fall. I killed him.'

'Then you have done the world a service, Mr Gibson. Come, do not dwell on it. It is history. You cannot change history.'

'Yes sir,' Keith replied. 'We must take the higher path. It is safe.'

Five minutes later, Keith halted outside a crevice in the rock face. He turned around to face the mountain opposite and waited for the rest to catch up.

'Is this it?' Nick asked.

For an answer, Keith pointed at some scratching on the rock face. Nick gently traced the outline of a K and a G with his fingers as if seeking confirmation that the whole story hadn't just been a junkie's hallucinations. He grinned widely, finally recognizing the truth of Keith's tale. It was turning out to be true after all.

'This tunnel used to lead up to the castle. It's blocked now, but there's a recessed room some six hundred and seventy-five heel-to-toe steps from here. The ground is sound, there're no pitfalls on the way. Better get some lamps lit though, it's pretty dark in there.'

And so they slipped into the tunnel, each man hyped up, adrenalin pumping like mad, nervous from the eerie shadows cast by the lamplight. Keith figured on four toe-to-heel steps being equivalent to about one normal pace, and counted them off in his mind as he went. He stopped at one hundred and ninety-seven, the wall to his left giving way to a recessed room.

'This is it,' Keith said pointing to an undisturbed rock-strewn floor. 'It's exactly the same as I left it four years ago. It hasn't been touched.'

Everyone smiled. They couldn't believe this was actually happening. Buried treasure. Man's eternal quest, and here it was, right here at their feet.

Lamps were placed around the sides of the old castle's dungeon floor. Except for Keith, Nick and his gang spread around the centre of the room and sank to their knees. Pieces of rock and handfuls of dust were sent scattering in all directions as they scrabbled away at the floor. Within seconds Geoff howled with joy as he reached a wooden surface. The crates were indeed still there. Keith stood back, looking down at his friends, frowning in apparent disappointment.

Within a few minutes all eight crates had been hauled out of the pit and opened. The kerosene lamplight caused the jewels to sparkle, and the gold to glint. Everyone was intoxicated by the sight, even the Chinese guards joined in the revelry. They screamed in ecstasy, shouted for joy, hugged each other, and shook their heads in disbelief.

Nick played like a kid with the jewels, letting the gems tumble through his fingers in sheer wonder. It was beyond the dreams of mortal man. The sight was just too fantastic to comprehend. There was so much of it. Far more than Keith had described, far more than he'd pictured in his wildest dreams. He caught John's eyes, and smiled. They had done it. They had finally found their way out of their humdrum sleazy existence. They had pulled off The Big One.

'Okay lads, calm down for God's sake,' Nick ordered, but not harshly. 'We'll celebrate later. Shut the crates up and let's leave. It's time to move out. We can't hang around here all day like a bunch of Girl Scouts on a picnic. Get those ropes and poles secured.'

As the wooden lids were being replaced, several greedy pairs of hands darted from crate to pocket. It was a now or never moment for Jook and Maliwan. It was as though they knew they may not get a second chance.

The eight crates were far heavier than anyone had expected, nigh on two hundred pounds each. It took four men per crate to cope with the strain of carrying them back around the mountain side to the main track. Poles and rope were used to create makeshift platforms between pairs of yaks, each pair laden with a crate for the trek back down the mountainside. The journey progressed slowly, the yaks noticeably disgruntled by their burden.

After a slightly easier downhill journey, the train of yaks, men and soldiers reached the outskirts of Shekar. The town was not as they had left it. It was quiet now, unnervingly quiet. No resident was visible; no one was going about their normal business. No movement anywhere. And no sound. Something was wrong. Both Nick and John sensed the tension at the same time. It was like the quietness of a jungle seconds before an ambush was sprung.

'Get to cover,' Nick screamed at the top of his voice, grabbing Maliwan and diving to the wayside.

Those who understood Nick's words reacted fast, and just in time. A hail of bullets took the Chinese guards by surprise. Most collapsed to the ground, blood spurting from their dying bodies, without a shot being fired in retaliation.

'Geoff,' Nick shouted, 'Get the general, we need him.'

'Fuck that,' Geoff retorted keeping his head down. 'I'm not getting shot trying to rescue some slit-eyed bastard.'

'Jesus!' Nick muttered. 'Then get the AK47s, will you? We'll need those if you want any hope of getting out of here in one piece.'

Geoff seemed to think the situation through. 'Right. My pleasure.' He ran to the nearest guard, crouched, pulled the soldier up in front of himself for protection and raced back to cover. Only then did he remove the AK47 strapped over the dead guard's torso and remove the ammunition belt.

'Very impressive,' Nick muttered. 'Don't suppose you'd care to do that again would you?'

Geoff smiled. 'No trouble Nick. Just like a spot of rugby practice.' And off he went, again and again, returning with armed, but dead, soldiers.

'John,' Nick said to his friend crouching close by. 'We need to get the general. He's wounded by the look of it. You up for it?'

'I don't think we have a choice. He's our ticket out of here.'

Nick passed an AK47 to Sean and jabbed a finger in his face. 'Cover us. Give a burst of fire as we run over to the general and bring him back.'

'Sure, Nick,' Sean replied.

'That means sticking your head up and taking aim, not just firing willy-nilly without looking. Right?'

'Yeah, Nick, I've got it.'

John grabbed another AK47 and handed it to Jook. 'Stay here with Sean, cover us please.'

Nick caught John's eyes. 'Right then, on the count of three. One . . . two . . . three, let's go.'

John and Nick jumped up and ran across the dusty track in a crouching position towards the general. Jook stood up calmly and sprayed fire at the windows, doors and rooftops of the nearest house some fifty yards away. Shutters splintered, tiles shattered, earthenware pots exploded. Encouraged, Sean fired too, but remained stooped. Jook reloaded whilst standing exposed.

Nick grabbed the general's arms, John his legs. Together they lifted him and ran back to safety behind the wall. 'You alright, mate?' Nick asked, dropping formalities.

'You came back for me, Mr Price. Why?'

'We're in this together, old son. And we still need you.' He looked down at the general's trousers, there seemed to be a lot of blood. 'You hurt bad?'

'My legs, Mr Price. They have both been shot.'

'Let's take a look.' John ripped material away from the thigh area. He studied the wounds for a few seconds before nodding satisfactorily. 'Superficial. Flesh wounds only. You've got two entry holes and two exit holes. You're a lucky man, General.'

'Lucky?' General Tsim replied. 'There must be another meaning to the word, gentlemen. I do not consider this pain to be lucky.'

'You're still breathing for one thing,' Nick muttered. 'That's more than can be said for your soldiers. I think there're only two left standing. The other eight look dead.'

'That is their fate, Mr Price. Now, it is time for yours. My men will tend to me, but it is your duty to try to get us out of this mess.' General Tsim tried to raise his torso to rest on his elbows. 'Ahh,' he cried out, clenching his teeth, 'but please be quick.'

'Hang in there, General,' Nick replied, 'I'm getting us out of here, don't you worry.'

Within ten minutes, Geoff had retrieved the eight dead Chinese soldiers. Their AK47s, revolvers and ammunition were shared amongst the survivors.

Mike Harwood undertook a count of the snipers ahead of them. 'I think there're only five of them,' he related to Nick. 'There're certainly only five positions where the fire is coming from.'

'Five? Is that all?' Nick responded. 'Why so few?'

'Perhaps they were counting on the element of surprise. Gun us all down at once,' Mike said shrugging his shoulders, 'guess they weren't expecting us to be so spread out.'

'Right then, two men per position. Let's divide ourselves up. One gives covering fire, the other advances a few yards. Got that everyone? Work as a team, for fuck's sake, or we won't make it. And don't waste ammo, there's not much spare.'

The small town of Shekar was a sniper's paradise. There were dozens of single storey whitewashed quadrangular complexes of houses, each with an entrance leading into an open courtyard so that the farming families could live with their animals. Flags, shredded and faded by the harsh wind and sun, flapped in the breeze. Wood, brush and dried yak dung were piled up high on rooftops. There were simply hundreds of places where a sniper could hide unseen.

The townsfolk of Shekar would never forget the frightful house-to-house battle that ensued that day. They cowered in their huts, children huddled tightly, praying that the wild gunfire would cease. Several families screamed in anguish as a fearsome looking body, dressed in army fatigues, dived through a window or crashed through their front door, rifles leveled ready to shoot.

It took Nick and his rag-tag bunch an hour to perform their mission. By the end of the hour, there were five dead snipers. Nick kicked the last one over with his boot. 'The prison warden,' he muttered, 'now what the hell is he doing here?'

'Guess he put two and two together,' John responded. 'It wouldn't have been difficult. Don't forget Keith gave him the ruby. Maybe some jeweller knew where it came from. Who knows?'

'Yeah, who knows? Who cares? Just so long as he kept it a secret between his friends here.'

Keith came up behind Nick. 'You called me?'

Nick shook his head. 'I was just saying, your mate the prison warden must have worked out where the ruby came from.'

Keith squatted down next to the body and started rummaging through the warden's pockets. Seconds later he stood up smiling, holding the ruby aloft. 'I've grown attached to this.' He put the gemstone in his pocket.

Nick muttered, 'I think it's cursed. It's brought us nothing but bad luck.'

John wheeled around and said, 'Not necessarily. Just think a moment. The warden and his friends must have come in on the plane I saw earlier.' He clicked his fingers excitedly. 'That means we have a way out of here.'

Nick looked at John astounded. 'A plane?'

'Yeah. You remember? Up the mountain this morning, I saw something shining down in the valley. I told you it looked like a plane coming in to land.'

'Sorry, John,' Nick replied. 'I remember you got spooked up there, but I wasn't listening. I was suffering too much.'

'There's a plane here I tell you,' John said like an excited schoolboy. 'It's our way out.'

The two ran down the main street, followed closely by a few of the others. After a few minutes they stopped dead in their tracks out of sheer disbelief. There, half a mile away, on the valley floor, was indeed a plane.

'I don't believe it,' Ronnie Nelson exclaimed. 'It's our plane, the Princes 3A. They must have patched it up.'

'How the hell did it get here?' Sean asked.

'Never mind the how, mate,' Nick replied, 'let's go back and get the others. We need to load up and get the hell out of here as fast as possible. Who knows who's going to turn up next. And Keith, mate, do me a favour, leave that ruby to me in your will. It's a good luck charm after all.'

Within no time, the yaks were rounded up, a stretcher made to carry the general, and the diminished party set off towards the Princess 3A.

'Christ, this is going to be a tight squeeze,' Nick mumbled as they drew up alongside the plane. 'Keith, do us a favour, will you? Get these smelly animals away from here, they're getting in the way. Pay the men off whilst you're at it.'

'Sure, Nick. How much?'

'Fuck knows. After what they've been through today, they deserve a handful of gold coins each.'

Geoff's forehead screwed up as though in pain. 'You're being a bit generous, aren't you Nick. They're only peasants.'

'Only peasants? The world goes round each day because of people like them, Geoff. They nearly died for us back there. They could easily have been shot.'

'Who would care?'

'Christ you're a bigoted bastard, Geoff. One day you'll get your comeuppance. I'd love to be around to see it.'

'I don't think so,' Geoff said smugly. 'Not where I'm going with my share of this.'

'Yeah? Well, we're not out of the shit yet. We're not celebrating for a long time to come, old son. A lot may happen yet. Come on everyone, let's get these crates on board, we haven't got time to hang around.

And so the plane was loaded. Or rather, it was overloaded. Seriously overloaded. No one, except Keith, had expected to find so much treasure. No one had realized just how heavy it would be.

The plane took a whole mile to take off and even then it barely eased off the ground by a few feet. It continued to climb slowly, foot by foot. The experience was agonizing for its passengers. Nick found himself sweating profusely with worry. Ronnie Nelson's initial cool declaration that it would be okay didn't allay his fears.

With each passing minute, Ronnie Nelson's coolness eroded at an accelerating rate. The plane may well have been at over ten thousand feet on take-off, but he would have to coax it a further eight thousand feet to clear the mountain range between them and freedom. The twin five-fifty horse power propellers of the Prince 3A aircraft were working flat out already, straining hard under the pressure. He knew the aircraft's specifications by heart; the plane had a ceiling of twenty-three thousand four hundred feet. He only needed to get it to eighteen thousand feet, but with all the extra weight, he couldn't begin to hazard a guess at how far the plane could rise.

Nick had flown the Princess 3A alongside Ronnie on several occasions. He had a reasonably understanding of its limitations and, at the present rate of ascent, he knew they were in trouble. He could see mountainside above them and out of both port and starboard windows. Worse still, dead ahead, right in front of the pilot, though still some miles away, a snow-clad peak loomed ominously. They were flying up a valley, a dead-end, no way out except onwards and upwards. Any fool could see they were heading into disaster and time was running out fast.

The tension in the plane was electric. Everyone sensed the predicament. For some reason, the two Chinese soldiers sitting towards the rear tightened their grip on their rifles. Their action was casual, unhurried and would have gone unnoticed under normal circumstances. But then the circumstances were anything but normal. Geoff raised his AK47 and pointed it in the direction of the soldiers.

'Geoff, keep your nerve, for fuck sake,' Nick shouted over the high pitched scream of the engines. 'Keep your finger off the trigger, it's fucking sensitive and you're on edge. This is not the place to screw things up.'

'Don't lecture me, Nick,' Geoff shouted back. 'If you hadn't screwed up from the beginning, we wouldn't be sitting here with these slant-eyed bastards itching to pull their triggers.'

'Save it, Geoff,' Nick shouted back, 'you want to fight over it, fine, but for fuck sake wait until we get back to Bangkok. This is not the place to pick an argument.'

Geoff continued to stare, moodily, at the Chinese guards.

With each passing second, the valley narrowed and narrowed until Ronnie Nelson finally appeared to realize that they had gone too far. 'We're not going to make it,' he screamed backwards to his passengers.

'What?' Nick screamed back. 'What the fuck do you mean, Ron?'

'Sorry, Nick, but this old crate can't do any better. We can't gain any more height.'

'What?'

'Height, Nick, we need more height or we'll crash into that fucking mountain.' Ronnie Nelson jabbed his finger at the monstrous rock formation directly in their path. 'Don't you understand?'

'Then do something,' Nick screamed back.

'I can't!' Ron screamed in panic.

'Jesus Christ, Ron, get a grip.'

'You chose this fucking heap of shit. I told you it wasn't good enough. I told you it wouldn't cope, but you just had to be right, didn't you. Christ Nick, this is your fault, we're all going to die.'

'Shit, get a hold of yourself, Ron. Snap out of it. You're a pilot for fuck sake, think of something to get this pile of junk over that fucking mountain top.'

But the aircraft was trapped; trapped within the confines of the valley by the pilot's own stupidity. Trapped like an insect in a spider's web, with its engines whining in a frantic effort to escape the inevitable.

'Get rid of everything surplus,' Ronnie Nelson screamed. 'Throw out what you can, for Christ's sake. It's our only chance, ditch everything you can out the door.'

Nick and his men looked at each other in horror, sheer panic on their faces. They reacted in unison. The aircraft door was yanked open, freezing wind howled in and the draught sucked the very breath from their lungs. In a frenzy, they ripped up everything they could. Seats, tables, cupboards, anything that looked superfluous was attacked. The strength of the desperate men was incredible. Objects that the aircraft manufacturers would have sworn couldn't be shifted were wrenched out of their sockets. Every object they could lay their hands on was frantically hurled out. The men fought in a blind panic, they would have thrown their clothes out as well had it not been so cold.

Eventually, there seemed nothing left to jettison. The plane was completely gutted. They looked towards Ronnie Nelson for confirmation that their efforts had succeeded. The pilot's face said it all; absolute terror.

'We need to lose a couple of thousand pounds,' Ron screamed at the top of his voice. 'We've got about a minute left. For God's sake chuck more stuff out.'

'We've ditched everything,' Nick shouted back.

'Find more. We're not going to make it. Dear God, we're going to crash.'

Nick looked down at the eight crates of treasure, realizing that the weight of the gold was going to kill them. He couldn't bring himself to suggest chucking it away, but what was the alternative? It was then that he noticed the Chinese soldiers still held their rifles. He gestured for them to chuck them out, but they stood rigid, defiant. He advanced towards them, hand outstretched, but the rifles were leveled to a firing position.

'Oh, for fuck's sake,' Geoff shouted at the soldiers. He lunged forward attempting to grab a rifle. The ensuing wrestle lasted a split second, abruptly ending with a deafening burst of gunfire.

'Jesus H. Christ,' Nick screamed as several people dived to the floor. 'You'll kill us all, Geoff. Leave them alone.'

'Oh my god,' John shouted. 'Mal's been hit.'

'What?' Nick shouted back. He turned round to see John kneeling over Maliwan, her blood already forming a pool on the floor. 'Mal!' he screamed, dropping to his knees by her side. 'Mal!'

'Nick,' Maliwan replied through her tears of pain. 'Oh, Nick, I'm sorry.'

'Mal?' Tears welled in Nick's eyes. Her blood was everywhere, seeping from more places in her torso than he could count. He cradled her head, placed his hand on her chest in a vain attempt to quell the gushing life fluid.

'Nick, I . . . Oh, Nick, it hurts,' she sobbed. 'Take care of my babies, please, Nick, I don't think . . .'

'No!' Nick screamed. 'No, Mal! Don't die, not like this, not now, please!'

Geoff turned to the soldiers and screamed, 'You bastards!' His face was red with a rage never seen before. He slammed a punch into the face of the soldier who'd fired the rifle, then wrestled with the other, freeing the remaining rifle. With lightning speed, he threw both soldiers out the door, then turned his attention to the general.

'Don't be an idiot, Geoff,' Des McAlister shouted. 'This is murder.'

But Geoff wasn't to be put off.

'No,' Des shouted and made to grab his friend's arm.

'Back off, Des,' Geoff screamed. 'Keep out of it. We still need to lose more weight.'

'It's not worth it, Geoff. You can't do this. You can't just chuck him out, it's murder.'

'Keep out of this Des. I'm not losing this opportunity for anything.' He made to grab the general's wounded legs, but reeled back in astonishment as the general pulled a revolver from his tunic.

'Get your hands off me!' General Tsim shouted.

Geoff stared at the gun in disbelief. Thwarted, he stepped back, his body shaking with rage, turned and stared down at the pathetic sight of Nick cradling Maliwan's lifeless body. In the heat of the

The Fourth Cart III

moment, he grabbed Maliwan's legs, gave a yank, forced her body out of Nick's embrace, and threw her out the door.

Nick failed to respond, he was frozen to the spot in shock, unable to comprehend events unfolding around him.

'No!' Jook screamed, jumping up from the floor and hurling himself at Geoff in rage. 'She's my sister.'

Jook's flailing arms, beating vainly against Geoff, failed to make any impression. 'You fucking fairy!' Geoff screamed. 'Don't you fuck with me!' He grabbed hold of Jook and flung him out the door into the freezing cold abyss.

Geoff turned on the rest of the group, visibly shaking, breathing heavily, his reddened face seemingly about to burst. 'Anyone else?' he screamed. 'Anyone else want to pick an argument with me?'

No one replied. They had all frozen in horror at the sight of a madman.

Chapter Twenty-Five

Magee had sat transfixed, hanging on every word Nick had spoken. Now Nick looked a broken man; huddled over, head bowed, his right arm clenching his stomach, his left hand wiping away the flow of tears teeming down his cheeks.

Magee was riveted, fascinated by the tragedy, knowing that he had been hearing the truth. Finally, he understood the grief, the pain, anguish, misery and wretchedness that would have stayed with the survivors for the rest of their lives. He waited, deep in contemplation, for Nick to compose himself.

'I'm so sorry, Nit,' Nick eventually spoke.

'For what?' his daughter replied kindly.

'For screwing up. For the death of your mother, that's for what.'

'It wasn't your fault,' Magee chipped in.

'Oh, but it was, Magee. I should never have let Geoff go to Tibet. He had been challenging my authority for weeks. I knew from the start he would fuck up, and he did. It was my call, my fault.' His head collapsed back into his lap and Nittaya put her arm around him.

Magee looked at John for help. 'I have to ask what happened afterwards. What went on in the plane next? How did it end?'

John took over recounting the story. 'Well, there was no sense of euphoria once we realized we were clear of the mountain. Only shock. The door was pulled to, the noise of the wind ceased. We all stood, or sat, in silence. I remember everyone staring from one to the other, trying to anticipate what Geoff would do next. He was so crazy we thought he might try to kill the lot of us. The general kept his gun pointing at Geoff for the rest of the flight. No one said anything, though. After all, what was there to say? It wasn't as though we could change what had happened.'

'And Geoff?'

'It was quite a while before he calmed down. No doubt he realized we were thinking ill of him. Maybe he thought we were thinking of chucking him out the door. Wish we had, actually. Wish the general had shot him. I felt terrible about Jook, and inconsolable about Mal. Nick just sat on the floor, trancelike. I'm surprised he didn't throw himself at Geoff.'

'You flew straight back to Thailand?'

'No, we headed back to Kathmandu, refuelled, collected our stuff from the hotel, then flew down to Chiang Mai. I remember hardly a word was said during the flight back to base. We left each other to come to their own conclusion about the episode. We were all thinking questions like, why did you do that? Why did you throw the two guards and Jook out? Why did you throw Mal's body out? Was it necessary? Was it worth it? All those types of questions, well, there seemed little point in even posing them. And that's the end, I suppose.'

Magee remained silent for a few seconds, composing his thoughts and studying the grieving man in front of him. 'Nick, I'm sorry, but you've never had closure have you? That must have been unbearable. No time to say goodbye, no funeral, no body to mourn.'

Nick looked up at Magee, his face red and puffy. 'I've mourned for twenty years,' he sobbed. 'Not a day goes by without me thinking of Mal. She was my life. I lived for her. She was my heart and soul. I've never stopped loving her. Her death was senseless. It's preyed on my mind ever since those manic seconds Geoff lost control.'

Magee could think of nothing to say. No words could console the broken man.

Nick withdrew a handkerchief and blew his nose. 'Sorry, Nit. This is the first time I've ever talked of the events on the airplane in detail. I find it hard to cope with.'

'Talking about it may have helped, you know, Daddy. It allows for a release of emotion.'

'I'm not the emotional type, you know that.'

Magee interjected, 'All men are actually, Nick, underneath the rugged exterior that is.'

'Maybe,' Nick reflected.

Magee turned his attention back to John Mansell. 'So, John, what happened once you got back to Chiang Mai?'

'Well, we arrived in Chiang Mai in the middle of the night, dumped the plane in a hanger and unloaded the crates into the van we'd brought up from Bangkok. Ronnie Nelson had some explaining to do about the state of the plane, but he promised a very large bung to compensate the Air Force for the damage. We never mentioned the treasure to anyone of course.'

'Speaking of the treasure, Mr Mansell,' Brigadier Armstrong interjected, 'just how much did you get?'

'Remember this is nineteen seventy-three we're talking about, a million was a million back then.'

Brigadier Armstrong's lip curled up in a wry smile. 'Come on, Mr Mansell, don't be bashful.'

'Gross, well, thirty-one million pounds, plus small change.'

'Good God,' Brigadier Armstrong gasped.

'Yeah, it does take your breath away, doesn't it? To think the Great Train Robbers got away with what, six million, just a few years before us. It must have been the biggest heist ever at that time.'

Brigadier Armstrong turned to Nick Price and said, 'No wonder you have such a highly respected reputation in the underworld.'

Nick Price shook his head. 'I told no one, Brigadier. Not a dickybird, not even a hint to anyone. Any rumour you've heard is purely conjecture.'

Brigadier Armstrong persisted, 'Yet you're known for getting away with millions, aren't you?'

'Well, I suppose that's been the word on the street. I've never denied it, but I've never confirmed it either. Guess everyone saw I had money and put two and two together.'

'So, Mr Price, just how much did you get each?'

'After auction fees and old Hans Schmidt's commission and expenses, there was just under two and a quarter million pounds each for the eleven of us. Eleven, that is, including the general, he settled for an equal share in the end.'

'My god,' Magee exclaimed. 'That was a hell of a lot of money back then.'

'It sure was. When I came back to England, I was paying staff around fifty quid a week. That puts it into perspective. You know, the football pools top payout was only a hundred thousand pounds at that time, it was like winning the jackpot twenty times over. That's how much it was then, an unbelievable fortune.'

'No wonder people were impressed. Flashing money around does that for you, I suppose,' Brigadier Armstrong said scornfully.

'You don't seem impressed though.'

'Not at all, but then I've been lucky. Family inheritance, you see. I've been able to choose what I want to do with my life.'

'Then you are indeed a lucky man, Brigadier. My money has never brought me happiness. Comfort, yes, of course, in the material sense. But the root of it, obtaining it, has left me with nothing but guilt, pain and frequent sleepless nights.'

'Mmm,' Brigadier Armstrong nodded wisely, 'I can see why.'

'I'm not proud of what I did, Brigadier. We were desperate at the time, young and foolish. We never thought of the dangers before we got involved in capers like our exploits in Tibet.'

'Capers? Plural? There were others?' Brigadier Armstrong was aghast.

'A few,' Nick replied frowning. 'Nothing like Tibet, though. We were living in a pretty wild era, don't forget. Some strange things were going on in Thailand at the time.'

'No more secrets to come out, are there? Nothing more that could embarrass the government?'

'I'd rather not say, Brigadier.'

'I wish you would.'

'Let's just say, then, nothing that would upset the current government.'

'Your word on it?'

Nick hesitated. He seemed to be reliving past events, mentally ticking off possible causes of anxiety for the Brigadier. 'Yes,' he finally acknowledged, 'my word.'

Brigadier Armstrong did not look reassured.

Nick turned to Magee and said, 'So, that's it. I don't think there's anything more to say. And as I said earlier, Khun Sa did not feature in that tale.'

Magee looked down at the notes he'd been taking. 'Just before Mal was shot, you said Ronnie screamed there was only a minute left. Presumably, he meant there was only a minute left before the plane would crash into the mountain?'

'Presumably so,' Nick replied.

'But you did, in fact, clear the mountain. Was the mountain angled or a sheer vertical cliff?'

Nick shook his head. 'I've no idea. I was in a panic. We all were. I can't say I noticed. It's not something I've ever thought about.'

'But it's possible it was angled?'

Nick grimaced. 'I suppose so. Why?'

Magee tapped his notebook with a biro pen. 'Well, if it was angled, and Jook was thrown out just moments before the plane cleared the mountain top, it's possible that he fell only a short distance. A matter of a few feet only, perhaps. And presumably the mountain top would have been covered with several feet thick of snow.'

Nick's jaw dropped. 'Christ!'

Magee nodded. 'That's precisely my point. It's possible that Jook survived the fall. Very possible. And you said he pocketed a few bags of jewels in the tunnel under the castle. That would have given him the means to get started in the drug business. And he would certainly have had a motive for the serial killings last year. Revenge for Mal's death.'

'You're still speculating, Magee,' Brigadier Armstrong said. 'I need proof. Absolute proof that Jook survived if we are to go any further down that route.'

'John,' Magee asked, 'Do you think Jook had it in him to become a killer? You portray him as a rather weak character, physically weak that is. Would he have had the guts to kill someone, close-up with a knife?'

John shrugged. 'I suppose that would depend on his reasons. He was close to Mal, really close. They were inseparable, as twins often are. I think Mal's death would have affected him pretty severely. Emotionally and mentally, that is. But enough to turn his mind? I don't know, that's hard to say.'

'That's what I would have thought,' Magee said. He fell silent for a moment, his mind adrift. 'Sorry, what did you just say?'

'I said I think Jook would have been severely affected by Mal's death.'

'No, before that.'

'Erm, I said, I think, that Jook and Mal were like most twins, inseparable. They did everything together. Almost like they were joined together.'

Magee sat unblinking for a few moments before muttering, 'Inseparable.'

'Are you alright, Magee,' John asked. 'You've gone pale.'

Magee stood up. 'I'm sorry, I need to make a phone call. Nick, sorry to intrude, is there a telephone I can use?'

'Sure, in the library. Paul, would you mind?'

Magee left the sitting room, following Paul into the library further down the inner hall. It was ten minutes before he rejoined the others who were by now enjoying a fresh pot of tea.

'Well, Magee,' Nick said. 'What now?'

'We wait,' Magee replied, as he poured himself a cup of tea and sat down.

'Wait for what?' Nick asked.

'Just wait. I'm expecting a phone call.'

It was forty minutes before Annie came into the sitting room with a message for Magee. She passed him a piece of paper on which there was a brief message, ready and waiting.

Magee looked at his watch. It was four thirty. He said, 'I'm sorry this has taken so long today, but if you'll bear with me a little longer, something important needs to be concluded.'

Nick looked quizzically at Magee. 'Sorry? What do you mean by that?'

'We're all going into Lewes. We have an appointment.'

As Brigadier Armstrong stood up, Nick turned to Magee and asked, 'What's this all about then?'

'I'm sorry, Nick. I can't say at the moment. Please bear with me. Can the five of you go in your own car with a driver? The Brigadier, Melissa and I won't be returning.'

'What the hell's going on, Magee?'

'Nick. I need to show you something. Give something back to you, actually.'

Nick looked puzzled. 'Like what?'

'Your life, Nick.'

'Pardon?'

'Trust me, Nick. Wait until we get there. I don't want you prejudging this.'

Ten minutes later, after the short drive from Cooksbridge into Lewes, Magee's car pulled up near the town's War Memorial. He indicated to the car behind for everyone to alight and left Melissa to find a parking space.

As Nick got out the car behind, he pointed to a funeral parlour and asked, 'We're going in here?'

'Yes, we're expected.' Magee herded the entourage into the building and into a quiet room in which there were six chairs placed next to a covered coffin, alongside of which stood DCI Ryan.

Nick appeared dumbfounded. 'What the hell is this about Magee? Who's in the coffin?'

'All in good time. Look, this is going to cause you more grief, I'm afraid, it's going to hurt you a lot.'

'Hurt? I'm not sure there's any hurt left in me, Magee. Not after what you've put me through today.'

Magee took a deep breath. 'You remember we talked about closure?'

'Closure? On what?'

'There's a matter that needs clearing up. Sorry, Nick, this isn't easy for me, I don't know how to put this into words.'

'I don't understand what you could possibly be on about.'

'Please, Nick. Hear me out on this, okay?'

'Okay, I'm all ears.'

'I need you to identify a body.'

'A body?' Nick pointed towards the coffin. 'That body? And what possibly makes you think I would be able to identify it?'

'Please, Nick. Don't argue, don't make this harder.'

Nick vented his anger.. 'You know I lodged an official complaint against you last year, Magee. This is the reason for it. Continuous fucking harassment. I don't give a shit who's in that coffin, it's got nothing to do with me. Don't you get it?' He turned away from Magee and headed for the door.

Magee turned to the others. 'John, please. Help me out here. Take a look, I beg you. Nothing's going to get resolved until Nick looks into that coffin.'

John Mansell shook his head and said, 'Magee, you're a sad man. This really is unbecoming of you.'

'Damn it, John,' Magee screamed. 'Just do it!'

The Brigadier intervened, nudging Paul. The two of them steered John towards the coffin. DCI Ryan pulled back a sheet that had been covering the body and indicated John to look down. It took John all of ten seconds to take in the sight of the mummified corpse.

'No!' he cried, 'It can't be, it's not possible!' He burst into tears, wrenched at his chest and looked back towards the man trying to leave the room. 'Nick, come back. It's her!'

Magee gave an audible sigh of relief as John bounded across the room and grabbed Nick. 'It's Mal, Nick. Magee's found Mal.'

'What?'

'She's here, Nick. Come on,' John said, grabbing hold of Nick as it appeared his legs had buckled.

'Mal? Here? What are you talking about?'

'Nick, really, it's her. It's Private Jugs, she's still got the uniform with that name on.'

'Private Jugs? You mean . . .?'

'Yes, come on.' John virtually carried Nick back across the room to the coffin.

Nick collapsed under the weight of emotion at the side of the coffin. Finally, his wish of the last twenty years, to be reunited with his wife, had come true; to be able to hold her hand one more time. The tears came like a waterfall.

Magee stood to the side of Nick. He waited until there was a lull in Nick's crying before saying, 'You need to hold a funeral for her, a proper funeral. With you, Nittaya, Somsuk, John and Paul beside you. To lay her to rest, to say your goodbyes. To weep at her graveside as you were never able to before. To visit her on a summer's day, to lay flowers on her grave, to remember the love you had for her . . .' Magee had to break off, unable to control the tears rolling down his own face. He took a step back and walked towards the exit where DCI Ryan had retreated to a respectful distance.

'That's a turn up for the books,' DCI Ryan said. 'That's Nick Price isn't it?'

'It certainly is. Go easy on him. That's his wife he's just identified. He's completely innocent of anything to do with her death or how she ended up in a Brighton flat. She died in an accident in Tibet years ago. It's her brother who's been carrying her body around.'

'Can you give me a name for him, and where I can contact him?'

'Well, his nickname was Jook. He died six months ago, but you'll have to take my word on that. He was the serial killer I was chasing last year, out for revenge on Nick Price and some of his old mates for the death of his sister.'

'Those knives with the carved handles were his signature?'

'Indeed they were. Ten in all. The last one, the one found alongside the Buddha statue, was meant for Nick himself.'

'So you can close a serial murder case file. Good for you, Magee.'

'It doesn't stop there, there's plenty in it for you, not just clearing up this case. You see, Jook was also Khun Sa, the drug lord from Thailand who was responsible for those drug gang killings earlier this year in Brighton. They were on your patch, I believe. He was also responsible for the arson attacks on Nick Price's business properties earlier this year, and they were your cases I seem to remember.'

'Wow! Nice one, Magee. That should boost my clear-up rate.'

'Unfortunately, you're going to have to keep most of this quiet though.'

'Really, that's a shame. Why's that?'

Magee grinned and motioned DCI Ryan to turn around. 'Let me introduce you to Brigadier Armstrong.'

Brigadier Armstrong held his hand out to Magee and said, 'Well done, Magee. I believe you've joined up all the dots.'

'I believe so too, sir.'

'You'll send me a copy of your report?'

'Of course, sir. May I introduce you to Detective Chief Inspector Ryan? The mummy is his case. He'll be processing the paperwork with Nick, so he's going to need names and explanations.'

Brigadier Armstrong gave DCI Ryan a warm smile. 'Of course. Before all that, though, we need to talk. National security, you see.'

Magee gave Melissa a wink, and went home exhausted.

Epilogue

Superintendent Vaughan looked bewildered. 'But what made you possibly think you knew the identity of the mummy? That's what I don't understand.'

Magee smiled for the first time in the hour it had taken to debrief his boss. At last, everything was out in the open; he had finally been able to explain his actions of the past eighteen months with the blessings of Brigadier Armstrong. 'It was only when it was mentioned that twins are often inseparable that it dawned upon me. It was the only satisfactory explanation as to why someone associated with Nick Price's life would carry around a mummified body.'

'But how on earth did the mummy get from a Tibetan mountainside to Brighton?'

'Well, by all accounts, the airplane was near the mountain peak when Jook went out the door. So, Jook survived the fall and must have come across his sister's body whilst climbing down the mountain. He probably covered her up with stones for protection from birds and animals, but he could do nothing else but leave her there. Some years later, when he'd made his drug fortune under the guise of Khun Sa, he must have gone back to Tibet to retrieve her body. That scenario is certainly consistent with the autopsy report.'

'So he carried her body around with him?'

'I think so, yes, sir.'

'The man must have been insane.'

'I believe he was. They were twins, Maliwan and Jook. Very close twins. I reckon Jook had thought of revenge for years, it was probably what turned him mad, certainly psychopathic. He couldn't let go of his sister. He probably took comfort from her presence. It's been known before, people holding on to their dead loved-ones.'

'So now you have the identity of Khun Sa, and of your serial killer. And it also proves Nick Price innocent of those appalling press allegations?'

'Yes.'

'But what of those arson attacks on Nick Price's business properties last year?'

'We can only speculate about that, sir. Jook died in Bangkok in May. The arson attacks stopped immediately, so it seems likely Jook was responsible for them. As to why though, who knows? Maybe he was trying to drive Nick Price over the edge, get him put away in a mental hospital.'

'For what purpose?'

Magee shrugged. 'To get access to Nittaya and Somsuk, I imagine. With Nick out the way, it would have been easier to step in as the long-lost uncle.'

'So why not just kill Nick?'

'I've thought along those lines too, sir. There is strong evidence to suggest that Jook may not have been able to bring himself to kill Nick. Perhaps it caused too much conflict for him.'

'Well, at least it ends happily, in the sense that Nick has been reunited with his wife and can now hold a proper funeral. And you, Magee, having proved that Jook survived, have solved several cases all at once. Talking of which, I have soon good news for you.'

'Sir?'

'I met Nick Price at his house in Cooksbridge yesterday. He's decided to decline the offer of a peerage, by the way, as he feels partly responsible for creating the monster, Khun Sa. He thinks it's for the best. Anyway, he told me he wished to withdraw the letter of complaint he made against you last year. In fact, he wished to exchange it for another letter. One of praise about you, Magee.'

Magee chuckled. 'I find that hard to believe.'

'High praise, I may add, although he did ask for the letter not to be shown to you. He said you might take it the wrong way and try to move in with him. I assume that was a joke?'

Magee smiled. 'I hope so.'

'It will stay on your personnel file in confidence, along with two other letters I received yesterday, one from Brigadier Armstrong and one from the Prime Minister.'

'Really? You jest, sir.'

'I do not, Magee. It's been made plain to me by those three gentlemen that we . . . I, rather, have done you a disservice these last few months. I think you should know that there have been hints from high above about the possibility of promotion.'

'Thank you, sir.' Magee couldn't resist a smug smile. He had his vindication at last. 'Whilst we're talking of commendations, sir, may I ask for DCI Ryan to get some form of acknowledgement for the part he played in my work. He stuck his neck out to bring me in on his case. I wouldn't have succeeded without his involvement. He should get credit for that.'

Superintendent Vaughan made a note on a pad of paper. 'Consider it done. Oh, one other thing, Magee. There's a certain young lady, a detective sergeant working here, who would rather like to be back working with you.'

Magee's face lit up. 'Melissa?'

'I believe she's settling back into her old desk, as we speak.'

###

Printed in Poland
by Amazon Fulfillment
Poland Sp. z o.o., Wrocław